I0668084

HEIRS OF THE ANCIENTS

BOOK TWO OF THE THREE WORLDS CHRONICLES

JAMES R NORWOOD

KJN PUBLISHING

Copyright © 2021 James R Norwood
All rights reserved. No part of this work may be duplicated or used without prior written consent from the publisher.

ISBN: 978-0-578-95896-5
Published by KJN Publishing
https://www.threeworlds.net

Library of Congress Control Number: 2021915425

For my mom, Georgia. I miss you every day. May your story always be told.

- A Trio of Worlds: Book One of the Three Worlds Chronicles
- Heirs of the Ancients: Book Two of the Three Worlds Chronicles
- Act I: A Middle School Drama Anthology

CONNECT WITH JAMES NORWOOD

- Twitter: https://twitter.com/jrnorwood
- Facebook: https://www.facebook.com/authorjnorwood
- Instagram: https://www.instagram.com/jrnteach/
- On the Web: https://www.threeworlds.net
- Subscribe to Newsletter: https://drjrn.com/newsletter

AUTHOR'S NOTE

As this book makes use of many more examples of the D'lai language, I included at the end, a glossary of terms that I used throughout the following pages. I figured it was the least I could do for you, as no one living today actually speaks D'lai, and the language only exists in my imagination with the help of an amazing website I found before I wrote *A Trio of Worlds*. If you are at all interested in conlangs, you should check it out - vulgerlang.com. Even if you're not interested in constructed languages, I'm hopeful that the glossary will help you to avoid that glassy-eyed stare and help you understand my characters a little more. Happy reading.

$\sim$ James Norwood

PROLOGUE

The ancients waited and watched as the ages unfolded before them. They laid their trap in a desolate corner of the galaxy, waiting patiently like a spider, while countless stars, planets, and civilizations were born, thrived, and died out. In the fullness of time, a desperate race of beings, fleeing from their home, was ensnared in their cosmic web, setting into motion a thousand-year struggle for survival, revenge, and dominance.

Without imagining the peril that lay before them, they forged ahead. Their motives and plans blurred the reality of their growing and swiftly approaching doom. Imprisoned by their own greed, the D'lai unwittingly fed the starving ancients, who grew in power and strength, until the day would finally arrive when their dark, consuming plan could be fulfilled.

Haunted by their lust for power, and consumed by their passion for revenge, the D'lai swept into space and were utterly destroyed by their own arrogance. Despite their failure, an ember still smoldered, and finally, emboldened and possessed by the rage and malice of the ancients, they struck once more.

The ancient game, played out over billions of years, would once more consume the galaxy, and this time, should they succeed, no being alive or dead would remain untouched. The final plan was in place, and the D'lai, the heirs of the ancients, were on the move.

PART 1

PART I - A GATHERING STRENGTH

CHAPTER 1

Cathar Prime – The Present

The Negotiator sat in the semi-darkened room, waiting for the arrival of The Emissary. Decades earlier the D'lai had been vanquished in the skies above Gathung'l and Earth. The shame and failure of Negotiator Ret D'iash left an immutable scar upon the D'lai consciousness. Those few survivors who remained, fled to the scorched and ruined planet Cathar Prime in a desperate bid to find a shred of peace. In systems all over the Orion Arm, countless D'lai ships had been disabled and destroyed, thanks to the discovery of smuggler Zea Windrow. Her FTL jump trick sent many thousands of D'lai to their doom in the stars they still believed theirs to rule.

Now, alone and virtually homeless, the D'lai remnant waited and planned for their triumphant return. It took years, but they rebuilt Cathar Prime in their own image. Any native Cathari who dared to defy their right to rule the scarred planet was banished into space. The D'lai meted out the same cruelty the Cathari imposed upon them centuries ago.

Cathar Prime had once been home to the vast Cathari Alliance, and boasted beautiful cities and graceful countryside. The Alliance crumbled after the war, leaving Earth and its allies to form the Three Worlds Alliance in its place. Now, twenty years since the violent conquest of the Cathar Prime, no corner of this once majestic planet was free of devastation. The planet's former capital city had never been rebuilt. The D'lai cruelly left its smoldering remains as a memorial, and a reminder, for the ordinary Cathari of their enduring shame, and crushing defeat. With time, smaller cities slowly sprang up out of the ruins, and the D'lai overlords and Cathari survivors now maintained an uneasy peace.

Among the successors of the D'lai, a new Negotiator arose. He studied under the disgraced Ret

D'iash, and expanded upon her cruel but cunning methods of conquest, command, and fear. Negotiator Brik Zat'ol had been aboard *The Spector* when the final battle was lost. He witnessed first-hand the barbarity of D'iash in not only implementing her conquest plans, but in how she dealt with the secretive cabal of Commanders that attempted to overthrow her rule. Zat'ol, then a junior officer on board *The Spector,* had himself been recruited to the cabal and worked to undermine her authority. Despite this, his greatest accomplishment in the final battle did not shower him in glory, but it did bring him personal pride. As he was traveling down a corridor of the ship, he stumbled upon the ill Negotiator outside her quarters, and after helping her inside, he murdered her with his bare hands. The dark memory of that moment still brought him undiluted pleasure.

Now he sat in this poorly lit room, awaiting the visit of an Emissary from the ancient Umawei Empire. Anticipation of the meeting thrilled him. Centuries in the past, when the D'lai had been expelled from Cathar Prime by a religious sect called the Däk'in, the D'lai encountered the remnants of the Umawei Empire in a system they called Ryi Bruai. Awed by the mega structures left by these mysterious aliens, the D'lai believed they found the origins of life on their planet.

The ancient Cathari long ago reasoned that a superior race of beings must have seeded all the habitable planets in this region of space with the building blocks of life. Their reasoning was simple. As they explored their region of the galaxy, they discovered that far too many species resembled each other in appearance and basic anatomy. A coincidence of nature? Probably not. They believed that if they could find the source, they could bring about a true galactic peace. The D'lai, on the other hand, held very different ideas around the source. They maintained that knowledge and possession of this seeding technology, if it fell into the right hands, would be an unstoppable source of unlimited power.

In an effort to prove their early theories of this ancient civilization, the Cathari sought them out with their vigorous exploration of nearby stars. As they explored, they encountered planets teeming with life comparable to their own. It grieved them, however, that only a few planets had advanced civilizations capable of space flight. Their travels through the stars increased their belief in the ancient aliens, however, they also began to realize that what they sought was a darker, more menacing, and immensely powerful civilization. They found scattered relics of this extinct culture in multiple systems, but none as enormous as those the D'lai encountered much later, after the schism.

As they fled Cathar Prime, the D'lai ran across an entire star system filled with planet and star-sized constructions. The discovery thrilled the D'lai, and enabled them to greatly advance their own technological prowess. D'lai leaders recognized that if they might ever recover from the horror of war and banishment, they needed superior knowledge. The Umawei Empire's remnants provided that ability. Unfortunately, due to the circumstances of their exile, the ancient D'lai never fully assimilated the abandoned Umawei technology. Their search for a home far outweighed the thrilling discovery. Centuries later, Zat'ol aimed to correct that early blunder. The D'lai would rise from the ashes of their failures, and assert their rightful place as masters of the galaxy.

As Zat'ol pondered the history of his people, something interrupted him. An aide approached and bowed. The Emissary had arrived.

Cathar Prime – The Ancient Past

"*VIUG! ROIŞ!* FATHER! HELP!" PULLED FROM THE arms of her father, and thrust into the air transport crammed with a dozen other crying children, the young Cathari girl screamed and kicked. Hours earlier, local Magistrates ordered Am'oll and his family to leave their home in Rai province – a home the family had owned and maintained since the time of the *Vdo Däk,* four centuries in the past.

Am'oll and his family were part of a breakaway sect of Cathari that called themselves the D'lai. Both spiritually and politically, Cathar Prime burned. Centuries passed since the first so-called divine religious leader, the *Vdo Däk*, taught the Cathari his particular brand of peaceful existence, and abhorrence of violence in any form.

"Life is sacred and cannot be violated," the *Vdo Däk* said.

Not lost on some congregants, pacifism made them wary. They believed that this new religion of the Cathari people would lead the planet into ruin.

The political leaders of Cathar Prime soon adopted this new religious movement called Däk'in, and in stunning fashion swept aside the multitude of religious belief systems that pervaded the planet. A small group of extremists refused to give up their beliefs and formed small secret cells all over the planet. At first, these cells were seen as harmless, and provincial and military leaders generally ignored them. Over time, the asceticism of Däk'in grew more extreme and permeated so much of Cathari society, that it became first immoral, and finally criminal, to believe anything else.

The small groups of breakaway D'lai grew and merged over time. The D'lai adherents saw most Cathari as being hypocritical in their beliefs. To use peace as a weapon could not be tolerated by the leaders of the D'lai. In an attempt at self-preservation, the D'lai faithful kept their religion hidden in the shadows. They developed ever more elaborate methods of greeting a fellow believer, and in time began to congregate on rural farms, in caves and abandoned factories, far from the prying eyes of the Däk'in.

The two rival faiths might have co-existed peacefully, with each secure in their own ideologies, if not for an inciting incident that not only exposed the D'lai faith to public scrutiny, but also endangered the Däk'in faith. In the four hundred years since the religious split between the two sects, the Cathari people as a whole explored with almost religious zeal nearby space in an effort to better understand the civilizations they discovered early in their observations of the stars.

Not long after the rise of the *Vdo Däk*, Cathari astronomers stumbled upon an erratically behaving nearby star. They discovered multiple planets based on the changing intensity of that star's light. They decided to point their radio telescopes at the nearby star, and reacted with astonishment when they detected sound waves emanating from one of the exoplanets. At first, they dismissed the detection as background noise. However, after careful study, they began to discern distinct patterns that could only be described with one word. Life.

Cathari scientists doubled their efforts, and began launching rudimentary space craft and satellites into orbit in an attempt to better understand their discovery. The Däk'in seized on the opportunity, and began morphing their religion to match the discovery of otherworldly intelligence. The *Vdo Däk* began teaching that the ancient Cathari gods were not spiritual beings. They were aliens. In time, the Cathari developed the ability to leave their own star system and began the long trek between the stars. Their discoveries would forever change the planet, and set into motion a chain of events that would eventually bring about their own destruction.

While the planet as a whole made tremendous scientific strides, The Däk'in and the D'lai grew ever more apart. Where the predominant Cathari religion believed in non-aggression and harmony with nature, the cast outs of the D'lai faith conformed to the belief that it is in the nature of all living beings to take what one required for survival, regardless of the consequences. D'lai ritual centered on the selfishness of life and threw aside all notions of peace and co-existence for mutual benefit. Living beings possessed the divine right to do as desired.

Cathar Prime orbits a red dwarf star and, like most planets in the galaxy, experiences seasons, day and night, and periods of increased solar activity. The Cathari evolved in cycles that closely matched their local star. Their religious activities mirrored those periods, and in time, despite a strong scientific awareness, their myths and superstitions still pervaded the advanced, space-faring society. Their missions to learn more about neighboring planets exposed the existence of other, less advanced civilizations. It also made the Cathari keenly aware of a much older, and darker community of aliens that seemed to have gone extinct but left its mark on multiple worlds.

Dozens of rituals evolved among the Cathari, including the annual celebration of Çäi, or summer. The ceremony became more elaborate in time, and after the teachings of the *Vdo Däk* began to merge with scientific discovery, Çäi became the most important day in the life of the Cathari people. However, a major problem soon emerged. The D'lai and the Däk'in held differing views on not only the importance of Çäi, but also on how to memorialize the day.

In the year 3710, a group of D'lai faithful celebrated Çäi in their usual fashion. The worshipers grew incautious as time elapsed, and allowed their secretive ceremonies to become more public. Incidents of intolerance between the religions grew far less frequent, and the D'lai became more comfortable practicing their faith publicly. The D'lai ritual surrounding Çäi involved the sacrifice of grazing animals called keṭ. These animals, a key ingredient of most D'lai rituals, offended the extremely peaceful Däk'in, and they found all animal sacrifice to be abhorrent. A group of Cathari happened to observe the opening scene in the D'lai celebration, and became so revolted by the slaughter, that they failed to remember their own ideals of pacifism. Enraged, they attacked the worshiping D'lai and in the act, killed a young boy who had been observing his first celebration of Çäi with his parents.

The leader of Rai Province, Varoth the Elder, incited further violence when, during a speech in front of the Cathari legislature, he declared "We must drive this evil from our cities!"

A loud stirring of assent could be heard among the gathered leaders. "We have tolerated the D'lai for far too long," continued Varoth. "It has infected our homes and filled our streets with a grotesque mockery of all we stand for!"

All over Cathar Prime, violent mobs began to form, intent on rooting out D'lai believers and in the process, exposing their own Däk'in faith as a lie. They abandoned almost overnight the peaceful ideals of *Vdo Däk*. Civil war was coming.

Earth – The Present

CORMAC GALLAGHER HAD A MASSIVE HEADACHE. The pounding kept him up all night, despite the fact that the next day was going to be overly busy for him. Leaders from Gathung'l and Mars were due to arrive for their semi-annual Three Worlds Alliance Summit.

"I've got to get some sleep!" Gallagher grumbled to no one. He tossed and turned and tried to count sheep, but sleep eluded him.

Several years earlier, after the successful cloaking of Earth and the defeat of the D'lai, Gallagher had been assigned as a military aide with then Secretary General Marsha Allen. She thought that by giving him such a cushy assignment, it would be a reward for his efforts at saving the planet. Gallagher disagreed.

He loved space and wanted to be back out there. To Gallagher, it didn't matter if aliens tried to kill him. He loved the adventure. Secretary General Allen, on the other hand, had other plans for the planetary hero.

"Gallagher, we need to put your face out there!" Allen said in one of their early meetings.

"My face...isn't there someone else who..." protested Gallagher.

"Nonsense! You are the hero of Earth!"

"Hero? All I did was follow some stupid orders and not be killed."

Allen smirked and then ordered Gallagher to report to the Office of Public Relations. Gallagher dutifully did as directed.

"Damn."

Now, rolling over in his bead, Gallagher decided to get up and do some work. Three years ago he had been unanimously elected as Secretary General. He didn't relish the idea of sitting in an office all day, but he figured why the heck not.

"Might as well get something out of this." He said to himself.

He sat down at a comfortable desk in the corner of his bedroom and scrolled through some messages on his pad. One particular message caught his attention, so he opened it up and smiled.

His old friend, Corey Hodges, had been working off-world helping to build a new orbital platform intended to replace the aging planetary cloak that protected Earth. While the old cloak worked well, and with routine maintenance did what intended, the limitations imposed by the old tech made communications and routine naval operations problematic.

As part of the new project, the old cloak had to be

taken offline and stored in a cargo hold so the new platform could be tested. Gallagher smiled as he read the message from Hodges while holding a picture of his old friend standing next to the slightly battered cloaking satellite they deployed around Earth. The caption said "Remember this?" Gallagher tapped out a brief reply, and reluctantly moved on to more important matters. He vowed to have dinner with Hodges on his next visit. It had been too long.

After he read and replied to a few more messages, Gallagher stood and groaned. His back recently began aching in the mornings, and he wondered when he had started to grow old. Only yesterday his younger self paraded around the galaxy. Now here he sat, a middle-aged dude with the beginnings of a spread around his stomach.

"Computer, remind me to exercise more," he said as he looked in a mirror. He grunted and then hopped in the shower.

Mid-song and soapy, Gallagher was startled when an alarm began blaring from his workstation. He tried to ignore it, but the software geeks that invented the system made sure the sound would not be easily dismissed. He turned off the water, wrapped a towel around his waist, and rushed to his console.

"Computer, shut off that damn noise!"

The computer complied. Gallagher sat down and read the message. He froze as he scanned the document. An instant later, the face of his military advisor came on the screen. She didn't seem fazed at all by the bare-chested planetary leader as she cleared her throat.

"Sir, we've just received word of an enormous explosion in orbit." General Janina Agda looked stern. An able commander, the 48-year old Swedish General stared back at him. Only urgent business would cause her to interrupt Gallagher's morning.

"Explosion? I need more details General Agda."

"Sir, the new cloaking platform is the source. We don't have much..."

"The platform? Damn." Gallagher's mind instantly went to the safety of his friend Hodges. "Survivors?"

"We believe no one has been critically injured, sir." The General said.

Gallagher breathed a sigh of relief. "I'm getting dressed. I'll be in my office in fifteen. I'll need a full briefing."

"Yes, sir." General Agda clicked off. Gallagher got dressed and left his quarters in less than five minutes.

Cathar Prime – The Ancient Past

Aᴍ'ᴏʟʟ ᴘᴀᴄᴇᴅ ᴛʜᴇ ꜱᴍᴀʟʟ ᴅᴇᴛᴇɴᴛɪᴏɴ ᴄᴇʟʟ ᴀꜱ ʜᴇ feared for the safety of his daughter and wife. A few days earlier he sat with his frightened family in their darkened home. The mobs of enraged Däk'in became increasingly violent and murderous as they sought out anyone who did not hold to their belief system. Am'oll, for his part, believed that his own D'lai faith mirrored the Cathari soul with greater authenticity.

"Shhh," said Am'oll to his cowering family. "I can hear them...outside."

The rowdy noises of nearby rioters emanated from neighboring streets. Am'oll did his best to barricade his small family inside their spacious home and hide their existence from the mob.

"So much for non-violence," said Suha, the wife of Am'oll. "I thought they wouldn't raise a fist in anger!"

"Suha, we've long understood that the pacifism of Däk'in is a sham. The Cathari soul..."

"Yes, yes!" Suha interrupted her husband. "I know!"

Suha and Am'oll held each other in an embrace as they consoled their frightened daughter. All Cathari valued their children. The D'lai taught that children embodied the *vdo hyëb*, or great spirit, of the Cathari gods. Until Däk'in became the major religion of the planet, they worshiped an entire pantheon of major and minor gods and goddesses. The *Vdo Däk* violently swept aside the gods as a child-like belief that an advanced society should shun. The D'lai still believed that the gods influenced their lives. They pointed to massive structures in a nearby star system discovered by Cathari explorers that could not be comprehended even now, as evidence of a superior intelligence.

The discovery of the ancient and seemingly extinct Umawei Empire rocked Cathar Prime. The subsequent discovery that the ancient civilization seeded its genetic material in primordial planets, including Cathar Prime, propelled the Däk'in believers to move beyond their past superstitions. This created conflict with the D'lai who still believed these ancient forebears to be gods, not beings like themselves. They believed that any sufficiently advanced civilization would destroy, not create. Nevertheless, the recent unrest on the planet threatened to undo all the advancements their society made scientifically.

Cultural and religious bias overrode the more reasoned and thoughtful leaders among the planets inhabitants.

Suha screamed when a particularly violent explosion rocked their hiding place. Am'oll attempted to soothe her to no avail. She dashed from their hiding spot and ran from the room. Am'oll would have gone after her if not for their young daughter. The violence outside threatened their safety, and he had no intention of leaving her unprotected to run after his foolish wife.

That violent night ended in his daughter being taken, and he and his wife imprisoned. Am'oll fumed. He also plotted. Unknown to all but the most senior Däk'in, Am'oll was secretly the leader of the D'lai. For decades, they planned for an event such as the one now overtaking the planet. Their mystics foresaw the phenomenon now engulfing Cathar Prime in metaphorical flames, and their leaders organized and developed worst-case scenarios.

Most Cathari possessed the uncanny ability to devise plans within plans. While the violent mobs of Däk'in faithful acted from pure impulse, the D'lai silently activated their long-term objectives. Even now, scores of them gathered in preordained locations and dusted off long abandoned, but meticulously maintained space craft. If necessary, the D'lai would leave Cathar Prime and venture into the stars. Am'oll hoped this would not be necessary. He still believed that the vast majority of the populace would come to their senses and avert the impending disaster.

A ruckus from outside the small holding area drew his attention. Am'oll expected that his fellow D'lai would mount a rescue attempt. However, if the plan failed, he believed the sect would survive without him. He understood that no matter how his life unfolded, the D'lai faith would go on.

"Am'oll, get down!"

The shouted warning startled Am'oll, but he knew better than to ignore it. He dropped to the ground and scooted under a bunk. An instant later, an explosion shook the holding area as dust and debris filled the air. Strong hands gripped him and whisked him from the wreckage of the cell. Blinded by sudden daylight, he closed his eyes while his rescuers guided him to the waiting transport.

After a few moments of adjustment, he was able to open his eyes and look around. Several dusty Cathari filled the small cabin. Among them, he recognized his cell-mates, and it relieved him to see his wife Suha crouching in a corner. She smiled at him.

"Suha...what...," Am'oll started to say.

"Just be grateful we got you out," said the driver of the vehicle, "we almost couldn't find you!"

The Cathari authorities tried to hide the where-abouts of Am'oll for just such a fear as an attempt to free him. They reasoned the D'lai movement would collapse without its leader. They could not have been more wrong. However, Am'oll's family and friends insisted upon attempting the rescue.

The air transport sped out of the city toward one of the D'lai gathering locations in a nearby cave system. They understood the importance of ushering Am'oll to safety. It would do no good for him to be recaptured. Am'oll sat back and grasped Suha's warm hand. The pair sat on the hard floor of the transport and smiled at each other. The odds were good they would not have many more opportunities for affection in the coming days.

CHAPTER 2

Gathung'l – The Present

The *Manchester* fled the nearby planet of Gathung'l after a nasty encounter with planetary security forces. Captain Zea Windrow, despite her promise to the former Second Dictator Bresu Xid to "go straight" and leave smuggling behind, found her life as an ordinary merchant to be less than fulfilling.

After Xid had been killed in an accident aboard *The Naomor* a decade after the fall of the D'lai Authority, Windrow decided she'd had enough boredom and weaseled her way back into the far more profitable smuggling business.

She had been involved for the past few years with a Gathung arms dealer who hired her to smuggle contraband between Gathung'l and Xiphus, a small, Earth-sized planet a dozen light years from the Gathung'l system. At first, Windrow balked at the terms. Xiphus was home to a markedly vile species of aliens called the Rozk. Invertebrates, the Rozk boasted arms and legs as well as four wings, and a short, thick tail they used to help them in flight and battle. Windrow told anyone who would listen that to her, they looked like giant bugs. They were however unappealing not just for their appearance. The Rozk, famous for their almost innate ability to build weapons, possessed no qualms about who they supplied their armaments to. They would gladly sell to both sides in a conflict, and had been a primary supplier of the D'lai.

After the fall of the D'lai, most planets shunned Xiphus and the Three Worlds Alliance refused to have any form of diplomatic relations with them. This didn't bother the Rozk. They had no problem working their particular black market. Plenty of smugglers and other undesirables could be found to do business with. Windrow was uncomfortable with the Rozk only because she was the sole cause of the destruction of much of the D'lai fleet, and therefore a major cause of their decline in revenue.

During the Battle of Gathung'l, Windrow discovered that an aborted FTL jump produced the right amount of background radiation to disrupt the computer networks aboard the D'lai ships. This knowledge enabled the Gathung and humans to destroy the vast fleets orbiting their respective planets. It also made Windrow persona non grata in much of the smuggling underworld that existed at the time.

A particularly tense encounter between *The Manchester* and a Scree smuggler after that epic battle almost resulted in the loss of her ship. As a result, Windrow vowed to leave smuggling behind while maintaining a few of her old connections, just in case. Years later and here she was, back in the thick of things, fleeing another disaster.

"Navigator, how long until FTL insertion?" Windrow asked as her ship fled.

"Unknown ma'am. I've not been able to plot a course."

"Why the hell not? Get us out of here Navigator!"

"I'm trying ma'am," said the stressed navigator. "The Gathung are interfering with our nav computers."

Windrow cursed. Ever since the destruction of the D'lai fleet, Gathung'l and Earth redoubled their efforts at developing better technology to enable them to easily outmaneuver any enemy in the future. Windrow herself helped Gathung'l further advance its own sensory abilities – including the ability to interfere with navigation and propulsion.

"I thought we locked down our own systems," Windrow said.

"Ma'am, we did," said the tactical officer. "They are using something we haven't seen before."

"Can we cloak?"

"Negative," came the reply from tactical. "However, I have an idea."

"Why are we waiting? Do it!"

"Yes, ma'am, it's just that..."

"Just what?"

The tactical officer paused, "Just that it could blow out our main engines."

Zea Windrow didn't even take a breath before replying, "Well, don't blow the engines!"

The tactical officer nodded tensely, and returned his attention to his work station. The minutes dragged on for an eternity before the tactical officer smiled in relief. On the viewer at the front of the bridge, the scene changed from the nearby Gathung ship and the planet Gathung'l in the distance, to a starburst effect as the ship rocketed away from their pursuer much faster than *The Manchester* seemed capable of doing.

Alarmed, Windrow turned to the tactical station, "Tactical, what the hell did..."

"Ma'am, we are traveling at sub-FTL speed. I was able to route the ship's energy capacitors that store power for the cloaks, FTL, and artificial gravity into the engine array. This gave us a burst of speed that outstrips that Gathung vessel and gives us time to..."

"I don't need a thesis on the subject!" Windrow snapped. "Will our engines hold out?"

"For another few minutes, yes. After that, we will be dead in space."

Windrow closed her eyes for a second before replying, "Make sure we aren't dead in space then!"

The officer nodded. *The Manchester* made a good enough distance from the pursuing Gathung ship when the tactical officer ended the surge. He gave a silent signal to Windrow, who turned at once toward the navigator.

"Navigator, how far until we are at an FTL point?"

"Ma'am, we can jump in...thirty seconds."

"Good. Get us to Xiphus."

As soon as the FTL drive engaged, Windrow left the bridge. Proud of her crew, she often wondered just how they came up with the little schemes that always saved their necks.

"I need a drink," she said to no one in particular as she made her way down the corridor. "Smuggling ain't what it used to be."

Earth – The Present

Cormac Gallagher strolled purposefully into the spacious outer office of the Secretary General in the United Nations Headquarters in London. An aide briefed him via comm link as he made his way from his flat overlooking Hyde Park, near Kensington Palace. It amused Gallagher that his home had a lovely view of the park and the nearby palace, while his office in the United Nations building had a view of not only the Thames, but also the Tower of London. Not much of a tourist, even he understood the references.

"You can live in luxury, but don't get too comfortable," he said aloud.

In his ear, the aide said, "Sir?"

Gallagher laughed. He had practically forgotten about talking on his comm. Despite that morning's news and his splitting head, he was in a generally good mood. "Nothing Shelly," he said as he entered his own office and noticed the packed room.

General Agda and several cabinet ministers, including the Minister of Intelligence, waited in his office. "Uh-oh," said Gallagher as he entered. "Who died?"

Startled, General Agda responded in her usual strait-laced manner, "Secretary General? As of this moment, we've not received reports of..."

"Joking, General," laughed Gallagher. "I'm joking. Just trying to lighten the mood."

The general did not seem overly amused at Gallagher's response, but she chose to overlook it.

"You all look like this is a state funeral." When no one replied, he shrugged his shoulders. "What's the status?" Gallagher asked the room at large. After spending years in the bureaucracy of Earth, he still always forgot no one really appreciated his sense of humor.

Intelligence Minister Hirota Renzo, a member of the Japanese parliamentary delegation to the United Nations, replied. "Secretary General, our orbital cloaking platform experienced a devastating malfunction that virtually destroyed the entire array. At this time, we cannot ascertain the cause, and damage reports are still being filed."

"Minister Renzo, I grasped that after I got out of the shower," said Gallagher. He ignored the look on the face of General Agda who earlier that morning directly observed him in nothing but a towel. "Can someone tell me something I *don't* know?"

Gallagher searched the faces of the room. When no one volunteered anything, he sat down behind his desk and waved them away. "All of you must have more important stuff to do." When no one moved to leave, he followed up by saying, "Let me know when you have something more." Gallagher dismissed the advisors with another wave. This time they seemed to have gotten the hint. As the room cleared, he groaned. His headache had not improved. He closed his eyes and held his head for a moment, and then punched a button on his desk, "can someone *please* get me some aspirin. And a coke?" He sighed and tried to focus on the ever growing pile of communications waiting for him.

Cathar Prime – The Present

A SHUDDER OF FEAR AND EXCITEMENT RAN through Negotiator Brik Zat'ol as the Umawei Emissary entered. Zat'ol once read accounts of previous D'lai who encountered this dark race of beings and despite the stories, he felt determined to make use of this new opportunity.

Almost three years ago, Zat'ol had been reading ancient D'lai records from the time of the *Vdo Zämi*, or Great Exile. The ancient D'lai leader Am'oll kept meticulous records which still survived despite the numerous catastrophes that struck his people in the ensuing centuries. Zat'ol stumbled upon an obscure reference to the Umawei Empire and an encounter with one of the ancient relics in a star system near Cathar Prime called Ryi Bruai. Close to the size of a small moon, the relic appeared dormant. However, as soon as the rickety space craft the D'lai were forced to flee in approached, the relic burst into life, emanating blue light and rotating rapidly.

D'lai scientists soon realized this object mimicked a pulsar a thousand light years distant. This discovery led the D'lai to more closely inspect the dozens of other massive constructs in Ryi Bruai. They realized the constructs replicated a solar system sized map of the galaxy. The thrilling discovery led them to a depository of what appeared to be an ancient library full of golden and rune-covered cylindrical disks. As the D'lai could not decipher them, they stored the disks aboard one of their ships, mapped the relics in the Ryi Bruai system, and continued their search for a habitable planet.

The Umawei Disks had not been decoded for roughly seven hundred years when a young D'lai researcher discovered the equivalent of a Rosetta Stone hidden among the runes on the disks. It took a further ninety years to fully uncover the mysteries they contained, and the immense knowledge they hid enabled the D'lai to massively advance their own civilization.

Perhaps the most consequential discovery made by the D'lai as they read and cataloged the vast knowledge, was the understanding of how the Umawei seeded hundreds of habitable planets throughout this region of the galaxy. The D'lai made dozens of attempts to contact the ancient race to no avail. Something was missing, and they could not quite figure out what. They could not have realized that the Umawei had been observing the D'lai and the Cathari for hundreds of years. As time went on without contact, conquest and galactic politics soon encompassed the D'lai imagination, and they relegated the disks to the history books. The disks were miraculously safe among the artifacts rescued when the D'lai sun exploded. Negotiator D'iash sidelined further study of the disks as she planned her conquest of The Three Worlds. Nevertheless, the secret cabal of commanders within the ranks of the D'lai Authority maintained their interest, and their study eventually fell to Zat'ol.

Zat'ol rose from his chair as the Emissary approached. Clad from head to toes in black robes, the Emissary's face, covered with an elaborate gold mask, betrayed no hint of the features beneath it. Zat'ol couldn't even be sure of the gender of his visitor.

"*Däz jdiä,*" greeted Zat'ol.

The Emissary came nearer, dipped its head in what resembled a nod, and then stood upright once more. It startled Zat'ol when the voice of the Emissary echoed not in his ears, but in his mind, *"Däz jdiä,"*

"You are telepathic, I did not expect this," Zat'ol said, slightly flustered.

"Yes, we abandoned physical form millennia ago. We wrap ourselves in these garments only as a courtesy."

Zat'ol motioned to a nearby seat. In response, the Emissary shook its head in denial. *"We do not require physical comfort,"* it said, *"why have you summoned us?"*

Surprised by the directness of the visiting alien, the D'lai leader got to the point. "Emissary, my people wish to learn more about this." Zat'ol opened an ornate wooden box and revealed an intricately carved silver orb inside it. The Emissary didn't appear to react.

"The Seed," the Emissary mind-whispered. *"A dangerous object."*

Zat'ol sat back and pondered. In the studies of the Umawei Disks, thousands of references to a seed were found among the tomes. "Why is this dangerous? Our scientists have studied it for…"

"Centuries?" Interrupted the Emissary. *"We have wielded The Seed for untold ages. You have no compre-*

hension in your infantile minds what this small cylinder contains."

The D'lai Negotiator studied the runes covering the surface of the small object and smiled. "No, but we wish for you to teach us."

"Be careful what you wish for. You may regret this moment."

Zat'ol smiled smugly. "I'll live with the possibility. Teach me."

The Emissary nodded once more. "As you wish, Negotiator."

Cathar Prime – The Ancient Past

IN THE DAYS AFTER THE RESCUE OF AM'OLL, events on Cathar Prime proceeded with stunning rapidity. Already, regional governors and Däk'in spiritual leaders were advocating for the eradication of the entire D'lai movement. Am'oll and his advisors hid themselves in naturally carved out living spaces beneath the Gray Mountains, a dozen kilometers from the capital city.

"We must respond to this *küad*," shouted Ryäi, a leading D'lai mystic and Am'oll's younger brother.

"Careful Ryäi," said Am'oll, "we must approach the Däk'in with patience, otherwise in their rush to judgment they may well destroy us."

"Nonsense," said Ryäi, "these *keṭ* do not frighten me."

"They may not frighten you, but they far outnumber us. We cannot risk..."

"Risk?" Suha interrupted the two men. "We cannot risk? Risk what? Our children? Our own safety?"

"Suha, you must calm yourself. We have to approach this carefully. I will not endanger our community unless it is necessary."

Suha snorted and left the room. Am'oll and Ryäi regarded her as she left, and then continued their argument.

An aide approached the two men as they talked. Am'oll looked up, annoyed, then froze at the expression on her young face.

"Am'oll, it's happening."

Am'oll and Ryäi looked at each other and jumped to their feet. Already, the sound of distant loud engines could be perceived approaching their hiding spot in these shallow caves. Am'oll realized this temporary hideout would not protect them for long, but he hoped to have formulated a long term strategy before the Däk'in found them.

As quickly as possible, the small band of D'lai outcasts rushed into sizable air transports and evacuated. Mere moments after they escaped the caves, explosions could be heard in the distance as the attacking Däk'in destroyed their hidden outpost. Am'oll directed the pilots of the aircraft to fly far out into The Voiceless Wasteland bordering the Gray Mountains. He ardently hoped his pursuers would not follow. Everyone on board the transport grabbed their prayer beads and chanted as Ryäi led them in a D'lai prayer for safety.

An hour after escaping the attacking Däk'in, the small group of air transports landed on an almost unnoticeable landing pad above another hidden system of caves the D'lai only recently discovered. The caverns here in the middle of The Voiceless Wasteland, far enough away from inhabited cities and towns, gave the D'lai no fear of detection. The only problem, they were so remote, Am'oll and his people could not keep track of the developments elsewhere on the planet. They were too far from civilization, and completely cut-off. Am'oll would have to trust that his own people would relay the news to him in a timely fashion.

After a few hours of rest and refreshment, Am'oll, Suha, and Ryäi inspected the major reason why the D'lai kept this base so far from prying eyes. Hidden in an enormous natural cavern sat a huge space craft abandoned by the Cathari Navy decades ago. Am'oll and his followers transported the vessel piece by piece from a nearby ship graveyard, and reassembled the vast craft inside this cavern.

The D'lai recognized that if matters grew worse, they may have to leave Cathar Prime to ensure the survival of their faith. The Däk'in were growing far too strong, and vastly outnumbered the D'lai.

It impressed Am'oll that his people were able to work so efficiently in reassembling this space craft. Walking inside the short corridors and cramped rooms onboard, he grimaced at the realization that this vehicle and half a dozen others like it scattered around the planet might one day be the only refuge of his small following. He vowed to himself to redouble his efforts. The D'lai did not believe in peace, but they did believe in co-existence with those less enlightened than themselves. They considered the Däk'in to be relative savages. However, if they hoped to co-exist, they needed to find a middle ground. Am'oll hoped he could find it before events fell out of his hands entirely.

He had no idea that it was too late.

CHAPTER 3

Near Cathar Prime – Present

Captain Zea Windrow attempted to get a little sleep when her comm unit chimed. Windrow groaned and turned over in her cramped bunk. Life aboard a smuggling ship could often be adventurous but not overly glamorous. The size of her quarters proved that.

She slapped the indicator button to silence the alarm and activated the comm.

"This better be good," said Windrow, "I was having a steamy dream involving a..."

"Captain, apologies for the intrusion," the tactical

officer said, "we've encountered...um...something... I think you need to see it."

Windrow checked the control panel on her desk console. "John, we are nowhere near Xiphus, I have a few more hours of sleep!"

"Captain, I really think you need to see this," said the officer once more. "It's um...well... um...enormous."

"Fine. I'm on my way." She slapped the comm unit shut and rose from the bunk. After a moment of stretching and shaking her head to clear the sleep cobwebs, she left the tiny room.

Windrow arrived at the bridge and grew alarmed at the state of near panic. She quietly scanned the room, planning which obnoxious crew member she would address first, when her gaze fell on the viewer.

"My god...what the hell is that?" Windrow said.

Turning toward the sound of her voice, the tactical officer replied, "Ma'am, that's just it. We don't know what it is. Sensors read it as a massive moon or small planet but so far out in open space that didn't seem possible," continued the officer, "after further analysis we've determined it is a space craft of some kind, but we cannot determine the origin of it."

Windrow sat in her command chair and pulled up

the data gathered so far. "That...*ship*...is almost five thousand times more extensive than *The Manchester*?"

The Manchester is considered small by most space faring civilizations standards. At eight thousand feet from stem to stern, the ship has eight decks and can accommodate a crew of one hundred.

Turning toward the captain, the navigator said, "That's not all, Captain. Sensors indicate it has almost no mass whatsoever."

"No mass, how is that even..."

Proximity alarms began blaring on the deck. Flinching, Windrow slammed her fist down on a control to silence them.

"Captain, we are picking up a D'lai vessel heading straight toward us."

Windrow shot out of her chair. "Cloak! Now!"

After receiving confirmation of successful cloaking, the tactical officer said, "Ma'am, we weren't detected. The D'lai vessel is not coming for us. It is going toward...*that*."

Several crew members were reacting with alarm at the sudden appearance of a D'lai ship. Windrow ordered the bridge crew to calm down, and gather as much information as they could.

"Why is a D'lai ship out here," she mused aloud. Windrow didn't expect a reply from her crew.

Several tense minutes passed as each crew member scanned their own workstations. Windrow passed the time by reading over sensor logs of the enormous alien *thing* that had drawn her from sleep. She found it incredible that such an enormous object possessed no discernible mass. The computer data would have seemed incomplete if not for Windrow staring at the object herself. A scientific officer interrupted her thoughts with an update.

"Ma'am, we cannot detect any recognizable compounds and the configuration matches no known ship configurations in our databanks."

"So, we don't know anything about this object?"

"Not quite, we do know a few things. For example," the science officer paused as he changed the view on the screen, "the object is both transparent and mutable." Windrow studied the screen. "In fact, I am gonna go out on a limb and theorize that the object is a projection."

"You mean it's not real?" Windrow asked.

"Oh no, it is real," said the science officer, "it seems to displace nearby gaseous matter, for the most part."

Windrow shook her head in confusion. She observed as the D'lai ship circled the object. "What is the D'lai ship doing? It looks like the thing is in *orbit*."

The science officer studied his pad. "Yes, it's orbiting for certain."

The crew stared as two more D'lai ships appeared and entered into orbit.

"What in the hell are we witnessing?"

The crew could only speculate. After an hour of the three ships orbiting the enormous projection, all three left and the object shimmered and vanished.

"Okay," said Windrow, "I'm officially spooked."

The crew nodded in agreement. They had no idea they had just witnessed the beginning of a new D'lai threat that threatened to sweep across the galaxy like a tidal wave.

Earth – The Present

AFTER GALLAGHER HAD TIME TO CLEAR HIS DESK, drink his coke and swallow a few aspirins, he felt ready to tackle the growing crisis in orbit. Pressing a button on his desk, he alerted his aide to recall his advisors. Surely by now they would have found sufficient time to gather intelligence that was useful.

Moments later, Chief of Operations General Agda entered the office with Minister Renzo. Gallagher grunted when he noticed General Agda looked just as stern now as she had a few hours earlier.

"General, Minister, what's the word?"

General Agda appeared to be slightly put off by Gallagher's informal tone. "Secretary General, we have evaluated further reports and have a status update."

Gallagher started to roll his eyes but stopped himself. "Be professional Gallagher," he muttered under his breath. "Continue, General," he said.

"Yes. Reports indicate there was no loss of life. All personnel are accounted for. Only minor injuries were sustained." General Agda said.

"We believe the cause of the explosion was a result of outside interference," said Minister Renzo. "We've not yet determined who or what caused it, but all systems were functioning normally when the incident occurred."

Gallagher nodded, puzzled. "If you had to venture a guess, you'd say..."

"Sir, I believe this was an act of sabotage."

"What is the status of our ability to cloak?"

General Agda replied, "On my orders we reinserted into orbit our cloaking satellite and it has been re-engaged."

Gallagher nodded. "Good. Now, let's get to the bottom of this sabotage as you call it Minister. We need to know who we are dealing with."

Minister Renzo nodded and turned to go.

"Minister, this isn't the D'lai, is it?"

Renzo stopped abruptly before responding. "Unknown sir. We've not received any reports of activity from the vicinity of Cathar Prime in..." Renzo checked his pad. "No reports in six months. The D'lai appear to be quiet."

"Thank you Minister. Keep me up to date."

Renzo nodded and left. Gallagher turned to General Agda. "Do you buy that?"

Agda sighed and indicated a chair in front of the desk. Gallagher nodded and she gratefully sank into it. "Sir, I don't buy anything the Intelligence Minister says. He is always trying to protect his own flanks."

Gallagher stared at the General for a long, uncomfortable moment before responding. "Me either. Something doesn't seem right."

"Yes, sir," said the General. "With your permission, I'd like to dig into it a little."

"You have it, General." Agda started to rise. "Oh, and General, about this morning..."

"Forgotten, sir." As she turned away, Gallagher could have sworn she winked at him.

Pleased with himself, Gallagher muttered, "Damn, I've still got it." He smiled as he got back to work.

Earth Orbit – The Present

COREY HODGES WAS MAD. HE HAD SPENT THE better part of six months building this orbital cloaking platform only to see it blow up in his face. He furiously reviewed any available data on the accident. No, not accident. Hodges refused to believe it was an accident. He was careful. His superiors and even his subordinates often groaned under the weight of his caution. Hodges liked his checklists, and he did not mind showing it.

Earlier today Hodges was reviewing logs from the previous days work when the ship he was in rocked violently. The blast from the orbital platform threatened to overwhelm the artificial gravity and stabilizers of the small ship. He immediately jumped to his feet and ran to a nearby window in time to see most of the orbital platform disintegrating with pieces flying in all directions from the force of the blast.

"What in the holy hell was that!" Hodges exclaimed as he ran from his small working office to the main deck of the ship. Another violent explosion rocked the ship and threw Hodges and other crew members off their feet. As the ship stabilized, Hodges stood and busily began reviewing the data streaming onto his pad.

"Let's find out if everyone is accounted for," said Hodges, "and someone report our status to Earth Command."

The few engineers and crewman onboard the vessel busied themselves. Hodges sat at a work station and reviewed more of the data. He was notified of an incoming message from Earth, so he opened the comm channel.

"Hodges here."

"Hodges, status report. What happened?"

"Colonel, we are trying to figure that out right now. Two gigantic explosions rocked the orbital platform. Visual inspection indicates most of the facility is gone."

"Are there survivors Hodges?"

"Um...one moment." Hodges muted the channel and asked a nearby crew member. After a moment, he returned to the channel. "Yes, we can account for the whereabouts of..."

"You're still muted," the Colonel said in mild annoyance.

Hodges laughed and unmuted the channel. "Sorry about that Colonel. You'd think by now I'd know how to use the..."

"Survivors, *Engineer*?" The colonel was not in the mood for levity.

"Right." Hodges looked down at a new status report that appeared on his pad. "We've accounted for all personnel. No one was on the facility when it blew apart."

"Update your status in one hour. I have to report this to General Agda."

Hodges nodded and closed the channel.

"Still muted...that's kinda funny." Hodges got back to work.

Cathar Prime – The Ancient Past

THINGS WERE GETTING MORE DANGEROUS ON Cathar Prime with each passing day. Am'oll received numerous detailed reports from his followers of the rising tensions. Dozens of D'lai faithful had been massacred in the past three days. Am'oll let it be broadcast to anyone who could receive his message that it was time to bring the fight to the Däk'in. The D'lai were done hiding in the shadows.

"I must caution you, however, follow the *Chäi kia Chlüi*. We will prevail but must not be like the Däk'in and abandon our faith." Am'oll said in his message to the faithful.

The *Chäi kia Chlüi* was the religious text passed down from long before the *Vdo Däk* corrupted the Cathari religion with his teaching of pacifism and neutrality. The *Chäi* instructed true believers on how to interact with the *flaibrawch,* or heretics of the true faith as the D'lai believe any outsider to be. All D'lai were taught that their primary interaction with heretics should be to ignore them. If a non-believer attempted harm on a member of the D'lai faithful, the *Chäi* taught that it was perfectly acceptable to seriously injure or even kill, to ensure self-preservation.

Despite this, Am'oll wanted to make absolutely sure that his followers only harmed another Cathari if it was truly necessary. If force was warranted, however, it should be delivered without mercy. That was the D'lai way.

The Däk'in professed peace above all, so this form of ritual murder by the D'lai should in theory not be required. Am'oll knew, however, that the Däk'in had abandoned their principles and blood would flow in the streets. The D'lai were ready and fully capable of defending themselves.

Over the course of the ensuing two weeks, the D'lai emerged from the shadows and took what they believed was theirs by divine right. They ritually murdered any Cathari who dared to oppose them. The bloodshed did not escape the notice of planetary leaders who, in a stunning act, outlawed the D'lai faith, and ordered that anyone who professed to believe, or follow Am'oll, would be held without trial until the peace of the planet was restored.

Am'oll raged against this edict. He had come to realize the time was now to strike. Over the course of the past dozen years, Am'oll and his close group of adherents had gathered munitions, air transports, and other assorted weapons. They would strike at the heart of Cathar Prime, in a bold attempt to assassinate the planetary leadership. Hours before the attack was to be launched, Am'oll received an anonymous report that he had been betrayed. He instantly knew who had turned him in – Suha, his wife.

Suha had been enraged that Am'oll had not spent more of his time in attempting to find, and rescue their daughter. Am'oll had tried to assure her that he was doing all that he could do, but from his hideout in the Voiceless Wasteland, it was proving difficult. Suha, reckless as ever, left the safety of the caves, and ventured on her own into the larger cities to find their child. She had never been the most devout D'lai congregant, and she presumed she would be safe, as long as she pretended to be a Däk'in. She was wrong.

Suha had only been in the Capitol for less than a day when, out of long habit, she greeted another D'lai faithful she happened upon, with the usual hand gestures. A local police officer marked the exchange, and arrested both women. Suha was not suited for torture, and with little duress gave up the location of Am'oll, and as much of the plan for the uprising as she had been privy to. The authorities, now on the alert, hastily put together an imposing strike force to take Am'oll and his followers by surprise. As for Suha, she was executed by burning the moment she was no longer of any use to the planetary leadership. Her last thoughts before the flames took her were of her small daughter and her utter despair that she would never see her again. The D'lai believed that only the faithful were granted an after life. Suha had denied the faith, and she would now be lost to the darkness forever.

Cathar Prime – The Present

NEGOTIATOR ZAT'OL SLUMPED IN HIS SEAT THE moment the Umawei Emissary left his ornate office. Their meeting lasted for several hours and even though Zat'ol found the answers to many of his questions on the origins of the Umawei and their admittedly dangerous seeding technology, he was glad the Emissary was gone for the moment.

Zat'ol fingered his prayer beads under his desk, attempting to calm his roiling mind. The Emissary was a frightening being, and communicating telepathically gave him an enormous headache. In numerous instances, the Emissary had been disappointed at the pace of their discussions. The D'lai mind was not built for mass amounts of data and conversation sent directly to the mind.

"*Communicating in this fashion is tedious,*" the Emissary had mind-whispered at least a dozen times as it tried to convey complex concepts with pictures instead of words. Try as he might, Zat'ol simply couldn't absorb it.

The matter had nominally been resolved when the Emissary had agreed to transfer the requisite knowledge to an experimental D'lai invention that imitated a living mind. In almost every conceivable way, the device the D'lai called the *awch jdiv*, or fake mind, was the closest their scientists had ever come to developing artificial intelligence so complex, the AI mind believed itself to be real and not a construct.

The Emissary had thankfully stopped flooding Zat'ol's mind, and instead focused its malevolent attention on the *awch jdiv*. Freed from the burden, albeit temporarily, Zat'ol ordered three D'lai corvettes to intercept, as instructed, the Umawei vessel in space on the outer fringes of the Cathar system. Unfortunately, that mission had not gone as planned.

An hour after the corvettes left orbit of Cathar Prime, he received a communication from one of the ship commanders.

"Negotiator, the Umawei vessel is not alone in open space. We have detected a ship of human design traveling in a nearby space lane."

"Were you detected, Commander," asked the Negotiator.

"Unknown sir. We believe the ship left the area, but it is likely they were investigating the Umawei ship."

"Acknowledged. Continue with your orders. I will notify the Emissary."

Zat'ol did not want to tell the Emissary that their secret rendezvous may have been seen by humans or some other alien. As it turned out, he didn't have to. Moments after disconnecting the communication with his commander, the Emissary mind-whispered, "*We are cognizant of the human ship. It is of no consequence.*"

The mind-whisper made Zat'ol want to scratch the back of his neck, but there was nothing there causing an itch. He shuddered and tried to return his attention back to the task at hand. The Emissary had instructed him to send three ships to their nearby vessel, and enter orbit around it. Zat'ol had been stunned at first. The vessel must be enormous that any ship could orbit it. He didn't know why the

Umawei wanted his ships to visit, but he also wanted that technology, so he was willing to do anything it requested.

In fact, Zat'ol had little understanding of The Seed technology at all. From his mind-conversations with the Emissary, he had gathered that the technology could both give life and take it away. This intrigued the Negotiator and made him almost giddy.

"*We can share that with this power, its possessor may either grant life to a dead planet, or take life from a living planet.*"

"You would share this with us? Why"

"*We share with whom we chose. Had we not found you worthy, you would have learned of The Seed...in a less than desirable...form.*"

Zat'ol shivered at the implications. His reading of the Umawei Disks had recounted in mind-numbing detail an account of The Seed being used on a desolate planet. The description enthralled him and forced him to search harder for a way to contact these almost god-like aliens.

He stumbled upon an obscure reference that had been cataloged incorrectly by a long dead researcher that indicated that the placement of the enormous constructs in Ryi Bruai were a star chart, and it was theorized that the map pointed to the homeworld of the mysterious Umawei Empire. Zat'ol was not an astronomer, so he delegated the follow-up to a trusted friend who had also been aboard *The Spector* when D'iash had met her *almost* untimely end.

Politics and other affairs had distracted Zat'ol, and it was a year before he heard from his friend and was given a location, based on the artifacts, of where the Umawei may have originated. The answer stunned Zat'ol and shook him to his core. From all apparent indications, the Umawei Empire originated on a small rusty planet in the Sol System. The empire that had seeded life throughout the galaxy, originated on Mars.

CHAPTER 4

Earth – The Present

General Agda sat alone in her overstuffed office three floors below the office of the Secretary General, and fretted. She liked Gallagher on a personal level. He was charming, funny as hell, and great in a crowd. All those charms could not outweigh her concern. Gallagher was not well suited to the life of a diplomat, and he most assuredly was not cut out to be the leader of the planet and the titular head of the Three Worlds Alliance.

Gallagher was a hero of some renown for his

efforts, along with Corey Hodges, in saving Earth from the D'lai invasion. His rise through the ranks took many years, but he relied on his brand to get him where he wanted to go. Agda wasn't certain Gallagher even *wanted* to be the Secretary General at all.

Nevertheless, he *was* the leader, and she had some unsettling news she was not one hundred percent sure how she was going to tell him. Her office had been monitoring the situation in orbit and grew more alarmed as time went on with regard to the explosion of the orbital platform. There existed no discerned threats against Earth at the time, and so all indications pointed to the incident being a terrorist event.

More troubling than any of that, however, was the terrorists who Agda believed were responsible were human. Over the past decade, a small but vocal minority of humans began loudly wondering why Earth needed a cloak. There was no threat from space, and the existence of the cloak complicated some rather ordinary and routine parts of planetary life.

For one, communications off-world were difficult. Despite streamlining of the harmonics the cloaking field emitted, it was still necessary to filter certain communication bands, and most of the time, those that were filtered were civilian channels. The Sol System was not a single planetary system. Humans lived on three planets in the system. Of course, classifying Titan as a planet was a stretch, but to most humans, it was a mere technicality.

Traveling off world was also a bit more labor intensive with a cloak in place. A ship could not "see" the planet, so it had to rely on complex coded communications to guide it into orbit. Those codes often changed, so a pilot or starship commander who was not paying attention could quite literally lose the planet.

Over the past several years, this small group of annoyed humans began to organize. Intelligence agencies now classified the group as a domestic terrorist organization. The group, calling itself Humans for Clear Horizons, rallied and protested at almost every government sponsored event. The HCH sent threatening messages to politicians who voted against its expressed manifesto, and even managed to get a small delegation elected to the planetary parliament in the last election cycle.

None of this would have made Agda feel anymore annoyed than if a fly was buzzing around her dinner. What worried the General was a recent revelation the HCH acquired craft capable of entering orbit of the planet. Intelligence Minister Renzo intimated in a recent briefing, the government should expect orbital trouble from the group in the near future.

General Agda, never one to keep her superiors in the dark, decided she had to let the Secretary General in on the news. It would do more harm than good if it turned out the HCH was responsible, and Agda had not informed the civilian government. She punched an icon on her console, and informed Gallagher's aide she wished to speak with him.

A moment later, the face of Cormac Gallagher appeared on her comm.

"General, to what do I owe the pleasure?"

"Mr. Secretary General, recent reports have indicated the explosion on the orbital platform may have been caused by a domestic terrorist group called the Humans for Clear Horizons."

Gallagher seemed to ponder this for a moment before asking, "Do we have evidence of this General?"

Agda was pleased at his response and lack of

humorous interjection. "We don't have a specific piece of convincing evidence. What we do have is all anecdotal and..."

"Excuse me General, have we *suspended* citizen rights?"

"Pardon, sir?"

"I mean, have we suspended the constitution, and we now accuse citizens of crimes without evidence?"

"No, sir. We have not suspended..."

"Okay, great. I just wanted to make sure." Gallagher said.

Flustered, General Agda continued, "What we do have, sir, is reliable anecdotal evidence that indicates..."

"Yeah, I heard you say that," said Gallagher. "Listen, I know you are probably right, but we don't need to stoke the flames any higher with accusations we can't *prove*."

Agda sighed. He was right, of course. "Dammit."

"What was that General?"

Annoyed she cursed out loud, Agda replied, "Dammit, sir. I know what you are saying. I'll dig deeper."

"Do that, General."

As Agda moved to end the communication, Gallagher said, "Oh, and General?"

"Yes, sir?"

"Good job. Let's prove it, and then we'll act."

General Agda smiled as she ended the communication. "Okay, maybe I was wrong about him." She went back to work, determined more than ever to prove her allegations.

"Let's flush you out."

Mars – The Present

WHEN HUMANITY FIRST BEGAN COLONIZING Mars and Titan, it had not yet discovered definitive presence of alien civilizations. Much of the buzz around aliens centered on scant videos captured by fighter pilots, crop circles, and the like. Even though aliens had surreptitiously been visiting for centuries, humans were for the most part blissfully unaware of it.

The first humans on Mars were more worried about setting up their habitats than they were about investigating possible signs of previous alien life.

Earth had for decades sent on and off world vehicles to investigate the Red Planet, and so far, turned up no conclusive evidence either way. There were of course the occasional anomaly that some conspiracy theorist or another would latch on to, but planetary authorities worked hard to tamp down any kind of invasive investigations.

Unfortunately for most inhabitants of Earth, their governments lied to them so regularly they had no idea at all what the truth was. The reality was that NASA and the European Space Agency discovered numerous sites on Mars that were, at the least, suspicious. One site in particular, near the largest mountain in the solar system, Olympus Mons, scared NASA so thoroughly they hid the truth from most of the men and women who would later colonize the planet.

One of the Martian Rovers had been dispatched to investigate the possibility of usable minerals near Olympus Mons. It seemed like an incredibly remote chance of finding a mineral deposit so far from the polar caps of the planet. However, an orbital satellite detected something strange, and so NASA did what it did best – it investigated the anomaly. What it found was so unsettling that an entire division of NASA was created by order of the President of the United States, tasked with sending direct human observers to Mars as soon as possible. The discovery was the major driving force that accelerated human colonization of not only Mars, but also of Titan. Among the first colonists to arrive at Mars, a team of them were tasked with the investigation.

The Martian rover, and later the human colonizers, soon confirmed what NASA inadvertently discovered. Buried under feet of dusty Martian soil was a cylindrical object made of a type of metal that Earth had never seen, and was most definitely *not* native to Mars. The cylinder was quietly excavated, and sent to Earth during a routine re-supply mission for the growing Martian colony.

Events on Earth soon overtook the discovery by NASA. Six months after the re-supply mission returned to Earth, war broke out planet-wide and most funding was diverted to the war effort. While most of NASA forgot about the odd cylinder, a handful of scientists became aware of its existence and routinely conducted unauthorized study of it. Among the scientists studying the canister was Josh Burke, a high-level astrophysicist. Burke would often tell made-up stories to his children of Martians and secret space craft. As Burke studied the object in more depth, he began to pepper his stories with small amounts of truth, to give what he believed to be more realism. He never imagined any of his children believed him. After all, everyone knew there was no life on Mars. However, Joseph Burke, his youngest son, did believe his father, and took at face value all the stories he was told.

The stories Burke told his children would grow into legend in his family, and over time, Joseph Burke began to create fanciful theories which evolved into full-blown conspiracies. Later in life, and years after the Cathari revealed themselves, Joseph Burke would help to found an organization protesting the use of Earth's planetary cloaking technology. The organization soon snowballed into a full-blown coalition of like-minded conspiracy theorists, called Humans for Clear Horizons.

Cathar Prime – The Present

A D'LAI SCIENTIST CALLED BRUILUS BUSILY studied the *awch jdiv* once the Emissary indicated it was finished dispensing the knowledge of the Umawei Empire. The vast amount of data that had been transferred to the fake mind device was overwhelming. Zat'ol pondered the implications of the data dump, and he wondered why the Umawei would be so willing to share their ancient knowledge with the D'lai. He assumed that much like his own race, they had hidden motives. It bothered Zat'ol, but he was willing to accept whatever the cost would be.

"Negotiator, it could take us decades to decipher all this," complained a dour Bruilus.

"Nonsense," declared Zat'ol. "The data is no doubt cataloged in some form. We need only work through those portions that are relevant to our current plans."

In the decades since the fall of the D'lai Authority, and their self-imposed exile on Cathar Prime, The Negotiator and his predecessors made extensive plans for their eventual return to galactic dominance. The D'lai were excellent long-term thinkers. It was this same ability that also proved to be their downfall in the disastrous battles against the Three Worlds. Zat'ol chose to ignore the past failures of D'lai Authority leadership, and focus instead on his future plans. He desperately wanted to use The Seed technology from the Umawei to avenge his people. He had to know how it worked and what would happen if he did use it against his enemies. The snail pace of discovery was maddening to him, and he fumed at his impotence.

For the Cathari, life was far worse than they could have ever imagined. The Cathari people that survived the massive planetary assault carried out by Ret D'iash were virtual slaves in the D'lai drive to rebuild its lost ships and technology. No Cathari could expect any civil liberties or mercy from their D'lai overlords. In fact, none were promised even their next breath. The D'lai were cruel task masters, and often without obvious cause, would violently strike out. As a result, the populace of Cathari was only a mere fraction of what it had been before the invasion.

To further spur on the massive D'lai push to rebuild, immense mining operations commenced on other planets, asteroids, and moons in the Cathar system. Cathar Prime itself was cannibalized of any useful scraps of metal and other mineral resources, leaving the native population to live in makeshift dwellings, near the ruined and once graceful cities.

With the access to vast ancient knowledge now granted to the D'lai by the Umawei, Zat'ol was more determined than ever to return to his civilization's former glory. The D'lai were on the rise, and nothing would stop Zat'ol and his minions.

"Negotiator, we need to know exactly what we are looking for if we ever hope to filter this data correctly," said Bruilus once more. "There is more information stored in the *awch jdiv* than in all the databanks we have, combined."

Zat'ol was impressed. The Emissary only spent three hours with the fake mind. He was also grateful, as that amount of data would have likely lobotomized living tissue. He sighed, and settled into a comfortable chair before addressing the scientist.

"Mmm...yes." Zat'ol gathered his thoughts for a moment. "What we need is all the available information on the Umawei seed devices. We must know how they are deployed, and the effects of using one on a living planet."

The scientist shuddered involuntarily but obeyed. Zat'ol was a hard master to please and many previous advisors and assistants had inexplicably vanished. He did not wish to be the latest victim of the Negotiator's ire.

"Very well, Negotiator. I will do what I can. I'll need..."

"You'll get me that information within twelve hours."

Bruilus gaped at the Negotiator, before remembering his place. "Yes, Negotiator."

Zat'ol relaxed back into the chair and allowed himself a moment of joy. Soon, very soon, the D'lai would rise.

En Route to Xiphus – The Present

THE CREW OF *THE MANCHESTER* PREPARED THEIR vessel for arrival at the planet Xiphus. The entire journey from the region of space nearest to Cathar Prime had been filled with rampant speculation about just what they witnessed.

Windrow was sitting with a few of her officers in the mess room, trying to scarf down a few morsels of food before they encountered the Rozk, and had to deliver their cargo.

Between mouthfuls, Window said, "That thing reminded me of a planet." Her second-in-command nodded. "It was certainly big enough. I mean, that thing eclipsed us in size!"

While *The Manchester* was on a mission, it was routine for the ships cooks to prepare only basic meals that met the minimum nutritional requirements of the various races on board. Today, however, was different. Windrow and her fellow crew members were pleased to find the cooks spent a little more time in food prep.

"Captain, it has been a day for sure," the head cook said as he handed her a plate filled with her favorite meal.

Windrow was pleasantly surprised that even out here, they could whip up some good old bangers and mash when the occasion called for it. The Captain heartily dug into the sausages, savoring their texture.

"My compliments to the chef!"

The cook smiled and returned to his duties. Other crew members were munching on delicacies of their own, including a particularly noxious meal being devoured by a nearby Gathung crew member. Windrow tried, without complete success, to ignore the sounds emanating from him.

"Now, we need to figure out what we saw, so we can... I don't know...report it to the proper authorities."

First Mate Theodor Kanner plopped down next

to Windrow. He was beaming with excitement as he tucked into his meal. "Where did cook get schnitzel?"

Windrow was far more interested in what her First Mate was enjoying than the foul *lyaw* fish on the Gathung's plate she was trying hard to ignore. Glancing at Kanner's plate, she commented, "I haven't had that since I was a young girl." All the smells and memories made her dizzy, and she shook her head to try to clear it. All this talk of food and other smelly alien delicacies was distracting her from what she needed to worry about. "I just can't fathom it. That thing looked like a planet."

Kanner slapped his head and shot to his feet, his half-eaten schnitzel forgotten. "Captain...my god... I remember what was bothering me!"

Alarmed, Windrow hurriedly followed the First Mate out of the mess room. "Kanner, wait up!"

Kanner slowed and turned to face the Captain. "Captain, that *projection*, you didn't recognize it?"

Windrow felt her insides go watery with sudden fear. "It did seem familiar but..."

"Captain...Zea...it was the spitting image of Mars."

The Captain swayed unsteadily as the implications hit her like a ton of bricks. "Mars...but...that could mean..." She dropped all pretense of calm and ran down the corridor to the bridge. First Mate Kanner grimaced and followed her.

Windrow burst on to the deck of the bridge out of breath. *The Manchester* was not an enormous ship, but running the length of it still was enough to push her athletic ability. "Navigator, stop the ship! Tactical, get me every piece of information we gathered on that encounter with the D'lai."

Both officers hurried to follow orders. Looking over her shoulder as she stared at her pad in disbelief, Kanner said, "Look at that...except for being transparent and covered in grid marks, I'd swear I was looking at Mars."

Windrow agreed. She turned to the communications officer and ordered him to contact Earth immediately. She then faced the navigator. "Cloak the ship again. Calculate a route back to the Sol System."

"Captain, what about the Rozk?"

"The Rozk be damned. If this is what I think it is, we have *much* bigger problems. Windrow hoped to god she was wrong.

"Please, let this be some kind of coincidence," she said under her breath as she waited for the connection to Earth." This far out, it would take some time.

"Navigator, engage."

The Manchester entered FTL and raced back to Earth. It would take at least a week. From the corner of the bridge, an unimposing crew member looked on and jotted a few notes in his pad. He had news to share, and he couldn't wait to give it to his handlers on Cathar Prime.

CHAPTER 5

Cathar Prime – The Ancient Past

Am'oll collapsed in grief when he received the news of Suha's brutal death. The fact of her betrayal did not lesson his pain. He understood that, as a mother, she did what she felt was necessary to protect the life and well-being of their daughter. Nevertheless, her betrayal stung, and it created enormous headaches for him. Now, facing the news of her torture and death, Am'oll was more determined than ever to make all Däk'in pay for this outrage with their blood.

Am'oll summoned his council, and upon their arrival in his chambers, he began. "Fellow D'lai. Long have we labored under the lie propagated by that snake, the *Vdo Däk*, and his idiotic followers." The D'lai advisors cheered these words. "The time is now! We must strike and remind the *chtuai,* the fools, who their gods are!" Am'oll shouted louder, and gesticulated wildly, as he worked toward his main point. "We must fulfill the *ëmshu chäi*!"

At these words, every D'lai fell quiet, stunned. In the close to five hundred years since the founding of the D'lai faith, no leader had yet implemented the most important and most secret of all oaths a D'lai must undertake upon attaining adulthood. The *ëmshu chäi*, or blood oath, was a promise so dire, any D'lai that broke it would be skinned alive in order to reclaim the blood that was stolen. In the history of the faith, only seven D'lai had suffered the *chleng uikir*.

Am'oll searched the faces of his followers, hunting for any sign of betrayal or fear. In their eyes he divined not only resolve, but something that both thrilled and frightened him. He saw, reflected in their own eyes, his own eternal hate.

After dismissing the council and delegating important tasks for the coming days, Am'oll grabbed his prayer beads and began the chant that would settle his mind and reinforce his resolve.

"Vdo chlüi, ḍoi fud riaẓ uisdaẓ. Jdaw riaẓ yuak flaibawṛ, vro ble riaẓ uisaṭ. Oh great god, to you I pray. Save me from the liar, and grant me victory."

After Am'oll rested for a few hours, he rose refreshed, and ready. As with every member of the D'lai faithful this morning, the first day of the Summer Solstice, he dressed in the traditional *sdawij* of his people. Together, each member present filed into the air transports that would deliver them as witnesses of their faith to the capital city of Cathar Prime. They traveled in formation along with three air bombers they had stolen from the Cathari military. The bombers were bristling with armaments and explosive devices that when dropped on the city, would rain death and destruction upon the infidels.

Am'oll ordered that the bombers would move in first, while the transports, filled with his followers waited in a holding pattern thirty miles from the city. Every D'lai that could be alerted had quietly left the area, and joined their fellow believers in whatever capacity they could. Every single follower understood their blood oath, and none of them wanted to suffer the agonizing death prescribed for blasphemy.

The first wave of bombers moved in on the capital, and delivered their devastating ordinance from three miles above ground level. In the first assault, a hundred thousand Cathari died. Most of them died as a result of the explosions, while many others died of secondary causes. The second wave delivered the most devastating blow of that day, and of all the days to come. The bomber dropped its payload and when it struck, it leveled an area of the city seven miles in diameter. Nothing survived. The enormous blast wave was visible, even from where Am'oll and his followers waited.

Smaller attacks were occurring all over Cathar Prime, though with much less destructive results. Ordinary Cathari had no warning and so did not fight back. Even the Cathari government, alerted to an imminent battle, were ill prepared to deal with the devastating onslaught of D'lai rage. The planetary leaders possessed no idea just how angry their D'lai constituents were. They simply could not comprehend that five hundred years of oppression and intolerance would result in the sheer loss of life now unfolding planet-wide.

On that first day of the Däk'in-D'lai War, over a million Cathari died while hundreds of thousands of others were injured and maimed. The D'lai had struck the first blow, but the Cathari military would not loiter long. They would strike back, and when they did, what would survive, was anyone's guess.

Earth – The Present

OF ALL THE DUTIES OF BEING THE SECRETARY General, none of them were more irksome to Gallagher than the long, *long*, briefing meetings he was subjected to on an almost weekly basis. While he didn't begrudge his staff, advisors, and military leaders their opportunity to fill him in on what he needed to know, he wished most of this talking could be done via email.

The Minister of Agriculture was just wrapping up her long diatribe on the effects of drought on planetary grain yield when Gallagher, suppressing a yawn, stood.

"Folks, I think now is a good time for a break." The gathered department heads and military leaders focused on Gallagher. Even though he *knew* that at least a few of them wanted to keep going, he could see a few smiles around the table.

"What do you think, forty-five minutes?"

Gallagher asked. He didn't expect a reply. There was one perk of being the guy in charge – people tended to let him have his own way.

The room emptied slowly as men and women gathered their pads or coffee cups and left. Gallagher was almost to the door when a hand was placed on his shoulder. Groaning at his near escape, he turned and was confronted by the attractive face of Margit Wold, the Minister of Transportation. Gallagher smiled. Another thing about being the leader of Earth that bedeviled him was the lack of opportunity to date. He was just so damned busy.

"Secretary General," began Minister Wold in her thick Norwegian accent, "a moment of your time sir?"

"Absolutely Margit...um... Minister."

The Minister smiled, the skin around her blue eyes crinkling a little, "Margit is fine, sir."

Gallagher was incredibly tempted to let her call him by his first name, but he sensed a few judgmental pairs of eyes on him, so he restrained himself. "Um... Margit, what can I do for you?"

Margit Wold motioned to a corner of the sizable conference room where no one was sitting. Gallagher and Minister Wold took seats opposite each other and

Gallagher had to consciously tell himself to stop smiling so much.

"God Gallagher, you're an idiot," he said under his breath.

Minister Wold pretended not to notice. She sat down gracefully, her long legs folding in front of her and did something that made Gallagher gulp hard in surprise. She reached up and released a polished wooden hairpin and let her surprisingly long blonde hair out of her bun, letting it fall around her shoulders. Gallagher crossed his legs and pretended to be oblivious.

"Is she...flirting with me," he said to himself. "Oh boy."

"I am sorry sir, but my hair was a little too tight and it was uncomfortable."

Gallagher nodded, trying and failing to control his breathing, and motioned for her to continue.

"Anyway, sir, I wanted to talk to you about some crumbling infrastructure in Africa that I think we need to work on." Margit held his gaze for perhaps a moment too long, before looking down at his lap.

Gallagher smiled so widely, he just knew she must think of him as a clown. He couldn't help himself. It had been a long time since a beautiful woman had taken him aside for a chat and even longer since one was so openly making a move.

"God, snap out of it man!" Gallagher whispered out loud without realizing it.

"Sir?" Gallagher looked away, embarrassed.

"Oh, nothing, please continue."

Margit lifted her arm as if intending to look at her watch all the while keeping her eyes on his face. "Sir, perhaps we can continue this...over dinner? That meeting went so long and I'm starving." She uncrossed her legs and leaned forward in her chair.

Gallagher didn't need any more persuasion. He called over his aide to tell the rest of the group that they could reconvene in the morning.

"It's late, let's meet in the morning." Margit smiled as Gallagher stood a little awkwardly.

Still smiling like a school boy, Gallagher led Margit out of the conference room. As they walked, they decided to have dinner in a little French restaurant near Hyde Park. Gallagher was pleased at this development – the restaurant was conveniently close to his flat. The only problem was, as Secretary General of Earth, he had a security detachment protecting him at all times. As Gallagher and Margit approached his private air transport, he pulled aside the head of his detachment for a brief word.

"Say, what would happen if things got a little... um...personal...?"

The security chief chuckled, glanced in the direction of Margit Wold, and winked. "Sir, you would not be the first world leader I've protected to get a little action and need some discretion and privacy."

Gallagher pretended to be shocked, but he couldn't convince even himself. He was unsurprisingly excited.

"Well, uh...yeah..."

"Sir, no worries. My men and I have kept much bigger secrets. You won't even know we are there."

Gallagher relaxed a little and blushed as he peered back at Margit and caught her watching his little chat, so he climbed inside and sat next to her. He leaned in just a bit when she placed her small but warm hand on his thigh as the transport lifted off.

"This is going to be nice," he said as the air transport left the United Nations headquarters.

En Route to Earth – The Present

"CAPTAIN, I HAVE EARTH COMMAND ON THE comm."

Zea Windrow stared up from her pad. "Put it on please."

The crew members on the bridge pretended to be busy with their own tasks as the Captain began speaking with Earth.

"This is Earth Command, Lieutenant Sparks. How can I help you Captain?"

Windrow cleared her throat before speaking. "Yes, Lieutenant. This is Captain Zea Windrow of *The Manchester*." Windrow scrunched up her face. "Of course he knows that," she thought.

"Yes, Captain. Please continue." Lieutenant Sparks sounded a little annoyed at being interrupted from what must no doubt be super important Earth stuff.

"My ship is conducting business between Gathung'l and some trade partners," said Windrow. She didn't want to explain to this low-level flunky just what kind of business she was engaging in. "We encountered an...anomaly or something just outside the Cathar System."

Windrow paused for a moment, trying to gather her thoughts and best describe what it was they had all seen.

"Yes, Captain?" There was that annoyance again.

"Lieutenant, am I keeping you from something?" Windrow asked, exasperated.

"No, no Captain. Sorry."

A little soothed, Windrow continued. "Anyway, this *thing* we witnessed wasn't so much a ship as a projection of...well...a planet," she said. "And well... we also saw three D'lai ships...orbit it."

"D'lai? Are you sure?"

"Yes, we recognized their configuration from previous...encounters." Windrow wondered if anyone even remembered the role she and her ship played in the downfall of the D'lai Authority. It made her feel old to realize this young lieutenant was probably not even born yet when all that went down.

"Can you give me more information? What were they doing?"

"Well Lieutenant, that's the thing. We don't know *what* they were doing, but we do know one more important fact."

"And that is..." asked Lieutenant Sparks.

"Umm...well. The projection, it was the spitting image of Mars." Windrow flinched as she said it.

"Get all the available data to us as soon as possible. What is your current position?"

Windrow checked the navigation computer. "We are a week out from Earth and en route."

"Good. Get here as fast as you can. We need that data."

Without even any closing remarks, Earth Command closed the channel. Windrow looked over at her First Mate who was observing from a small workstation near the bulkhead.

"That was...terse."

"Yeah, I'm sure they didn't really want to hear the D'lai may be active again." Kanner smiled. "Of course, that bit about the Mars lookalike might have spooked him as well."

Windrow nodded as she picked up her pad once more. Kanner understood what needed to be done and no command from Windrow was required. They had spent years working together and knew each other well. Kanner got to work gathering all the data while Windrow continued her reading. She was curious if any of the library files reported anything like what they had seen out there. She was intrigued, and scared. For all she knew, Mars was in major trouble. She had no idea just how right she was.

Mars – The Present

LIFE ON MARS WAS NOT SO BAD, THOUGHT JAKE Davis, as he worked in his small bake shop. Jake had spent the past few years building up a booming bakery that supplied peckish tourists to the Great Dome. Tourism was a major source of revenue for the Martians ever since the planet was the site of the signing of the Three Worlds Alliance. Humans, Gathung, even Scree and other assorted races spent their hard-earned money in shops and business all around the Red Planet.

Jake was also something of a local legend. A year earlier, a prominent Gathung leader had ordered one of his cakes and almost choked on an almond. Not knowing all that much about Gathung biology, and perhaps a little foolhardy, Jake jumped over his counter and performed the Heimlich maneuver on the extraordinarily stunned leader. His entourage gasped in horror. Apparently Jake didn't know that you just didn't touch a Gathung and you certainly didn't grab him.

Nevertheless, the Gathung leader realized his life

had been in jeopardy and whatever it was that Jake had done, saved his life. He motioned his people to stand down as he turned, paler than was usual for a Gathung, and smiled. Jake had never seen a Gathung smile, and he sincerely hoped he'd never see it again. It wasn't a smile so much as it was a frightening grimace.

"You saved me young foolhardy human."

Jake tried to return what he hoped was a smile. "I only did what anyone else would do... I couldn't have an important person like you choke to death on my cooking!"

The Gathung leader laughed. That was another thing Jake hoped he'd never experience. The Gathung were not celebrated for their cheerfulness.

The Gathung left Jake's shop. It didn't take long for word to spread that a Martian baker had saved the life of the Fifth Dictator of Gathung'l. The Dictator was on Mars for an Alliance meeting, and wanted to explore the shops on the outskirts of the Great Dome.

After the encounter with the Gathung Dictator, Jake's business was so busy that for the first time he had to hire help.

"Life is good indeed!" Jake inspected his small domain with pride. He was half-way through writing up the menu for tomorrow when he heard screaming coming from the causeway outside his shop. Jake ran outside, panicked. People were running in all directions. Something serious was wrong and Jake feared the worst.

A loud klaxon began blaring as a female voice came over loudspeakers placed all around the causeway. "Citizens, find a safe location and go there at once. A crack has opened in the Dome. I repeat, find a safe, airtight location, and take cover. A crack has opened in the Dome."

Instinctively, Jake looked up. The Great Dome was vast, and he couldn't see any obvious problems with it. He recognized he couldn't ignore the call to action, so he re-entered his shop and closed the outer doors. He was thankful that his father had built this location to be airtight. Mars was, after all, deadly to anyone not protected from the thin atmosphere and solar radiation.

Jake went into the backroom of his shop, and tuned his comm device to the local emergency broadcasts. What he saw chilled him to the bone. Outside the Great Dome, Jake counted no less than seven immense space craft firing their energy weapons at the dome. The facility had been built to withstand a lot of abuse, but Jake didn't think it was built to survive a sustained onslaught from attacking space ships.

On the screen, a commentator was addressing stunned Martians watching the events unfold.

"Ladies and Gentleman, what we are witnessing is beyond belief. The Great Dome is under direct attack. Martian air defense forces have been mustered, but there are gigantic cracks already appearing in the dome itself." The announcer looked away from the camera for a moment before turning back. "I'm being told that air defenses are returning fire. Yes, look at that! The ships are breaking formation and appear to be leaving the vicinity of the Dome."

Jake stared in stunned horror. He was *inside* that dome, and he comprehended what awaited everyone outside of it. Every Martian had been taught since childhood what would happen if they were caught away from the protection of the habitats and structures.

Loud sounds of metal and shattering glass could be heard outside the shop now as Jake kept his gaze on the screen. An enormous section of the dome seemed to have collapsed, and he could see bodies writhing on the ground, exposed to the Martian atmosphere. The camera abruptly cut away from the scene as Jake reached out and shut the device. He felt safe in this shop, but he was afraid for his friends and family. The dome would self-seal, but not before lives were lost in the unfolding disaster.

From orbit, the D'lai Commander smiled. He appreciated his ships had only done comparatively minor damage, but that was the point of the attack. Not only was it unexpected, but it was a diversion. The true mission of the D'lai was near Olympus Mons. While his ships attacked the Great Dome, a smaller detachment of cloaked vessels entered Martian airspace and descended unnoticed to the surface. All they needed was little more time, and the D'lai have what they came for.

All was going according to the Negotiator's plan.

"Excellent."

CHAPTER 6

Earth – The Present

The United Nations Space Operations command center was in chaos. Moments earlier alerts had come blaring in of the devastating attack on Mars by the D'lai. The command center was routinely run by lower-level officers overnight and so, with staffing low, no one expected that a crisis would develop that would require the direct attention of General Janina Agda.

The General marched into the command center just as more reports came flooding in of the devastation of Mars' Great Dome and the loss of life. Even though Mars and Earth maintained separate governments and militaries, Mars was still dependent upon Earth for any kind of off-world defenses.

"Report!" General Agda barked to the Lieutenant Colonel currently commanding the facility.

The Colonel stood and saluted before replying, "General, from all available accounts, seven D'lai vessels entered the atmosphere of Mars and attacked the Great Dome." He indicated a display screen in the center of the room.

"D'lai," said Agda, "and we didn't see them coming?"

"Negative, General. They flew in under cloak and evaded our sensors."

After the almost disastrous D'lai invasion of the Sol System twenty years ago, Earth and Mars had collaborated on increasing their ability to detect alien space craft entering the solar system. Earth deployed extensive sensory nets near the most common FTL insertion points in the system. Mars had declined the installation of a planetary cloak, deciding instead to rely on its relative unimportance. Earth leaders decried that choice, but ultimately it was not up to them to protect every planet in the galaxy.

"Has the Secretary General been notified?" Agda asked.

"No ma'am, we thought it best to wait for you to..."

Agda sighed. "You thought it best for me since you'd rather I be the bearer of bad news."

The Colonel nodded a little sheepishly.

"Very well." Agda looked at a chronometer on the wall and then turned to a communications officer. "Somebody please wake Secretary General Gallagher."

Agda felt sure that he would not be all that happy. His sneaking away from the briefing with Minister Wold had not gone unnoticed. She looked back at the chronometer. 0230 hours. The General motioned to her aide once more and mimicked holding a coffee cup in her hand. The aide, a lithe and dark-skinned Malawian woman of almost thirty smiled and went in search of coffee for her boss. After a few moments, she returned with an overlarge and steaming cup. Agda liked her coffee with cream and sugar. The bitterness of black coffee made her irritable. The General smiled as she held the warm cup in her hands and waited on communications with Gallagher. While she waited, she ordered the surrounding officers to give her up to date reports. She did not wish to wake the Secretary General and then have nothing for him.

"Ma'am, the D'lai vessels were able to evade detection from the sensor grids. Mars has no orbital security to speak of, but those ships still should not have been able to get so close to an Alliance world without us seeing them."

Agda pondered that piece of intelligence. "We need to figure out how they..." A beeping from her console indicated that Gallagher was on the line. She put down her coffee and opened the channel.

"General Agda, I hope this is a social call." Gallagher said. His hair was rumpled from sleep, and he was quite displeased at being interrupted. Agda could see that Gallagher was not alone, and she winced at the obviously bad timing. Gallagher glanced over his shoulder at someone in the room, before replying. "Every time we talk, you always seem to have more bad news."

"My apologies sir," said Agda. She felt bad about waking him up, but this couldn't wait. "Less than an hour ago, multiple D'lai vessels attacked the Great Dome on Mars. At this time we know that there has been mass casualties. The Dome is still standing but is seriously damaged."

Gallagher whistled and rubbed his forehead. "D'lai? Those buggers again?"

"Yes, sir. Also, indications are that they entered the system undetected and..."

"We didn't see them? How is that possible?" Gallagher said.

Agda snapped her fingers at a nearby tactical officer to get his attention. "Sir, we are attempting to gather that information as we speak." She pointed at her comm device and then at the tactical officer, miming orders for him before continuing. "However, my gut tells me they've figured out most if not all the layers of our security protocols, and have been able to adapt accordingly."

Gallagher felt the bottom of his stomach drop out. "General, that means that..."

"Yes, sir. The D'lai could be anywhere at all in the system, and we may not be able to figure out where."

"I'm on my way back to headquarters. Get everyone, *everyone*, together. We need to address this matter now!" Gallagher paused a moment then added, "First the HCH and now the D'lai. What next? No, don't tell me."

Agda nodded and clicked off the communications. She stood, her coffee forgotten, and activated the alert system that would bring all department heads, civilian ministers, and chief military commanders back to the United Nations headquarters. She allowed herself a brief smile as she realized that at least *one* cabinet minister could catch a ride with Gallagher. This was going to be a long day.

General Agda's aide grinned mischievously at the ensuing chaos.

"Perfect," she said softly as the General left the facility. "Just...perfect."

Mars – The Ancient Past

THE UMAWEI EMPIRE AROSE EARLY IN THE LIFE of the Sol System on a small red planet that once boasted vast oceans teeming with life. Three billion years before humans learned to write, the Umawei first traveled the stars in vast ships. Their civilization had evolved at a time when few other planets in the Orion Arm had even begun to reproduce as single celled organisms. The silence and immense emptiness of the vast oceans of space they encountered, led the Umawei farther from Sol, toward more ancient regions of the galaxy.

Mars itself was a planet in flux. It was just barely

in the habitable zone of its own solar system and yet, for its distance from the central star, life thrived. Most life on Mars was aquatic, and few land animals emerged from the deep seas to bask in the weak sun. The Umawei themselves, amphibious and comfortable in both sea and on land had no natural predators. They possessed rudimentary eyes capable of only sensing shades of light and dark, and they developed no auditory senses whatsoever. Their lack of hearing did not hinder them, and their weak eyesight was not an obstacle, for a species that did not require those senses for its own safety.

As a result, the Umawei were telepathic, and what little external communication they exhibited, was in the form of vibrating the air or water around them.

Despite their dual nature, the Umawei found themselves to be natural space travelers. The technology to leave their fragile planet developed slowly, but once it did, almost every one of them left Mars and never looked back. Their life spent partially below the seas adapted them to the harsh conditions of space, and they traveled the stars with ease.

As the Umawei explored the galaxy, their technology evolved with extraordinary speed, and in time, they mutated so much, they shed their mortal bodies. They no longer needed flesh and bone to protect them. In every alien civilization they encountered, they assimilated everything, and their knowledge and technology blossomed.

Millions of years after the Umawei first left their home, a massive ecological disaster struck Mars and forever altered it. A rogue planet entered their solar system and the gravity of that foreign body stopped the rotation of the planet's molten core. Soon, the Red Planet's magnetosphere would weaken and much of the thin atmosphere would be stripped away by the harsh solar winds. Most of the liquid water on the surface evaporated, and all life on the planet died out. Afterward, the unprotected soil and dried up oceans were buried in deep layers of dust, hiding away all traces that life ever existed at all.

The surviving Umawei were hundreds of light years from Mars, and by the time they discovered the horror of the disaster, it was far too late to act. In their grief, they built immense structures in dozens of star systems, memorializing for all time their home, their technology, and their pain. As the millennia rolled by, the Umawei lost all interest in further exploration, and grew ever more inward looking. They realized that without a home, they were doomed to be forgotten. Civilizations past and present would not remember them. Their vast knowledge, and incredible technology would be lost to the ages. As a result, they devised a plan that would forever alter the course of the galaxy, and almost all life that would emerge as a result.

The Umawei bio-engineered their own DNA into dozens of forms – some aquatic, some terrestrial – and began to seed this engineered DNA on thousands of worlds throughout the galaxy, as a final gesture of their immortality. On planet after planet, Earth, Scree, Gathung'l, Cathar Prime, and so many others, they planted their seeds and sent Emissaries to watch over these fragile worlds and prepare them for life. The Seeds they planted did not always succeed. Some planets were too old, while others were far too young to support life. They even tried to restart life on their own now dead world. Two seeds were planted near Olympus Mons, but The Seeds only rested there, never activating. Life was too fleeting, and Mars could seemingly no longer accommodate it.

The Umawei moved on. They watched as life grew from the dregs. They had no qualms about influencing the life that blossomed on their seeded worlds.

To many planets, they were seen as gods. They rejoiced in triumph where life exploded, and mourned lost opportunities on others. Further millions of years would pass, and eventually, their generosity and vitality turned to malevolence and rage.

Before the Umawei withdrew completely, and abandoned their work, they devised a trap to lay in wait for some unsuspecting civilization. Their creations no longer needed them, but the Umawei refused to go silently into oblivion. It was time to move on and wait until the trap was sprung. The Umawei, with all their infernal desires, would not re-emerge again for thousands of years when the D'lai would inadvertently be caught in their web.

Cathar Prime – The Present

ZAT'OL CLOSED THE CONNECTION WITH HIS commander in the Sol System. He was overjoyed at the initial success of their first mission as they climbed their way back to galactic dominance. The minor attack on Mars, and the subsequent landing of D'lai vessels on the Red Planet, were good first steps in the more ambitious plans the Negotiator had for the foreseeable future.

Already, the Umawei data in the *awch jdiv* had given up copious amounts of valuable information on the origins of The Seed and the effects of deploying it. From what Zat'ol had been told by his scientists, The Seed was capable of terraforming and inserting basic DNA structures into any planet or moon that was capable of sustaining water in any form on its surface. This meant in theory that if a planet had ice and even a thin atmosphere, it could be a viable candidate for The Seed.

As Zat'ol waited for more news from Mars, he read with awe galactic history as told by the Umawei Empire. Their utter power and complete dominance of the early galaxy thrilled him to his core. To think that a civilization that had existed for untold billions of years would share its knowledge with the D'lai – a civilization that was a mere embryo by comparison. If only the D'lai could attain some small measure of that strength, he and all his predecessors could accomplish their final goal.

For a moment, Zat'ol recoiled in despair as he pondered why a race like the Umawei would deign to give him their wisdom. What were the D'lai to them but a mere pawn in an eternal struggle? He pushed that thought away, and fingered his prayer beads. What did it matter if the gods were willing to shower their attention on him?

He was disturbed from his grand thoughts by the ever pouty Bruilus. "Negotiator, I've found it."

At first Zat'ol puzzled over what Bruilus was talking about. Seconds later he snapped his full attention to the present and stood, excited. "You found it! Show it to me!"

Bruilus pulled up on an oversized screen in the center of the room a schematic of a metallic cylinder. Data flowed on the screen but Zat'ol ignored it.

"This is The Seed?"

"Yes, Negotiator. This unobtrusive looking silver cylinder is the source of life," said Bruilus. Zat'ol sensed a "but" was coming, and he was not wrong. "But, we don't have near the technological ability to replicate it."

Zat'ol was not surprised. The D'lai may be technologically superior to most of the races in the Orion Arm, but it could not hold a candle to the immensity of the Umawei.

"Did we find either of the abandoned Umawei seeds on Mars?"

Bruilus looked as if he wanted to run away. "No, Negotiator. The first was not where we were told it would be, and we've encountered trouble finding the second."

Zat'ol was thunderstruck. How could that seed not be there? It would have been buried beneath millennia of dust and Martian soil and virtually undetectable. As he railed, he realized with sudden clarity just exactly where that seed most likely was.

"Earth!"

Startled, Bruilus cowered. "Sir?"

"Earth has it! They must have found it when they colonized that planet!"

"Sir, if Earth has it, we'll never..."

Zat'ol whirled on Bruilus, enraged. "We must! That seed is our salvation!"

The Negotiator quickly ordered the ships near Mars to re-engage if necessary and search for The Seeds again. "If either is on that dusty planet, we must have it!"

Bruilus was not privy to the plans the Negotiator had made, and he had no idea what bargain he had struck with the Umawei.

"Surely, the Umawei have more?" Bruilus said.

Zat'ol started to laugh. "They abandoned physical form so long ago they don't even have real ships."

"But the projection near the heliosphere…"

"Is nothing more than that. They used their minds to make it."

Bruilus seemed to deflate. "If we can't find a seed, and they can't give us one, why are we bothering at all?"

"Because, you fool, if we possess a seed, we can dominate the galaxy with the mere threat of its use!"

"What do the Umawei want, then, if not The Seed?"

Zat'ol glared at Bruilus with a look that froze his blood.

"Us, Bruilus. The Umawei want us."

"Sir?"

"They are tired of life without bodies. They want ours."

"That's…"

"Yes, I know. Why do you think we've allowed any Cathari at all to live?"

It was as if a light bulb turned on in Bruilus's brain. He smiled at Zat'ol. "You've known of this plan far longer than any suspect, Negotiator." It was a statement, not a question. Bruilus looked at Zat'ol with renewed adoration.

"You get it now? We may have failed to seize control of the galaxy, but there is always a plan B."

Both D'lai grinned and laughed. Unseen nearby, and shed of its garments, the Emissary monitored them. The plan the Umawei had hatched a thousand years ago was finally coming to pass, and it would not stop with Cathar Prime.

Earth — The Present

JOSEPH BURKE WAS A MAN WITH A MISSION. THE successful destruction of the new cloaking platform in orbit of Earth was just the beginning. He and his comrades were determined to free the planet from the oppressive regime that forced the planet to hide itself from the stars and inconvenience millions of the planets inhabitants.

Burke believed that Earth should not hide itself from the galaxy and that in so doing, it was conceding to anyone who cared enough to listen that it was too afraid to earn its place in the galaxy. He and his friends in the HCH wanted Earth to stop being an observer and do something to make the galaxy pay attention to it.

Burke was too young when the Cathari first appeared to understand the implications, but he was an adult with his own life when the D'lai tried to invade. He understood why the leaders of the planet at the time did what they did, but to him, it was sheer folly to keep doing it. The D'lai were gone! It was time to rejoin the universe.

"We must free ourselves! This tyranny must end!" Burke said to a crowd of HCH supporters. "This *mandate* is oppression! End the cloak!" The throng cheered his words.

Burke also just happened to be a pawn in someone else's game. Naturally, he had no idea at all. His idealism was so single-minded that it proved useful to a more mature, far seeing organization, to shield their own actions behind his public and foolish endeavors. Allowing the HCH to take credit for blowing up the orbital platform was an amazing smoke screen for their own plans.

The organization had operated in the shadows of Earth politics for decades and had one singular goal in mind. Its members had come to the planet when the

Cathari first established their diplomatic ties with Earth's nascent planetary government. When the Cathari Alliance fell apart, and Earth hid itself, this group of aliens remained on the planet, hidden in plain sight. After all, who would suspect an unobtrusive group of hard-working Gathung to be dangerous? The Gathung were friends and allies with Earth.

Ever since the D'lai captured and enslaved Gathung'l, it fostered a loyal cadre of its inhabitants as a form of spy ring. These faithful Gathung would serve the D'lai long after the end of the occupation, and even well after the fall of the D'lai Authority, at the end of their disastrous war.

Now living on Earth, they would remain in covert contact with the remaining D'lai on Cathar Prime, and work to undermine Earth from the ground – a feat the D'lai could not accomplish. All Cathari had been banished from Earth for fear there were D'lai among their ranks. The Gathung, however, were welcomed with open arms.

No one on Earth suspected that anything was amiss. The secret Gathung group, the *Sriam Yë,* had received orders from the D'lai that they needed to find something called a seed, and they needed to do it now. The Gathung weren't entirely sure how to proceed, but fortunately their D'lai masters had given them two clues: NASA and Josh Burke.

Members of the *Sriam Yë* got to work deciphering the clues. They knew about Joseph Burke most definitely, so learning more about his father should not be too hard. Getting into NASA would prove more difficult. Thankfully, they had the HCH to help them. They would find this seed, if it existed. Failure was not an option. The D'lai must be served, and they must be satisfied.

PART 2

PART II - RISE OF THE D'LAI

CHAPTER 7

Saturn Space Hub – The Present

The *Avenger* undocked from the Saturn Space Hub and moved away from the station. Captain Arvesp Erth sat in her command chair and beamed with pride as her efficient crew maneuvered the aging but still magnificent ship away from its berth.

A month earlier, after spending almost twenty years at the helm of the Gathung ship, she had been promoted to the rank of full captain, and given command of the vessel. Her former captain, Qik Ziqna, was back on Gathung'l in an effort to be chosen as the next Dictator of Gathung'l. Arvesp was proud of her former commander, but she was more thrilled at her own current assignment.

"Navigator, take us to the FTL insertion point, full speed." Arvesp ordered as soon as the ship received clearance from the hub.

"Affirmative, Captain," said the navigator.

Arvesp beamed with pride as her navigator executed her duties flawlessly. She had even more reason to be proud than for a job well done. Like Arvesp, the navigator was from the Gathung'l southern continent of Sumor. When Arvesp had been given leadership of *The Avenger*, she intentionally placed a Sumorian *My* in her old berth.

Arvesp studied her pad for a long moment, as she considered the mission she was about to undertake. Earth and Gathung'l had grown incredibly close in the decades since the failed D'lai invasion, but they did not keep up the same pace in protecting their own systems. Earth advanced by leaps and bounds, while Gathung'l stagnated. Rapid turnover in planetary leadership was to blame. After the death of First Dictator Kwiu Zig during the invasion, and the elevation of Bresu Xid as Second Dictator, Gathung'l was, for a moment, politically stable.

Unfortunately, stability only lasted for a decade.

During a routine training mission aboard *The Naomor*, Xid had been killed when an errant shuttle pilot recklessly slammed his smaller craft into the hull of the much larger ship, buckling several bulkheads, and exposing three decks to the vacuum of space. Xid, alone in his quarters at the time, had been one of the victims blown into space when the crew deck was severely damaged.

Naturally, that shuttle commander was summarily executed, but that didn't resolve matters at home. A rapid progression of Dictators came and went, delaying any advancement in protecting Gathung'l space, and fraying the edges of the Three Worlds Alliance. Martian and Earth governments were far more stable, and they bristled at the brisk change in leadership the Gathung people were experiencing. Implementing policies and treaties was challenging on any given day, however, it was far more burdensome when one never knew who was running the place.

Arvesp, secure in her new position as Captain, brushed aside the memory of all the turmoil on her home world and continued with her own brand of leadership.

"Navigator, what is our current heading and mission?"

The Navigator cleared her throat. "Ma'am, we are en route to the FTL injection site. Our course is planned to take us near Cathari space for routine monitoring."

In quick succession, Arvesp drilled the other members of the crew on the bridge. She believed it was imperative to keep her people on their toes at all time. Captain Ziqna grew lax over the years, and the ship paid the price. It took sixteen months to refit the aging vessel before Arvesp was willing to take it out of dry docks and on this sort of maiden mission of the refurbished, and more technologically superior, ship.

The Captain continued her drilling of the officers right up until they reached their FTL site.

"Captain, we have permission to jump," said the navigator.

"Let's go," Arvesp said, smiling. "What is our ETA to the Cathar system?"

"Ma'am, we should arrive at station in..." the navigator checked her console, "...nineteen hours."

Arvesp whistled. Before the upgrades, courtesy of Earth, it would take the ship three days. "Impressive," she said aloud to no one in particular. "Navigator, you have the bridge." Arvesp stood and exited.

In addition to the major upgrades of the ship, Arvesp made one more critical change. She assigned only Gathung and humans to the crew. After the experiences of the past, she didn't trust other alien races to have the best interests of this ship in mind. To Arvesp, it didn't matter so much what Gathung'l needed, it was what *this* ship needed. Her loyalty to the home planet slipped slightly, owing to the constant chaos in the civilian government. Of course, this was a civilian ship, so it didn't answer to the Gathung'l military.

Arvesp made her way to her quarters. She maintained the same bunk as she had when she was the navigator. She'd grown accustomed to her surroundings, and the roomier suite the captain enjoyed wasn't all important to her. Besides, her quarters were conveniently close to the mess hall, and she loved to eat. It was a win-win.

Arvesp entered her quarters and tossed aside her pad and kicked off her boots, when her comm console began beeping urgently. Sighing, she sat down before answering.

"Yes," she said.

"Captain, sorry to bother you. We've received a coded communication from Alliance headquarters on Earth."

"Why would the Alliance be...never mind. Patch it through."

"Yes, ma'am." The navigator disappeared from the screen, replaced by a grim faced human.

"Captain Arvesp Earth of the Gathung ship *Avenger?*"

"The ship is called *The Avenger*, um... Mr...?"

The human rolled his eyes before continuing, "Under Article XVII of the Three Worlds Alliance, I am authorized to commandeer your vessel, and place it under the military jurisdiction of the Three Worlds."

"Whoa, whoa there...um...human," Arvesp could not detect a rank and was not sure how to address this flunky trying to steal her ship out from under her. "You can't just..."

"Captain, we do *not* have time to waste. Your ship is now under the command of General Janina Agda of Earth Space Command. I am sending new coordinates to your navigator. You will arrive there in six hours and at that time, you will rendezvous with *The Terran*. Further orders will be provided at that time."

Arvesp was about to protest once more, but she was cut off by the rude human. "I'm sorry, but this is far more important than anything you had going." With that, he abruptly ended the call.

Arvesp glanced out of the window of her quarters, cursed loudly at the room, and returned to the bridge. She groaned in frustration as she realized she neglected to put her boots back on. Before she could even step on the deck, she heard nervous shouting from the other side.

"I can't... I have no control..." shouted the Navigator. Everyone on the bridge whirled in the direction of the door as it swooshed open and Captain Erth entered.

Half a dozen voices erupted at once, all vying for the Captain's attention. Arvesp remembered with a sudden wry humor, a similar situation in a corridor of this very ship, when she and several others had been shouting to be understood after the D'lai captured their ship. Captain Ziqna had not been pleased and roared in anger. She liked Ziqna, but his fierce temper could frighten even the bravest crewman.

Not one for yelling, she chopped the air with her hands, silencing the rabble. "One at a time. Navigator?"

"Ma'am, these blasted new upgrades...they've taken control of the ship and I can't change course!"

Arvesp wasn't terribly surprised the gift from Earth was more of a Trojan horse than anything else. "Of course they did..." She demanded status updates from the other crew members, and sat once more in her command chair.

Despite the chaos, it was the little things that pleased her, and she had been super happy the old command chair that was sorely abused by Ziqna's girth, had been replaced. Now though, she wished he was in charge, and she was the navigator. Arvesp briefed the crew on their new objectives, and ordered them to calm down.

"We'll get through this. Something is up, and we are mere pawns in a galactic game of chess."

When her crew gaped at her in puzzlement, she chuckled. Arvesp spent several years with humans, and some of their mannerisms and customs rubbed off on her. "Never mind, let's do what we can."

In six hours, the next adventure would begin, and Arvesp had some reading to do. "What kind of ship is *The Terran,*" she mumbled to herself. She would soon find out.

Earth – The Past

"WHAT IN THE HELL ARE WE LOOKING AT?" DR. Josh Burke asked? He and a group of NASA scientists were studying a metallic cylinder that arrived from Mars a few weeks ago.

"I'm not sure Josh, other than the obvious fact it was found on Mars, buried under ten feet of dust..."

"I know all that Mike, but look at this readout." Burke pointed to data gathered from the mass spectrometer. "This is made of an element we've never seen before."

Dr. Michael Wyatt peered at the printout in stunned silence. "Surely this is a mistake, I really thought this cylinder just...well...dropped off one of our landers or satellites."

"I thought so too Mike, but listen," he checked for who might be listening before proceeding, "I've checked this data three times. It's legit."

The implications of their discovery was staggering. "Are you saying, this cylinder is extraterrestrial in nature?"

Burke stared at Wyatt for a long moment, "No,

I'm not saying that. What I *am* saying is, I don't know where this came from."

"Okay, let me run a few tests of my own, let's see what we find out."

Burke nodded and tried to focus on his other projects. Neither he nor Wyatt were tasked to examine this artifact. NASA established procedures and protocols for everything, but when it first arrived in the lab, both men had been immensely curious.

Wyatt worked on several Mars missions and was familiar with most if not all the technology developed by NASA, SpaceX, and others, in their push to conquer the Red Planet. This cylinder didn't match up to any recognized configurations, but Wyatt was not a believer in all that Martian hoopla it seemed was running rampant in recent months.

It didn't take long before both men became preoccupied with studying the cylinder, and eked out more and more time to devote to the topic. Neither scientist was involved with any current missions, and so it was easy to find a little time here and there.

A week later, Wyatt approached Burke and, after getting his attention, led him to a small unused office nearby. Burke was shocked at Wyatt's haggard appearance.

"Have you gotten any sleep at all man?" Burke asked with alarm.

"Yeah, a little." Wyatt glanced over his shoulder, then walked over and locked the door. "Listen, I found something I can't explain and..."

Laughing from the hallway halted the discussion. Wyatt in particular seemed to be fearful of being overheard.

"Geez man, calm down. What is wrong?" Burke asked.

Wyatt placed a hand on his chest in an attempt to calm himself before continuing. "Josh, this thing...er cylinder...the thing's not empty. I was able to scan it and...well...it is full of a non-Newtonian fluid."

"You're saying the damned thing is full of *slime?*" Burke started to laugh but the look on Wyatt's face stopped him dead in his tracks. "Why are you so alarmed by slime?"

"Josh, the fluid...it's moving inside the container."

"Holy...it's alive?"

"Yeah. We brought back something alien...something alive...here on *Earth.*"

Burke flew from his chair. "We have to alert the administrator!"

Wyatt grabbed his arm, "No! Think this through man! We are the first scientists to discover *alien* life!"

Neither man was aware the universe quite literally was teeming with alien life. The Cathari had not yet made their first appearance in the skies over the planet. That wouldn't happen for another fifteen years. This discovery of potentially alien life was the most important discovery either man would ever make. They had to handle this properly to avoid losing control.

"Shit, man. We aren't even supposed to be *looking* at this thing, let alone making scientific discoveries about it!" Burke said, crestfallen. "We can't alert anyone without exposing ourselves to…"

"Forget all that Burke! We've got a much bigger problem."

Burke realized with sudden horror what exactly Wyatt had done.

"Oh…my…god…you opened it didn't you?"

Wyatt nodded slowly. "Yeah, just a fraction of a millimeter, so I could examine the interior better."

"What on Earth would possess a Harvard educated astrophysicist to open an unknown alien device to see what was inside of it?"

"Josh…it told me to."

Burke understood now his friend Wyatt simply lost his freaking mind. "We have to seal it, bury it, this cannot ever get out."

Wyatt nodded sadly. "It told me you'd say that, but I didn't believe it."

"You are off your rocker! The device *spoke* to you, it *warned* you? What is wrong with you?"

Without warning, Wyatt stood, reached inside his lab coat and pulled out a Smith and Wesson nine millimeter handgun from a concealed belt holster. Burke froze in place, the sight of the handgun pushing aside all thoughts of alien artifacts and NASA administrators.

Burke didn't have to worry, however, as Wyatt opened his mouth and inserted the barrel of it inside. Wyatt closed his eyes, and Burke watched in a kind of slow motion horror as Wyatt's index finger pulled the trigger.

A split-second before the gun went off, Burke thought he heard Wyatt say "We are all going to die." The report of the gun echoed in the small room as a spray of red splashed on the wall behind him and Wyatt slumped to the floor. Burke stood there in shock, and even when security arrived to the scene of the suicide, all he could do was stare at the corpse of his friend.

Mars – The Present

"Mars Command, this is Lt. Colonel Vadim, please respond."

"Colonel Vadim, this is Mars Command, we read you."

"Mars Command, we have eyes on Olympus Mons. Estimate closest approach in thirty seconds."

"Acknowledged Colonel. Mars Command Out."

Lt. Colonel Artur Vadim led a small fighter wing of four reconnaissance anti-gravity fighter jets suitable for the thin Martian atmosphere. Their current mission was to deploy to the base of Olympus Mons for a visual inspection. Mars Command received scattered reports from eye witnesses of aerial disturbances nearby. In light of the D'lai attack on the Great Dome, it was thought that as a precaution, deploying fighter jets to the vicinity would be a wise move.

Vadim, a fourth generation Martian, was hopeful this mission was not a waste of time. He would much rather have been deployed closer to the population centers of the planet to aid in the defense, if necessary, from the D'lai. Mars Command, however, saw fit to send him, and three other pilots to this remote region of the planet.

The anti-gravity jets deployed on Mars were marvels of human engineering. Designed to fly at altitudes of anywhere between ten and thirty thousand feet above the red Martian soil, the jets had a maximum cruising speed of just under six hundred miles per hour, or approximately the Martian speed of sound. Lt. Vadim and his fighters could travel from their base on Amazonis Planitia to Olympus Mons in just over an hour.

The flight from base had been uneventful. Vadim expected nothing less. Prior to departure, he had been briefed on the cloaking technology of the D'lai, and he did not expect that even if his wing encountered them, they'd see them visually, but he was confident their onboard detection systems would pick them up. The jets were equipped with search and track sensors that could, in theory, detect any kind of airborne craft. Additionally, the technology was capable of detecting disturbances in the air that might indicate a hidden craft.

Vadim activated his search and track sensors or STS, checked that everything was functional, and after confirming with the other pilots, initiated a search grid around the enormous mountain.

Fifteen minutes into the active search, Vadim's radio crackled to life.

"Colonel, my STS is picking up a disturbance 30 degrees to the left."

Vadim adjusted his own instruments. "Acknowledged. Adjusting sensors...whoa!"

Proximity alarms blared in Vadim's cockpit as soon as his sensors resolved. He couldn't see the alien ship, but his STS and infrared cameras told him it was there. He pulled up hard to avoid a collision, and was relieved to see the other pilots in his wing following suit.

An instant after he re-oriented his jet in the direction of the hidden craft, his onboard warning receiver trilled that an active weapons lock had engaged. Vadim maneuvered his fighter in an evasive pattern, as an amber beam of light shot out from the now uncloaked D'lai vessel, narrowly missing his wing.

"Goddamn," yelled Vadim as he tried to evade the ship. A brilliant flare of flame from his right told him the D'lai weapons connected with at least one of the other jets. Vadim twisted his head to try to see it, to no avail.

"Colonel, I'm hit," shouted one of his pilots. "I've lost flight control. I'm ejecting."

Vadim didn't have time to respond, as another amber bolt was flung in his direction. He whistled in relief as he was able to avoid it yet again. He raced to higher altitude in an attempt to flee the D'lai, engaging in a wild flight pattern. After a moment when his heads up display didn't show the ship, Vadim sent an automated distress call to Mars Command, and ordered his wing to retreat.

Vadim made visual contact with the remaining fighters when a third amber bolt lit up the sky. This time, it connected with Vadim's jet. Vadim did not have time to scream before his cockpit exploded outward and Vadim's body fell from the tumbling jet into the deep-frozen Martian night.

Cathar Prime – The Ancient Past

THE WAR BETWEEN THE D'LAI AND THE DÄK'IN dragged on for months with small victories on both sides of the battle. Am'oll was growing disheartened at their lack of success. He believed the righteous cause of the D'lai would far outweigh the feckless Däk'in, and they would surrender without much fight. He seriously underestimated their so-called peaceful religion.

Am'oll also never anticipated how devious his opponents could be. It shouldn't have come as much of a surprise to him, however. D'lai and Däk'in were one race. If one group was capable of intricate planning, certainly the other would be. Nevertheless, Am'oll allowed his biases about the Däk'in faith to blind him to the obvious fact he and his followers were being led into a trap. A trap that would not end well for the D'lai.

"We've surrounded a large group of enemy soldiers holed up in the center of Rai province," said a D'lai commander in his report to the leaders of the D'lai.

"Excellent, we are running short of munitions in that sector, we need to be sure we can take them out with what we have," said Am'oll. "It's time we end this war."

"Am'oll, I'm not sure this battle will end..."

"Kiat," said Am'oll, "the destruction of this cadre

of Däk'in will loosen any remaining resolve among their troops." Am'oll stood and walked to a map of the region. "By our calculations, this is one of the last significant strongholds they possess."

"That is all true, Am'oll, but we must be prudent."

"Prudence be damned!" Am'oll shouted, startling those in the room. His ordinarily calm demeanor was shattered by this outburst. "I'm tired of these *chtuai* and their hypocrisy! It is time we end this and win Cathar Prime for ourselves!"

Everyone in the room avoided eye contact with the obviously angry leader. Kiat walked over to his friend and leader and placed a hand on his shoulder. "Am'oll, friend," he said, "find the peace you require. We have fought long and hard, and we will win." Am'oll glanced at his friend and breathed heavily.

"You are right Kiat." Am'oll returned to his place at the head of the table. "Continue. What is our objective?"

Mission commanders continued the briefing. The plan was to lure the soldiers to a plaza in the center of the city by making the outskirts of the area inhospitable with strafing fire, small explosives, and the like. Once all the soldiers were gathered in one place, D'lai bombers would fly overhead at a high altitude and drop the largest remaining bombs on the unsuspecting people below.

Am'oll had no qualms about murdering his enemies in this fashion. The D'lai believed in taking what was needed, and he believed this was a necessary evil. After this battle, there would be so few fighters left the Däk'in would have to surrender.

The gathering broke up and each man went to his own private quarters. Despite the ongoing bloodshed, the D'lai were extremely religious and each man and woman followed a strict pattern of prayer and other religious observances. After their evening prayers, Am'oll and his combatants went to bed to try to catch some sleep before the ultimate and hopefully final battle.

Am'oll slept fitfully and arose not refreshed. He was midway through his morning prayers when the ground shook so intensely, Am'oll believed the caverns above him were collapsing. The sheer magnitude of the shaking toppled everything in the room. He quickly ran outside and into the central cavern. All around him men, women, and children ran screaming from their own quarters.

After what felt like minutes, the ground stopped moving and Am'oll was able to proceed to the command center. D'lai commanders and soldiers were running around trying to ascertain what happened.

"Am'oll, that was not a quake, it was something else entirely."

Am'oll looked at a few screens that managed to stay upright in the shaking. He was frantically flipping through various pages when one caught his attention. He froze, his mind numbed by the sight. On the screen, an enormous mushroom shaped fireball was rising near the cavern system he was currently hiding in.

"Kiat...our base..."

Kiat turned and stared. He punched in something on a console and scowled at his friend. "Am'oll, it's gone. Our bombers, our soldiers, everything."

"What could do that?" Am'oll was afraid he knew the answer. He locked eyes with Kiat, and saw reflected in them confirmation of his worst fear.

Kiat took a long breath. "The Däk'in used a thermonuclear device." He somehow managed to sit in a nearby chair without falling. "We avoided using them, yet they...poisoned their own planet...to try to stop us."

Am'oll studied the room filled with the men and

women he led through the horrors of war. If the enemy was willing to kill their own planet in an effort to stop a religious uprising, the D'lai lost and nothing would save them now.

Am'oll turned to Kiat. "Signal Cathari High Command. Send them this message." Am'oll stopped talking for a long moment. When he resumed, he was barely able to speak the words. "Tell them, we surrender."

The war was over. Now all Am'oll and his followers could hope for was a quick, painless death. They could not have anticipated the cruel fate the Däk'in had in store for them. As it turned out, the D'lai were far more peaceful than their enemy.

CHAPTER 8

Cathar Prime – The Present

I t was time. A few minutes ago, Zat'ol received word from his battleship commanders near Mars of the successful recovery of one of the two seed devices the Umawei deployed in a desperate attempt to rebuild their lost civilization.

Zat'ol wanted to find both seeds, but he was thankful the blasted humans seemingly found just the one. His agents on Earth, the *Sriam Yë*, were working to locate the second seed. The Negotiator did not want Earth to have the means to undo the plans laid out over the past twenty years. It was encouraging, however, that the *Sriam Yë* were unable to easily locate The Seed. Zat'ol believed this meant Earth may not know what they had in their possession.

Zat'ol swept grandly into the expansive command center, as all eyes focused on him. He was eminently pleased at the progress, and today was a momentous day. Today he would order the vast fleet, assembled in silence, to fill the skies of the Cathar system.

"Negotiator, we await your command," said the D'lai Operations Commander. He motioned to a seat in the center of the command center. Zat'ol beamed with pride as he took the throne-like chair and looked around the room at all he accomplished in a short time. His grasp of the newly formed D'lai Authority was complete.

Zat'ol searched the faces of his fellow D'lai. He found no reason for concern, but saw only pride mixed with fear. Good. He wanted his people to fear him. As he continued his observations, he glimpsed a D'lai mystic hovering nearby. He invited the priest to perform a ritual of thanks. As every believer in the spacious room fingered his or her prayer beads, the priest waxed at length, reciting from the *Chäi kia Chlüi*.

When the D'lai mystic at last finished, Zat'ol

stood from his chair, and loudly declared, "Commander, order the fleet into orbit."

"Yes, Negotiator." The gathered D'lai in the room beat their chests in the usual D'lai form of applause.

From one hundred underground bases all over Cathar Prime, the second planet in the Cathar System, hundreds of D'lai warships rose boldly into the blue sky. A similar scene was occurring on Cathar III, the only other rocky planet. The D'lai spent much of their exile rebuilding their lost fleet. When the deployment was complete, five hundred D'lai warships filled the Cathar system.

Zat'ol was awed by the simple fact, according to the preserved history found in the Umawei Disks, this D'lai armada was the largest gathering of hostile ships in galactic history. This naval force would sweep aside the puny defenses of the Three Worlds Alliance, and usher in an era of complete D'lai dominion over the civilized galaxy. Zat'ol naturally didn't even take into consideration any plans by the hidden Umawei.

With a single unspoken command, every ship in the D'lai fleet cloaked in unison. Zat'ol's engineers and scientists had carefully studied the data from their disastrous defeat, perfecting their technology to avoid the same ignominious fate. Their cloaks were now more impenetrable, and their ships hardened from FTL radiation. That dastardly trick from Zea Windrow would not succeed a second time.

Over the course of the next week, each of the D'lai vessels would begin a secretive journey first to Ryi Bruai and then to their final destinations: Earth, Gathung'l, Scree, and Mars. Unknown to the humans, Mars was their primary target. The cloaked Earth was an obstacle to their plans, but Mars, having refused a cloak, was an easy target. It was also a fact the D'lai wanted very badly to dig more into the origins of the Umawei.

The fleet would travel while under cloak, an impressive technical accomplishment no other civilization had so far mastered but it had its drawbacks. Jumping while under a cloak would considerably slow their progress, and inhibit the effectiveness of the FTL drives. That didn't matter to Negotiator Zat'ol. Time was on the side of the D'lai. This surprise attack would rain fire down on the major civilizations of the Three Worlds Alliance. Nothing would stop the D'lai now.

Zat'ol laughed, and laughed, and laughed. Every

D'lai within earshot cringed in fear. The Emissary, hidden still, spied the scene with unaccountable joy.

Earth – The Present

ORDERED CHAOS WAS HOW GENERAL AGDA would describe the scene in Earth Command Headquarters. The recent attacks on Mars, the news from the Cathar System, and the attack in Earth orbit of the new orbital cloaking platform all worked together to create a perfect storm of events.

Three distinct task forces were working on the major crises of the moment, and each one of them required more time in the day than Agda had to spare. She was a good delegator, but tasks of this level of importance required at least a good amount of her time.

She stalked into the command center a little before seven in the morning, blazing cup of coffee in hand. "Report."

Several heads snapped in her direction. It was customary for the reports to be given in order of rank – the most junior to the most senior. In this case, the most junior officer with a report was a full colonel. She gave a succinct update on the Cathar System.

"Ma'am, nothing new to report at this time with any specificity. *The Manchester* is due in Earth orbit within twelve hours. We expect we will have more information once we can confer."

"Why did we not gather the data remotely?"

"Ma'am, that ship is outdated and the remote transfer of data was proving too unreliable."

Agda stopped her urge to roll her eyes. She looked at the next officer, this time a General.

"General Taylor, an update?"

"Ma'am, we are gathering physical evidence from the site of the Mars attacks." The General consulted a pad in his hands before continuing. "Also, we believe the D'lai were doing some digging around Olympus Mons. We found huge bore holes where excavation lasers could have been sifting through the top soil."

"Looking for what?"

"Ma'am, that we do not know. We are doing a deep data analysis and a records search for anything that may have been discovered by previous expeditions in that area. I will update you when I have something tangible."

Agda focused her attention on the remaining officer to report out. "Admiral, HCH?"

Admiral Inowe stood straighter as she addressed the Commander in Chief. "General, we have infiltrated, with the assistance of our intelligence services, HCH. We believe a group of Gathung are coordinating much of the efforts of HCH."

"Gathung?" Agda shook her head as if to clear it. "Explain."

The Admiral returned the gaze from General Agda. "Ma'am, several communiques we intercepted from HCH leadership were in Gathungi." Gathungi is the native language spoken by only a handful of Gathung. When the D'lai conquered Gathung'l, their language was outlawed. In the hundred years of slavery, most Gathung began speaking D'lai natively.

"Gathungi? I thought that was an extinct language."

"Yes, it is generally extinct. Most living Gathung don't speak it. However, we believe it is used for covert communications since it is so rarely used."

The Admiral pointed a handheld control at a wide display as she manipulated it to reveal several charts. "I did a brief history search when I discovered the use of the native language. It seems First Dictator

Kwiu Zig used Gathungi to communicate with his insurgents during the rebellion against the D'lai."

General Agda pondered this new information. "What does that tell us?"

"General, I believe a group of Gathung are coordinating for some unknown purpose against our interests." General Agda opened her mouth to ask another question, but the Admiral had more. "In fact, ma'am, from what I can ascertain, the D'lai used Gathung cells similar to this to work against their own people."

"Admiral Inowe, you are saying we have Gathung on *this* planet spying against us?"

"Yes, that is my belief, backed by strong circumstantial and tangible evidence."

The room was silent as everyone in it pondered the massive implications. Agda paused for a very long time before she looked straight ahead, rolled her shoulders back in determination, and walked to the communications officer.

"Colonel, initiate Code Black."

The military officers in the room barely reacted to the order. Their long years of training kicked in and each man and woman in the facility began working on prearranged tasks that should be carried out if Code Black was ever initiated.

Several things happened at once. In orbit, the cloak around Earth was confirmed as active. Every ship of the line within two astronomical units of the planet was recalled and ordered to take up a defensive orbit of the planet. In addition, every ranking military commander, cabinet officer, and the Secretary General himself, were transported to the secure bunker below the United Nations headquarters.

Code Black had never been implemented, so the final part of the protocol was new and no one really knew how it would play out. As part of the orders, every non-human on the planet was placed under house arrest. All off-world communications were halted, and any alien found to be in non-compliance would be imprisoned without trial until the end of the declared emergency.

Agda hated the concept of initiating this Draconian order, but if the Gathung on Earth were truly plotting against humanity, she had no other choice at all.

Saturn Space Hub – The Present

Nine hours after the Code Black was initiated, Zea Windrow and *The Manchester* arrived ahead of schedule at the Saturn Space Hub. Windrow had initially expected to exit FTL closer to Earth, however en route she was given alternative orders to dock at the hub. Earth, it seemed, was in some kind of lockdown.

"I wonder what is happening at home?" Windrow said over a cup of coffee she was trying to enjoy with First Mate Kanner.

"Who can tell," said Kanner. "It must be kinda important though, I've never seen so few navy ships at the hub."

Windrow thought about this for a minute as she looked out at the immense orbital space station. The rings of Saturn could be seen in the distance. Ordinarily, she would find the view breathtaking. She loved being out here in the system. The planets were massive and each one was incredibly striking up close. Saturn was by far her favorite.

Today, however, she felt a sense of unease. She too had noticed the usual hustle and bustle around the hub to be muted. "Do you think Earth recalled all their ships?"

Kanner sipped his coffee. "Hmm...could be."

Windrow forced a smile. "Well, whatever it is, I'm sure we won't find out first hand, and we'll have to do some digging of our own." She winked at Kanner. In a previous life, Kanner had been an operative with one of the major intelligence bureaus on Earth. Windrow suspected he was probably already working his contacts to gather intel.

Kanner pretended not to see the wink as he practically licked the bottom of his coffee cup clean.

Windrow laughed, "You, sir, are a caffeine addict!"

"Am not! I just love a clean mug!"

Both of them chuckled as they stood and reluctantly headed back to the bridge. "I guess we should finish the docking process and find out who to report our observations to," said Windrow. Kanner nodded as they entered the small command deck.

The navigator turned toward Captain Windrow as she entered, "Captain, we've just received permission to dock."

"Good. Let's try not to scratch the paint this time navigator."

The navigator looked away sheepishly. The last time they had docked at Saturn she had gotten a little too close to a boom arm that was transferring cargo from an enormous nearby carrier ship.

"Yes, Captain. I don't see any booms this time."

Everyone on the bridge smiled at the levity. Windrow was pleased that her crew could be so at ease with each other despite the obvious tense issues they were facing. That whole hullabaloo out near Cathar Prime and their recall back to Sol was enough to make anyone age a bit more than usual.

Windrow sat in her command chair and waited for final docking to be completed. A moment later her communications officer reported that they had an incoming message from the hub.

"Put it on."

"Aye, Captain."

The speakers crackled for a moment before a strong feminine voice came over the channel. "Captain Windrow of *The Manchester*, this is Colonel Faris at Earth Command."

Windrow was shocked that a colonel was hailing. Usually she got some second lieutenant. "Colonel, to what do we owe the...um...pleasure?" She winced at her poor choice of words.

The colonel didn't appear fazed as she continued. "Captain, events on Earth are tense. As a result, we found it was more appropriate for your...ship...to dock at Saturn. The skies over Earth are quite crowded at the moment."

"We appreciate that, Colonel." Windrow started to go on but she was interrupted.

"Captain, Earth is aware of your nefarious past, and we are also knowledgeable of your role in the D'lai War."

Windrow smirked at the comment. Of course the higher ups wold be concerned about a smuggler.

"Nevertheless," continued Colonel Faris, "we believe that your unique status is an asset and not a hindrance in this case." She paused and another voice could be detected. "Captain, first we need to gather the intelligence you reported on from the Cathar system. Additionally, engineers from the hub are going to be performing some...minor...upgrades on your ship."

Windrow was shocked. "No, Colonel, they are not."

An audible sigh came over the speakers. "Captain, I don't want to pull rank, but I do have the authority to commandeer your vessel in a time of war or a state of emergency."

Windrow bristled, but she relented. "Fine, Colonel. What kind of upgrades?"

"Yes, the upgrades are improvements on your ability to transfer data remotely as well as a minor upgrade to your cloak and your FTL drive."

"Colonel, what is the purpose of all of this?"

A long pause ensued before the colonel replied. "Windrow, we need you and your crew to get back to Cathar Prime. We don't want to send one of our destroyers because we believe that a *smuggler* will not raise the attention one of our naval vessels would"

"Well, colonel, that makes a certain kind of sense. Why?"

"The reasons are classified, but I am able to read you in enough to tell you we believe war is imminent with the D'lai. We need to verify a few things, and we have to do it quietly. We do not want to jump start things by being foolish."

Colonel Faris and Captain Windrow talked for a few more minutes about the logistics of the upgrades and the mission they needed *The Manchester* to perform. Once she was satisfied, Windrow gave her permission.

Things were about to get a lot more interesting. In

sixteen hours, she was heading back out there, and she had no idea at all what to expect.

"Wow," was all she could say as the communication ended. Kanner watched her, and nodded.

"Wow, indeed," said Kanner. "Well, let's get started."

Windrow agreed.

Deep Space – The Present

THE *AVENGER* ARRIVED AT ITS PREDETERMINED coordinates to find absolutely nothing nearby. The crew took detailed sensor readings of surrounding space as soon as they exited their faster than light jump. This region of space was barren. There were no nearby stars or planets, no nebulae, nothing.

Arvesp waited a bit impatiently for a report from her navigator. After an eternity, the navigator reported. "Captain, from what I can tell based on star charts, we are in a region of space called The Barrens."

Arvesp was stunned. "The Barrens? That's a problem." Everyone on the bridge turned to look at the Captain. "We passed through a portion of The Barrens thirty years ago. We were nearly stranded here. It took us weeks to get out."

The navigator was going to respond when the communications officer notified Arvesp of an incoming hail.

"Can we put it on the viewer?"

"Yes, putting it on."

The screen came to life and the oldest human Arvesp had ever seen came on the screen.

Arvesp literally began laughing at the absurdity. The human on the screen did not seem quite as amused.

"Captain Erth, I am Rear Admiral James Christopher." The Admiral bowed slightly as he spoke. "I am tasked with bringing you and your crew safely through The Barrens."

"Admiral...um... Christopher...why exactly are we here?"

"Captain, Earth found something out here, and we don't have enough of an understanding of the D'lai to figure out what it is."

"Oh, and so you figured you'd ask a Gathung about them? How original." Arvesp snorted her disbelief and was sorely tempted to end the transmission.

She turned to the navigator when the Admiral stopped her.

"I know, this is not what you wanted to be doing. Your people suffered immensely during the occupation."

"You want to call it an occupation? Why not call it what it was. Genocide. *Millions* of my people died. Countless more are *still* enslaved. They'll never recover from that horror."

"Yes, I do understand, at least a little but Captain, this is something you can do to help...lessen the pain... of your people."

Arvesp sighed and relaxed into her chair. None of what happened to her civilization was the fault of this or any other human. Humanity had not even met an alien until long afterward.

"Admiral, what did you find?"

The ancient admiral smiled and stood. "Captain, we found ancient ruins. Ruins that pre-date even the Cathari."

"Okay..."

"Right, but the reason why we needed *you* Captain was we also found what appears like an ancient D'lai ship among them," said the admiral, "and, we can't read D'lai."

"These ruins, they're huge, right?" The admiral nodded. "I mean, more than huge, they are planet sized?"

"You've heard of them before?"

"Yes, the stories are legendary. A thousand years ago when the Cathari and the D'lai parted ways, these ruins from some long dead race were the catalyst of the D'lai civilization." Arvesp was excited now. "We thought these were myths the D'lai told us to keep us in chains. You found them?"

"Yes, thanks to you." The puzzled look on Arvesp's face told the admiral he needed to explain. "Your ship was trapped in this region of space thirty years ago. The dark matter clogged up your FTL drive, remember that?"

Arvesp nodded slowly, "Yes, we found a way through."

"Yes, thanks to Major Gallagher. He theorized it wasn't just dark matter...it was a form of anti-radiation generated from something in the system, but he didn't know what. After the D'lai war, we decided to come looking and, well, we found the source."

"You found the Umawei?"

"We don't have a name for it. The D'lai vessel we found is old. Every indication is that it suffered some kind of massive damage and was abandoned. We've recovered some kind of writing that seems to be in ancient D'lai. We obviously can't ask *them* to translate. Want to see it?"

Arvesp smiled. "Yes, though my D'lai is rusty."

"That's okay, mine is even worse. Let's meet. Bring a shuttle."

"Admiral, a shuttle to where?"

The admiral laughed again. "Right." He turned to speak to someone off camera. "We remained cloaked, just in case you weren't friendly."

"Not friendly? Half my crew is human."

"You wouldn't have heard then about the problems on Earth."

"No, what problems?"

"Earth has gone silent. We don't know why."

That seriously worried Arvesp. Something was up. "I'm on my way, admiral."

CHAPTER 9

Cathar Prime – The Ancient Past

"Surrender? Why would we do that?"

Am'oll contemplated the question for a moment. "Ryäi, we surrender because we must!"

None of the D'lai understood why Am'oll would so quickly give up. True, the Däk'in had demonstrated their willingness to destroy the planet in an effort to stop them, but they had choices.

Am'oll pondered his next words before addressing his loyal followers. "*Riaẓ jdiä*, my friends, the Däk'in will not stop at poisoning the planet once. They have shown their faith to be a lie. I love Cathar Prime. It is my home. I love my faith. It grounds me and guides me." Am'oll stopped and pushed back a wave of tears. "If I must choose one, I will choose D'lai!"

The room erupted in cheers. The gathered followers understood the stark choices that lay ahead. "D'lai, we have planned for this. We are ready for this. If the Däk'in want this planet so badly, let them have it!"

The assembled D'lai fell silent at the implications. "Am'oll, our ships are ancient, they won't support us." Ryäi said.

"Wrong, they must support us. If we remain here, not only do we die, but D'lai dies with us." Am'oll gathered himself for one last reminder. "If you choose to remain, you break the *ëmshu chäi*. The consequences you know."

Everyone in the room knew that to break the blood oath was to suffer the *chleng uikir*. No one wanted to be skinned alive. One by one, each D'lai present removed a dagger from their belts and ritually cut themselves, mingling their blood together as a reminder of what every single one of them swore.

"Ryäi, *riaẓ ftialchuaṭ*, my brother, summon the faithful. It is time to leave."

The D'lai had attained a dozen old star ships in

several locations around the planet. Every D'lai who was able to go gathered in one of the diverse locations. Timing was imperative. Am'oll did not believe the Däk'in would simply let them leave. He feared that as soon as their ships blasted into the skies, the Cathari military would shoot them down. Instead, he planned to make them believe it was their idea that the D'lai were leaving. If they *wanted* them to go, his people would be able to leave in peace.

As the D'lai gathered for their journey off planet, Am'oll activated a plan he put into place long before the current conflict. During the conflict, several prominent Däk'in teachers tried to convince their followers that only with the D'lai dead or off planet would Cathar Prime flourish. One teacher in particular who styled himself as the spiritual successor to the *Vdo Däk*, was actively encouraging planetary leaders to banish the D'lai and erase them from the history of the planet.

Am'oll seized on this and sent a broadcast in which he declared that the D'lai would target any Cathari who preached or spoke urging their banishment. The broadcast had the desired effect, and within days, the trickle turned into a torrent. Soon almost everyone who had a voice in Cathari leadership was demanding the D'lai be sent off world forever. Am'oll had achieved his goal. He signaled to his followers that it was time. They would leave Cathar Prime and venture into the stars to seek out a home where they could worship as they pleased.

For the next thousand years, every D'lai would believe they were forced from Cathar Prime. Am'oll never revealed that he had engineered their banishment in a noble attempt to salvage their faith. He had unintentionally done to the D'lai what the Däk'in had done to their own faith. He had turned every one of his followers, now and forever, into hypocrites.

Earth – The Present

Secretary General Gallagher chafed at being virtually locked up in the underground bunker. He had just started to get somewhere with Minister Wold when, once again, all hell broke loose.

"This is becoming the story of my life," he said to Margit Wold in one of the few moments they could sneak away."

"Cormac, relax, this isn't as bad as floating in

empty space." Margit tried to calm Gallagher by placing a soft hand on his arm, but he resisted.

"Margit, I never wanted this job. I was perfectly happy teaching at the Naval Academy. Those cadets..."

"I'm sure they hung on every word, Cormac." Margit smiled at him and leaned in closer, "To tell the truth, I'm much more comfortable with you in charge then some other person. You understand the common man."

"Common man...that's bull. I don't understand them, I *am* a common man. I'm not cut out for this."

Margit tried to relax Gallagher, but she knew most of his self-doubts were marks of a humble man. "Hun, you are the *only* one that can lead us right now. We need someone who's actually been out there and defended us!"

Gallagher returned the affection Margit was showing. "You're right. I'm just...nervous. What if Agda is wrong?"

"Questioning yourself won't help."

Gallagher drew in a long breath and his face brightened. "I'm glad I met you." He leaned in and softly kissed her. Gallagher was a confirmed bachelor and already in his late fifties, but he felt for the first time, he was falling in love.

After another moment hidden away, Gallagher and Margit returned to the main conference room. Everyone in the room pretended not to notice their return, but more than one person present smiled to themselves. It was about time Gallagher found some happiness.

"General, do we have an update?"

General Agda checked over her pad for a few seconds before looking up at Gallagher. "Sir, *The Manchester* has left Saturn and is en route to Cathar Prime to begin their monitoring of the system. We've maintained a communication blackout for any ships outside of the Sol System so until we lift the Code Black, we won't know the full extent of what they find."

Gallagher still wasn't sure why Agda had enacted Code Black. He understood there was possibly some spying going on, but to blind themselves at a time when they needed every scrap of intelligence they could get was madness.

"Agda, when do you anticipate lifting the code?" Gallagher as a civilian leader had no authority over the military and could not countermand the orders of the Commander-in-Chief.

"As soon as Military Intelligence confirms we have locked down the attempts by HCH and the Gathung spies, we'll lift the orders in stages."

Gallagher shook his head but there was not much he could do. "General, I hear that you have ordered my old ship *The Avenger* into service. What's that about?"

"Mr. Secretary General, we have discovered some ancient alien technology, and we needed someone we could trust to have a look at it."

"I'll need a full briefing."

"Of course, sir."

Gallagher looked over at Margit Wold. She was off in a corner of the conference room talking to an aide. He didn't really know why the Minister of Transportation needed to be in the secure bunker, but he was happy she was here. Margit Wold for her part also wasn't sure why she was required to be here either. She couldn't imagine there were a lot of transportation emergencies that required an underground military bunker. She caught Gallagher's attention and smiled. At least she had a decent reason to stick around.

Margit was just about to walk over and mention dinner to Gallagher when alarms began blaring in the room. Alarmed, she looked at the panels and froze.

On the screen, an extensive section of New York City seemed to be on fire. Every pair of eyes in the room beheld the scenes unfolding with dread and horror.

Gallagher whirled around and shouted to the room, "What in the hell is going on? Find out, now!"

Angered by the lockdown and the Code Black, HCH had intentionally detonated an underground gas line in the Williamsburg neighborhood of Brooklyn. They wanted to send a clear message to the planetary government that they were able to create chaos wherever and whenever they pleased.

"Sir, HCH has taken credit for the attack," Colonel Faris said, "We received an encrypted message just after the gas line blast. They demand we lift the Code Black and deactivate the cloak."

"The blast damaged a subway line beneath the city, trapping hundreds of commuters."

Gallagher looked over at Margit. At least now she definitely had a good reason for being here. She returned his stare with muted horror, and then turned back to a group of aides to see what she could do to help.

"Rescue crews have been dispatched, and we've sent in air and ground support to assist with the cleanup," said Colonel Faris. "Sir, what is our response to HCH?"

Gallagher turned to Colonel Faris, a look of determination on his face. "Message received." He didn't need to say anything else. They'd bring the fight to HCH directly. They had no real choice.

Near Cathar Prime – The Present

NEVER BEFORE IN RECORDED HISTORY HAD SO many ships crowded the stars of the Cathar System. Zat'ol took his command chair aboard the newly rebuilt flagship of the D'lai. *The Spector*, the largest ship in the D'lai fleet, headed a column of ships headed for the Ryi Bruai system.

Before embarking on the conquest of Earth, Zat'ol first wanted to visit the remains of the first great D'lai ship *The Faithful*. Almost a century had passed since any D'lai vessel of renown had visited the fabled final resting site of the greatest leader in their long history, Am'oll.

According to legend, Am'oll had led his people from Cathar Prime after the government banished all traces of the D'lai faith. The Cathari discovered the Ryi Bruai system long before those tumultuous events, but Am'oll wanted to bring his people to this cradle of civilization where the Umawei left massive structures scattered among the planets of that long abandoned solar system.

As he sat on his bridge, Zat'ol idly wondered why the Umawei never seeded Ryi Bruai. He made a mental note to study the planetary bodies. The Negotiator understood some planets, like Mars, were incapable of sustaining life or reacting to a seed.

"Negotiator, we are approaching the FTL insertion coordinates."

"Very good navigator. Alert me once the entire armada has arrived."

The Spector was capable of traveling substantially faster at sub-light than most ships in the D'lai fleet. Zat'ol had no wish to be aboard a ship that could easily be left behind. In fact, his paranoia had grown over time. With this new mission and the plans ahead of the D'lai Authority, he started to see enemies everywhere. Even now, sitting on his own command bridge, his security stood guard over him.

Not lost on his crew, the widening mania of the Negotiator caused consternation and doubt. Those among the D'lai who had been a part of the previous war did not wish for a return of the instability of Ret D'iash. Nevertheless, all D'lai past and present were still bound by their blood oaths and would obey.

Zat'ol was unaware of his crew's wariness. He plowed ahead with his scheme. He also could not have been aware that the Emissary still watched. The Umawei were pleased at the progress he and his followers made. Their malevolent plans were nearing completion as well. In only a matter of time, the Umawei could reclaim what they lost all those eons in the past.

The voice of the navigator startled Zat'ol from his thoughts. "The armada has arrived Negotiator."

"Very well. Engage the FTL drive and signal the fleet to do the same."

The moment of triumph approached as the massive group jumped. Other than some preliminary testing of the new FTL drives, this would be the first time the new D'lai technology would be used. Only recently, their scientists believed entering faster than light while cloaked to be impossible. New upgrades, courtesy of the Umawei, changed all of that.

The armada now on its way, would arrive at Ryi Bruai in less than three hours. Zat'ol left the bridge, and secluded himself in his spacious quarters. Even though they had rebuilt this ship, portions of it remained from the original vessel that had carried the previous Negotiator. Zat'ol made certain his quarters were the same as those that once belonged to D'iash. He relished the memory of choking the life out of her.

The Negotiator relaxed on an overstuffed chair in the center of the room. In these quiet moments, memories of past glory were mingled with those of past ignominy. Zat'ol, like most D'lai before him, treasured his early life. Long-lived, members of his race often spent their first thirty years in adolescence. Zat'ol had been designated from an early age to be trained in star ship command. He had been assigned on a small corvette near Scree, when life for all D'lai changed forever. His civilization had been massacred when the D'lai star went supernova. Sadly, Zat'ol's entire family had been on D'lai, and did not evacuate in time. The disaster changed the momentum of the D'lai Authority, pushing it toward that final, fateful battle in the skies over Gathung'l. Despite what he told himself, the loss of his family gutted him on a level he would never understand. The shock wave from that star, still expanding into neighboring systems, changed galactic history forever.

Zat'ol grabbed his nearby prayer beads, and chanted quietly to center himself. He needed all of his wits about him in the coming days. Paying homage to Am'oll and the first D'lai was only the beginning of the epic story he had so delicately crafted for himself. Soon, the galaxy would once again fear the name D'lai.

Unknown to him, the Umawei had a different plan. If he had realized, it would have been more terrifying than he might ever imagine. It was some small mercy, therefore, that he remained unaware. The eye of the Umawei never wavered.

The Barrens – The Present

Arvesp Erth's shuttle docked with *The Terran* an hour after she and the admiral had ended their intriguing conversation. Arvesp was awed by the size of *The Terran* from the viewport of her small shuttle. Earth designed their star ships to be grand and this impressive specimen did not disappoint.

The Terran measured nearly six thousand feet in length and boasted no less than twenty decks. Under normal conditions, the battleship could harbor a crew of over three hundred.

Arvesp wondered why humans made their ships so big and what made them design them in the peculiar fashion they did. The ship boasted a massive saucer shaped super structure over the large FTL engines on both sides of it. She had watched what Gallagher called "classic SciFi" with him and it amused her that Earth liked to model their ships after those plastic and metal models used on the ancient videos.

Her shuttle docked in the vast hangar bay at the rear of *The Terran* and she was greeted by Admiral Christopher himself. It alarmed her that the admiral was rather diminutive and used a cane to walk with. Nevertheless, physical appearance was only one measure of someone, and she brushed her thoughts aside.

"Greetings Captain Erth," said Admiral Christopher. He extended a hand in greeting. Familiar with human customs, Arvesp did not hesitate and grasped the mans hand. His grip was surprisingly firm for a man of his advanced age.

"Admiral, it is a pleasure," she said. "I am happy to be aboard your magnificent ship."

"Thank you, Captain. When we have time, I'll make sure to give you a grand tour."

The admiral gestured to a waiting conveyance nearby. "I'm old and the corridors are long. We can walk if you prefer."

"Don't be ridiculous Admiral, of course we will travel in whatever manner is most comfortable for you."

As they traveled the ship, Arvesp had a funny thought and laughed. His curiosity piqued, the admiral asked, "Something funny?"

"Hmm...oh... I was just wondering. I bet I'm older than you."

"No fair, the Gathung people have much longer lives than us puny humans. I'm ninety-three but I already know how old you are." He winked at the Gathung who took no offense at the human's old-fashioned manners. "However, it would not be very gentlemanly of me to reveal it."

Arvesp giggled a little at the thought. She liked this elderly gentleman.

They soon arrived at their destination and the admiral gingerly stepped off the conveyance. Arvesp offered to assist him but he refused. "I have my pride *young lady*," he said in an obvious joke.

Once inside the spacious conference room, Admiral Christopher and Captain Erth settled into seats opposite each other. On the table was a holo of the derelict D'lai ship they were heading toward.

"You can see by the looks of it, this ship is in rather bad shape."

"It's no wonder, considering it has lain in this system for well over one thousand years."

"However, what interests us is not the ship itself, but what is *inside* the ship."

Arvesp studied the holo. She manipulated the display to zoom in and take a closer look. "What *is* that?"

"That is what we want you to help us find out." The Admiral punched a button and the holo of the ship vanished. The object inside replaced it, magnified.

"It is some kind of cylinder. I've never seen one like it. That isn't D'lai inscribed on it, though."

"I feared as much," said the admiral. "Some of my

people believed it to be an ancient form of D'lai runes."

"Admiral, when I was a young lady, back on Gathung'l, I studied linguistics. Did you realize that our First Dictator Kwiu Zig was also a skilled linguist?"

"I did not know that. Fascinating. Do go on."

"Yes, well. One of the things that fascinated me the most was ancient runes. I've seen these symbols, or something like them, before. I'm not sure..." Arvesp trailed off in thought.

Admiral Christopher gave her some time to think. He was interested but unfortunately this far out from Earth and on this particular mission, he had not thought to bring a linguist or anyone even similar with him. His goal had been simple. Find what Gallagher suspected was out here. The admiral found all of that and much, much more.

After a time, the admiral cleared his throat in hopes of getting Arvesp's attention. She looked up at him. "Admiral," she said, "I need access to a data console that can interface with *The Avenger*. I have some files there I need."

The admiral made a sweeping gesture of the room, "Anything you need is yours my dear." He stood and made his way carefully to the door. "I'll leave you to work. Please let me know when you've found something more."

Arvesp nodded as she worked her fingers over the console and accessed her personal files. The admiral smiled as he left but inwardly, he was not smiling.

"I hope she can decipher the symbols before too much time has passed." The admiral was fearful that if they tarried too long in this system, their presence might be noticed. He had no way of knowing that the D'lai were mere hours from entering the region. All hell was about to break loose, again.

CHAPTER 10

En Route to Cathar Prime – The Present

The *Manchester* left the vicinity of Saturn after a minor refit and was now approximately seven hours from arriving in the Cathar system. Captain Windrow was reading over the schematics of the new upgrades Earth Command had insisted in putting on her baby. They impressed her. Not only did Earth increase the speed of her FTL drive by over fifty percent, but the ship was now capable of transmitting data over the vast distances between the stars.

"Listen to this, they even installed new wiring in the gym." Windrow chuckled.

"Why did we need that?" First Mate Kanner was amused as well. "Some of the details they put into a very fast and supposedly very simple upgrade are kinda ridiculous. New routers for our bathrooms?"

The two of them were enjoying some time off duty on the mess deck, one of Windrow's favorite places. She stood and stretched, "Well, it's been real. I should get some sleep before we arrive in the Cathar system."

Kanner stood as well, his easy smile and green eyes on Windrow. "Sure, Zea. Good idea." He faked a yawn which Windrow found to be cute, and together they left the dining area. Their quarters were in opposite directions but neither wanted to leave just yet. Windrow sighed. If she wasn't his commanding officer, who knows what might happen. She patted him on the arm and walked away before she did something she would regret. Maybe she wouldn't regret it, but she definitely didn't need any more complications right now.

Windrow didn't even remember hitting her bunk when the alarm went off to wake her up. Had she been asleep for four hours already?

Groggily, she mumbled, "Computer, stop." The alarm ceased and the lights turned on. She really hated the automatic lights, but she also realized that without them, she'd probably oversleep a lot more often.

Rising, she took a quick shower which refreshed her. She pulled on a clean uniform and left the small quarters. Windrow barely remembered a life before this ship. She'd been its captain for so many years, anything prior was a blur. Windrow had been raised on Titan before going to University on Earth. She missed her family but, out here, her crew was family now.

She made a quick stop by the mess deck for a cup of coffee then headed toward the bridge. They should be arriving in Cathari space soon, and she wanted to be on the bridge and alert when the time came.

Windrow greeted the crew on the bridge as she settled in and was updated on the mundane details of the previous shift. It was kind of boring, but such was the life of a captain, even when that captain was a smuggler.

"Captain, we should be entering the Cathar system in about an hour," said the navigator. She double-checked her readout then responded, "Correction, forty-nine minutes until we exit FTL."

The accuracy of her navigator amused her, but

they weren't recognized for their sloppiness. A messy and untidy navigator would probably jump them into a star. Windrow shuddered involuntarily at the thought.

"Great. I've got some reading to do. Let me know when we exit." Windrow started to lift her coffee cup to her lips then remembered something else. "Oh, tactical, make sure we are ready to cloak the *instant* we emerge. We don't need any surprises."

Windrow continued browsing the upgrades. One particular entry caught her attention. "What the hell is an inverse detection field?" No one on the bridge knew what it was, so she bookmarked the page so she could dig a little deeper later.

Right on schedule, *The Manchester* exited faster than light. Tactical was spot on and reported that the ship was cloaked thirty seconds later. Windrow ordered a full sensor sweep of the area. "Let's see if anything is out there," she said to her crew.

Sensor sweeps were often labor intensive, but another upgrade from Earth was an improved interface. The upgrades pleased her crew. They could carry out this duty with only one or two keystrokes, and it was also much faster. It felt like no time passed before her tactical officer reported.

"Ma'am, I've performed an initial sweep and well, something strange."

Windrow turned toward her tactical officer, her left eyebrow raised in curiosity. "What's up?"

"Well, ma'am, from what I can tell, an enormous number of ships have recently passed through this region of space. I count dozens...no...hundreds of plasma trails."

"What? Can we trace the source?"

"Yes, a moment." It took some complex calculations but after a few minutes, the report came back. "Ma'am, it appears that most of the trails originate from the vicinity of...Cathar Prime."

Windrow shot to her feet. "Red alert! All hands to battle stations!"

Everyone shot into battle ready mode. The evidence of a vast fleet of ships coming from the vicinity of the D'lai home was seriously alarming.

"Captain, some of the trails also come from Cathar III."

"Can we tell how long ago they passed this area and where they may have been heading?"

"Negative. All I can say for certain is that these plasma trails are decaying at a fast enough rate that it must have been at least a couple of days. All of them look to be heading to our FTL insertion point in the system."

"Let's try out this newfangled communications gear. Get in contact with Earth command. Let them know we suspect the D'lai are active and on the move."

Windrow looked longingly at her empty coffee cup. "Maybe someone can refill this for me?" It was going to be a busy day.

Cathar Prime – The Ancient Past

"The D'lai must go!"

The chant grew louder in the *Ë Iuv*. Members of the planetary parliament grew increasingly vehement over the mere presence of D'lai on Cathar Prime. In stunning fashion, a majority of the five-hundred seat *Iuv* voted to expel from the planet anyone that adhered to the heretical faith. They disregarded their own government's use of a thermonuclear device near the main D'lai hideout. All pretense of peace now abandoned, they sent a clear message. Follow the *Vdo Däk*, or leave forever.

Am'oll was pleased with the outcome. His intent was not to force his followers to leave the only home they had ever known, but to keep them safe it was a viable option. Preparations for this eventuality consumed a major portion of his thoughts and long-term planning.

Now, with action by the planetary parliament, Am'oll knew it was time. He thanked the *vdo chlüi*, or great gods, that he and his colleagues on the D'lai council exhibited the foresight to winnow away derelict craft. Thanks to their wisdom, they had enough space going vessels to evacuate every D'lai on Cathar Prime.

Am'oll stepped into the extensive command center, intent on ordering the retreat of his people.

"Am'oll, the news, it's horrible," said Ryäi the moment he saw his brother.

"Peace Ryäi."

Others in the room gathered around the D'lai leader. All of them were aware of the hidden fleet squirreled away all over the planet, but none of them fathomed the immensity of leaving Cathar Prime forever.

"Where will we go?"

"I have given this some thought," said Am'oll. "I believe our first destination will be Ryi Bruai."

Gasps and sounds of shock filled the room. "Ryi Bruai," said Ryäi, "why?"

"Our *vdo chlüi* have given us the clues we will need to find a new home. I believe we will find that answer in Ryi Bruai."

Preparations began in earnest to gather all the surviving D'lai in one of the eleven launch sites. When the war began, the D'lai numbered seven million. The devastation cratered their numbers and now they would leave Cathar Prime with a population of seventy-thousand. As part of the planning for this massive undertaking, D'lai scientists organized the survivors so that each vessel would contain enough biodiversity to ensure the survival of their religion. The possibility existed that not every one of the eleven ships would make it to a new homeworld.

In addition to securing an abundant gene pool on each of the generation ships, large sections of each vessel were set aside for food production. The flora and fauna on each craft needed to be enough that each could sustain itself without relying on any other ships in the fleet. Oxygen generation, artificial gravity, heat, and water were all essential to the life of each craft. Every inhabitant of the enormous vessels were assigned a role.

It was understood that those with families would live together, and any unpartnered D'lai was mandated to reproduce. However, the ships were finite and could only sustain a maximum of fifty thousand each. Planning would need to be meticulous to avoid overpopulation. Fortunately, the D'lai were master planners, so despite the enormity of their task in searching for a new home, they were determined to thrive in the cold outer darkness of space.

A week passed without any further hostilities on either side. The D'lai agreed to their banishment while at the same time laying a curse upon the Cathari. They swore in time they would return and reclaim their lost home. The Cathari would answer for their murderous abandonment of their own so-called peaceful religion.

The Däk'in for their part began moving past their own shame. Mystics and teachers urged the masses to return to their peaceful ways. The D'lai had not even left the planet. It was an insult to Am'oll and one he vowed would be avenged.

Chaos reigned the morning of the departure. Getting everyone on board the vessels was an enormous undertaking. Throngs of curious Däk'in gaped at their soon to be banished cousins. The air was more of a carnival than of a time of despair.

Despite the disunion, ninety-five percent of the surviving D'lai were accounted for when Am'oll ordered the massive doors to be closed on each ship. The intended departure time approached. In a symbolic gesture, each of the massive craft would hover over the planet for ninety-three seconds before blasting into orbit. Numerology was an important part of both Cathari religions. For the D'lai, the number ninety-three represented death. Essentially, in their final act on the planet, the departing Cathari were sentencing the planet and its inhabitants to an eventual extinction.

Upon liftoff of the eleven D'lai vessels, they hovered and then blasted into orbit of the planet. Wailing and moaning could be heard throughout the corridors and decks of the departing space craft. In contrast, cheers filled the streets of every major Cathari city. Neither civilization would find lasting peace. The ensuing centuries on Cathar Prime would be filled with attempts to forget, but the D'lai would never forgive, never forget, and they would one day seek their vengeance.

Am'oll turned from the small window on the bridge of the newly christened ship *The Faithful* as he verified the successful orbital insertion of the D'lai ships.

"Leader, all eleven ships survived the launch and report stationary orbit above Cathar Prime."

"Good. Transmit our course to Ryi Bruai to all commanders." Am'oll ordered.

The ancient D'lai ships were slow and could not travel faster than light. Their maximum cruising speed was seventy-five percent of light speed. Their destination, Ryi Bruai, was eleven light years distant. Am'oll was saddened but resolved, as he understood this first journey of the now banished D'lai would take almost fifteen years.

It was time to settle in for a prolonged voyage.

Earth – The Present

MASSIVE POLICE AND MILITARY RAIDS WERE occurring all over the planet in an attempt to uproot the HCH and stop the violence once and for all. Despite his aversion to the use of force, Secretary

General Gallagher authorized his government to find and imprison any supporter or sympathizer of the HCH.

Already, the arrests numbered in the thousands. As part of the Code Black directives, many civil liberties on the planet were suspended. This had the practical effect of ensuring the jailed HCH members would remain behind bars without a trial for the foreseeable future. Plans were being made to relocate many of the so-called traitors off-world to a penal colony established on the moon.

The irony of this move to eliminate the HCH was not lost on Gallagher. He intimately understood the implications of removing from the planet a group of rabble rousers, and the parallel history on Cathar Prime in the distant past. Nevertheless, with the possibility of war looming, it was vital Earth try to remain united. The HCH were disruptors and jeopardized the planet's security.

"Sir, we just captured Joseph Burke near Scranton."

Gallagher was relieved that, at the very least, the leader of Humans for Clear Horizons was in custody. "Is the Minister of Justice nearby?" He didn't see the tall minister among the throng of people in the conference room.

"I'm here, sir," said the minister.

Gallagher turned to the minister. "Neal, I know Code Black is in effect, but this guy," he pointed to a screen with the picture of Burke on it, "needs to be publicly tried."

The Minister of Justice nodded his head in agreement. "I agree sir. If we are going to restore order..."

Gallagher interrupted the minister. "It *has* to be a fair trial. No kangaroo court Neal."

"Understood. We must adhere to our charter."

The leaders discussed plans for the trial and how to safely transport Burke while maintaining operational security for the remaining raids. It would do no good to lop off the head of the HCH but leave the roots of it still out there to regrow.

After the Minister of Justice went off to huddle with his own people in a far corner of the room, Gallagher looked around for Margit Wold. She was the only ray of sunshine in these rough days. Her ready smile, elegance and wit made Gallagher weak at the knees several times a day when he thought about her. It was a pity he was so damned busy that he didn't have time to run off with her more often.

Margit was deep in conversation with an aide and didn't notice Gallagher's longing stare at her.

"My god, she is gorgeous," Gallagher said to himself. He shook his head in an attempt to clear his thoughts. He needed to focus on the issues at hand.

Two days ago Gallagher asked his old buddy Corey Hodges to return to the planet. He wanted to catch a few moments of relaxation and maybe down a few beers together. Even though things were moving at lightning pace, he still needed to recharge. Slowly, Gallagher was learning to delegate. He didn't need to be at every single boring briefing.

Standing, he walked over to Margit and kissed her cheek. "Sweets, I'm gonna take off for a few hours. Corey just landed and..."

"Of course Cormac." Gallagher was a little hurt that she had not used any endearing term to address him, but he also understood that the room was filled with eyes that saw everything and wagging tongues that loved to gossip.

Margit squeezed his arm lovingly and then returned to the task at hand. Dismissed, Gallagher left the room, trailed by his ever present security detail. Hodges would be escorted to Gallagher's private quarters in the bunker.

"Guys, make sure I have some beer and munchies," he said to his detail. "Grab enough for yourselves too." The security officers chuckled, even though they knew none of them would be imbibing this evening.

Hodges had just settled into an overstuffed recliner when the door swished open and Gallagher strolled in.

"Buddy, it's been an age!"

Gallagher beamed at his old friend. "Too long Corey. How the hell are ya?"

"Can't complain," said Hodges, "things are rough but as some famous writer said, 'at least I'm still above ground.'"

The pair settled down, beer in hand, and spent the next hour catching up. After they'd chatted for a while, Gallagher finally felt himself relaxing.

"Buddy, I've missed this. Life aboard *The Avenger* was much simpler."

"I know what you mean Cormac," said Hodges. "Now, what's this I hear about a new lady in your life?"

Gallagher grinned from ear to ear. "Yeah, Margit."

"Margit, she sounds lovely."

"Yeah man, she's a stunner."

Gallagher and Hodges each grabbed more beer and a handful of pretzels. The rest of the evening was their time to relax and forget. The world would be waiting for them when they were ready.

In an unmarked ground car near Scranton, Pennsylvania, Joseph Burke was en route to a detention center in Baltimore, Maryland. Events were unfolding that would shape the foreseeable future of Earth, and the Three Worlds Alliance forever.

The Barrens – The Present

THE TERRAN AND THE AVENGER TRAVELED together in formation through The Barrens en route to the derelict D'lai ship. Arvesp and her crew felt almost like children in a candy shop with each discovery on the journey deeper into the region the D'lai called Ryi Bruai.

Massive structures littered the star system. One particularly fascinating artifact was the size of Gath-ung'l, itself an overlarge planet. Arvesp marveled at the feat of engineering that must have been involved in building something so massive.

"Captain, from my readings, that relic is composed entirely of a mineral that is nearly identical in molecular structure to the crystal onyx."

"Onyx, something *that* big?" Arvesp was stunned at how long it must've taken whomever built these structures to gather enough crystal. "What is its purpose?"

"Unknown, ma'am. I have a theory though."

Interested, Arvesp turned to face her scientific officer. "Well, what's the theory?"

The scientist paused a moment then continued, "I believe that structure, like a few others we've encountered on the way in, is designed as an enormous communications array or repeater of some sort."

"Fascinating. I wonder who they would be communicating with that would require something so enormous."

"Based on my initial scans, it could be capable of sending signals as far as fifty light years. I wonder how they overcame the Odic Paradox."

At the mention of obscure scientific problems, Arvesp's mind drifted. To her it did not matter how this ancient civilization did things. It mattered that the civilization existed at all.

"I wonder where the creators of all of this went?" Arvesp said aloud.

"These structures are millions of years old at the very least. They could have simply died out."

"Perhaps."

Arvesp went back to watching the display screen as her ship moved closer to the abandoned D'lai vessel. While she was on board *The Terran*, she had worked to decipher some ancient runes that the human admiral thought were D'lai in nature. Her linguistic abilities were a little rusty, but she was certain they had not originated with the D'lai.

True, the patterns in the runes were similar to D'lai writing, but there was something more alien about them. She could not quite place her finger on the problem. She couldn't decipher the runes either. Frustrated, she had returned to her own ship and together the two vessels made their way deeper into the system.

"Captain, we are approaching the coordinates we were given by *The Terran*."

"Very good. Slow us down and prepare to stop."

Arvesp watched the display screen as the ancient vessel came into clearer focus. Despite the nature of the mission, it was thrilling to get a chance to study

D'lai origins and how they traveled the stars in the early days after their banishment from Cathar Prime.

Most Gathung knew the stories of the *Vdo Zämi*. The D'lai liked to tell anyone who would listen of their historic nightmare. Arvesp was never convinced, however, by the stories. She always believed they either omitted or didn't know major portions of their own story. Any legend so old could be obscured by the mists of time.

"Captain, incoming hail from *The Terran*."

"Put it on the viewer."

The wizened face of Admiral Christopher appeared on the screen. "Captain Erth, we're here."

Arvesp tried at least three times while on board his ship to get the admiral to call her Arvesp. She didn't like formal titles. Unfortunately, protocol was so ingrained in the behavior of the old man that he could not bring himself to use a familiar term with her.

"Yes, admiral. It was quite a journey. All those old relics."

The admiral nodded. "Yes, Captain. It will take us years to study all of them. We could..."

He was cut off mid-sentence by an aide rushing up to him. The admiral turned and Arvesp couldn't hear his response. When the admiral looked back at her, his grim visage told her something was very, very wrong.

"Captain, I'd advise you to cloak. Immediately."

Arvesp whirled and issued the command. The timing was perfect, because just as she received confirmation of successful activation, her tactical officer shouted. "Ma'am, we have long-range contact with...my gods...hundreds of ships."

Remaining in communication with the admiral, Arvesp issued a series of commands to her freaked out bridge crew. After a few minutes, she focused her attention on the similar scene occurring on *The Terran*. "Admiral, we might want to move away from our present location. It is about to get very crowded." Arvesp looked down at her pad to confirm some information. "It looks like whomever that is, will be here in just over an hour."

"Agreed, captain. A moment." The admiral muted the connection for several tense seconds. "Captain, I'm sending over new coordinates. We will rendezvous there in three hours." With that, the comm channel was closed.

Arvesp made the necessary orders and *The Avenger* moved quietly but quickly away from the derelict D'lai vessel and to the new coordinates. Admiral Christopher had suggested they use the mass of a nearby moon to hide themselves, so they could regroup and figure out what was going on.

Deep inside, Arvesp knew exactly who had come. "Who else but the D'lai?" Everyone on the bridge of *The Avenger* feared that she was correct.

The massive D'lai armada moved inexorably closer to the remains of *The Faithful*, hopefully unaware they were not alone in Ryi Bruai.

CHAPTER 11

Ryi Bruai – The Present

After a brief journey from Cathar Prime to Ryi Bruai, the massive D'lai armada began exiting FTL and returning to normal space. On the bridge of *The Spector*, Zat'ol watched as the region came into focus on his ships sensors.

"Tactical, scan for unknown vessels."

"Yes, Negotiator. Scan in progress."

Zat'ol did not expect that other ships would be this far out in deep space. The Ryi Bruai system was remote, but it was also barren. His fleet was capable of traveling through the region at FTL speeds when required, thanks to the discovery of the region a thousand years in the past by the ancestors of the D'lai, and also to the technology shared in recent months by the Umawei.

His forebears kept the discovery of this region to itself. Most star charts excluded this region, solely because of the unusual properties that prevented most ships from traveling at greater than light speeds through it. Much like a map inscription used by ancient seafaring vessels warning of dangerous obstacles, the Barrens, as most civilizations called it, was marked as perilous. No sane pilot would wish to enter a region that would increase his travel time from hours to months.

Zat'ol waited for the scan for nearby ships, and took advantage of it to call up on his pad some deciphered writings from the Umawei Disks. According to the Umawei, this region of space was chosen for the mind-numbingly enormous artifacts they built in the ancient past precisely because of the odd characteristics that made the star system off limits. They took advantage of these properties to help them build the relics that memorialized their ancient and forgotten civilization.

Unknown to everyone, the Umawei were in Ryi Bruai as well. The Umawei made their home on a small planet close to the central star. It was the only habitable planet in the Goldilocks zone where life was possible. The planet had been seeded by the ancient Umawei but a space faring civilization never developed. The inhabitants of the planet, called the Voli by the Umawei, never advanced beyond basic combustion engines. They also worshiped the Umawei as gods.

Deep below the surface, the Umawei hid a trove of additional disks. These disks detailed the true history and plans of their civilization and were never intended to fall into the hands of any other race. Their disembodied spirits hid the planet inside one of their vast constructions, protecting the Voli and their secrets. Any passerby would be convinced that the mass and gravity was a product of that artifact.

"Negotiator, our scans indicate that at least one vessel exited FTL near our present location, but we cannot detect if the ship is still present in the system."

"Mmm. Interesting. Dig deeper into the scans," said Zat'ol. He peered over his shoulder to the communications officer, "Order the fleet to remain cloaked and proceed to the ruins of *The Faithful*."

The cloaked D'lai fleet moved stealthily onward. Despite the news that another ship recently traveled through the region, the Negotiator was not worried. No doubt it was a foolhardy captain that traveled too close to the system and became trapped.

An hour after entering the system, *The Spector* was within visual range of the floating graveyard of Am'oll and many other early D'lai. From records maintained through the generations, *The Faithful* miscalculated the effects of the region and was severely damaged while trying to mine ore from the nearby asteroid field. The remains of the ship drifted too near one of the large constructs and was forever trapped by a periodic energy wave it emitted that mimicked the singularity or black hole at the center of The Milky Way galaxy.

Every ship in the D'lai armada fell silent as crew members beheld the scene. Am'oll's ship was gigantic. A generation ship by design, it was possible to house fifty-thousand, though none of the ships of the *Vdo Zämi* ever reached their full capacity. This particular vessel protected somewhere in the vicinity of ten thousand D'lai refugees when it met its horrific end. Of the thousands aboard her, less than half were rescued. Am'oll, was not among the survivors. The remaining D'lai designated the ruins as a memorial.

Not wishing to meet a similar fate as *The Faithful*,

the armada maintained a comfortable distance. The ancient Umawei relic was silent, but no one knew if or when it would reactivate. Even imitating a black hole could pose a major disaster for the Negotiator. However, he believed that on board the ship were artifacts he needed before he could continue his conquest of the galaxy.

Despite the fact that the D'lai were excellent record keepers, their history was so long, holes existed. The precise location of the original scrolls containing the religious text of the D'lai faith were believed to be on board Am'oll's ship when it was abandoned. None of the survivors were able to rescue them, and so Zat'ol fervently hoped he could free the *Chäi kia Chlüi* from its resting place. The Negotiator believed that the scrolls contained hidden knowledge that could be used to further decipher the Umawei Disks. He was desperate to rival the ancient gods of his people and dominate them. Of course, the possibility was strong that he was a fool leading his people astray.

Near Cathar Prime – The Present

AFTER ZEA WINDROW NOTIFIED EARTH OF THE mysterious evidence of D'lai movement near Cathar Prime, the waiting game began. With the upgrades to *The Manchester's* communications gear, Windrow expected to hear back from Earth in a few hours.

She decided to kill the time by digging in to the latest novel from her favorite author. These days she didn't find much time for herself, but there was really nothing to do until she received additional orders from Earth. Windrow curled up on a sofa in a recreation room, turned on the holographic fireplace, and sipped her coffee as she read.

Windrow allowed herself to escape into the world of the novel and did not at first hear the communications alert beeping insistently on her pad. She preferred the feel of printed books over the digital versions favored by almost everyone else, and so her pad was on a table across the room.

A nearby crew member who was also enjoying the holographic fireplace cleared his throat, trying to alert her. After he realized she was not paying any attention, he said, "Um... Captain?"

Startled, Windrow glanced up. When she realized there was an incoming communication, she exhaled, dog-eared her book and closed it. The annoyingly helpful crewman handed her the pad. His face showed that he was genuinely sorry for disturbing her. Windrow nodded tersely at him, dismissing him.

When she was sure she was alone in the room, she activated the pad and punched the communication icon. "Windrow here."

A new human face she had never seen before appeared. "Captain Windrow, this is Admiral Kelly Austin," the admiral said. "We've received your report and are transmitting further orders...now." The admiral stared down at her own device for a moment and Windrow could see her finger moving past the camera as she transmitted them.

Even though this communication was three hours in the past, the additional orders appeared at the same time. Windrow chuckled to herself. She knew the admiral could not see her. The view of the admiral was replaced by a readout of the updated orders. She rubbed her eyes for a moment as if what she was seeing could not be accurate.

"What the actual hell?" Windrow raced from the recreation room and ran at full speed to the bridge. "Please be there!" She did not know the location of her First Mate, but she prayed he was on the bridge.

The second the doors opened she spied Kanner in

a corner of the bridge conferring with a junior member of the crew. Windrow sighed in momentary relief as she walked over to him. She touched his elbow to get his attention, and he looked up into her face and his easy smile vanished.

"Zea, what's wrong?"

Fighting back tears, Windrow handed Kanner the pad. After a moment, his eyes closed, and he stood. He reopened his eyes and ran them around the room with such profound sadness, anyone watching would have feared that death was imminent.

"We need to discuss this...not here." Windrow said as she led Kanner off the bridge to her private office nearby. As soon as the two of them entered, she whirled on him.

"What in gods name does this mean? Tell me now before I put you out an airlock!"

Kanner regarded Windrow with profound regret written all over his face. "Zea... I..."

"Don't call me that. It's captain to you!"

"Captain, not according to this it isn't." Kanner pointed at the pad in his hand.

"You've been ordered to relieve me of my command? What the fuck?"

Kanner flinched at her use of profanity. In all

their years working together, the worst he had ever heard was a damn or a hell. "I can explain."

Windrow turned her back on him. "Don't bother yourself. That data file says it all."

The orders from Earth were clear. First Mate Theodor Kanner was a member of Earth's peace-keeping force. More specifically, his assignment was in the intelligence bureau. For the past seven years Kanner spied on Windrow and reported back to his superiors her actions. Now that war was approaching, Earth felt it could no longer hold back. As part of the seizure of her ship under Article XVII of the Three Worlds Alliance, Earth was empowered to remove her from commanding her own ship, and place whomever it wished at the helm.

"The crew won't back you, you know." Windrow said. She half raised a hand to slap him, but controlled herself.

Kanner waited for the slap that didn't come. He moved in a few inches closer to her. His scent and closeness threatened to overwhelm her. To think she once considered being more than just a friend and colleague sickened her. She leaned over and retched. Kanner flinched as some of her vomit splashed on his shoes.

"The crew will support me if you order them to."

"Why the hell would I do that? You're stealing *my* ship out from under me!"

"Zea..." Her eyes flashed, so he rephrased. "Captain, I'm doing no such thing. Earth is."

"If I tell them you've been *spying* on us," she wiped away tears forming in the corners of her eyes, "they'll tear you apart."

"Yes." Kanner met her gaze and his sudden seriousness rocked Windrow to her core. "If you tell them that, they'll kill me. What do you think Earth will do to you then?"

Without even thinking about it, Windrow knew. Smuggling was a crime. She knew if she disobeyed, Earth would lock her and the rest of her crew up for the rest of their lives. Sighing heavily, she slumped in defeat.

"Fine. You're going to have to confine me to my quarters, *Captain*." Windrow knew she could not be a part of the mission without endangering the crew she valued much more highly than this piece of shit standing in front of her.

"Agreed." With that, Kanner turned and left the room. Alone, Windrow ordered the computer to extinguish the lights as her tears overwhelmed her.

She could only hope Kanner would not get them all killed.

Near Cathar Prime – The Ancient Past

FOUR DAYS AFTER DEPARTING THE SURFACE OF Cathar Prime, the D'lai generation ships broke orbit and headed away from their former home. The fifteen-year journey to Ryi Bruai was a brutal reminder of how far the D'lai had fallen since the start of the catastrophic war. None of the inhabitants of the eleven ships felt any sense of hope or joy at the prospect. Nevertheless, despite the immense slowness of their fleet, each D'lai settled in to a new routine. Every adult, and adolescents over the age of twenty, were assigned to work details designed to maintain the gargantuan ships, and provide for their futures.

On *The Faithful*, even Am'oll was not above mundane tasks. Every D'lai would be required to work in order to guarantee their success. It took those early ships nearly six months to exit the Cathar system, and begin the journey through interstellar space. Eleven light years was seemingly insurmountable, but Am'oll was convinced they would find their future among the relics of the ancients who had built them.

From almost the moment of departure, small and sometimes big emergencies filled his days when he wasn't working in the arboretum. The generation ships were fragile, and were decades past their useful lives when the D'lai were forced to flee in them. As such, ships in the fleet would suffer minor malfunctions. One ship had explosive decompression and killed a dozen D'lai laboring on food production. Another vessel lost its star drive altogether, and required assistance to get it working again. Even Am'oll's ship had its share of annoyances. The artificial gravity on one of the lower decks consistently gave out, forcing those in the area to use bulkheads and handles on the walls to get around.

Am'oll hoped in time these issues would be resolved, and the fleet would be more capable of the journey ahead. Despite all that happened to his people, he was an optimist, and always strove to see the positive in every situation.

One of his first commands upon disembarking, was to make sure the D'lai in the fleet were able to find ample recreation, as well as maintain their adherence to the faith. Replicas of the *Chäi kia Chlüi* were on each of the ships, and D'lai mystics led daily rituals to keep the faithful grounded in their ancient religion. Am'oll believed that despite all the hardship behind and ahead of them, their faith would sustain them.

Time passed slowly on the ships, but soon everyone settled in to their daily grind, and their moods improved. As the vessels were repaired and improved, and as the distance from Cathar Prime increased, joy and hope began to bloom among the D'lai once more. Each ship developed its own microculture, and the first children began to be born, slowly but inexorably increasing the population of the refugees.

Am'oll, widowed when his wife Suha had been executed by the Däk'in, followed his own orders and began co-habitating with an attractive widow whose husband died during the war on Cathar Prime. He soon found a sense of happiness with her, and life began to feel more normal.

Fifteen months after the D'lai left their home world, Am'oll's new wife Rexha bore a healthy son to him. Am'oll did not believe he could be any happier. The D'lai celebrated with their leader the birth of his baby, and a rare holiday was declared on board each of the eleven generation ships. Men, women, and children were allowed to take part in the merriment. The event gave them even further hope for the future.

Am'oll's joy was short-lived, however, when his son grew increasingly fragile and soon died. This embittered the D'lai leader, and he spent much of the following months isolated and alone. He pored over the *Chäi kia Chlüi* for any sign as to why his infant child died. Eventually, Am'oll became convinced his great lie to his people about the true reason for their banishment was to blame. He vowed to never again procreate, and buried his original sin so deeply it would never be exposed. After a year alone in the depths of his ship, he emerged a changed man. His ardor and zeal for the D'lai faith only grew during his self-imprisonment, and his people suffered as a result. Harsh penalties for minor infractions were imposed, and over the ensuing years, the D'lai faith morphed from one of optimism to one of self-centeredness and greed.

The original teachings of the *Chäi kia Chlüi* in the end were discarded, and the scrolls were buried deep inside *The Faithful,* where they would remain for the next one thousand years.

Earth – The Present

JOSEPH BURKE, LEADER OF THE HCH, SAT ALONE in a small and windowless cell in a detention center on the outskirts of Baltimore, Maryland. Hours earlier he was fleeing New York City after the successful attack on the city.

The Deputy Minister of Justice, Sela Grant, arrived at the detention facility to oversee the handling of this particular high-value prisoner. The Ministry of Justice did not want there to be any hint of impropriety in how Burke was treated which could stain his upcoming trial.

Under the auspices of the Code Black implemented planet-wide, a trial would be held within twenty-four hours. Minister Grant was tasked to act as the prosecutor in the case and to ensure Burke retained qualified counsel. There being no shortage of lawyers willing to take on this case, she waited while the wolf pack of them outside the facility figured it out on their own. She had no interest in assisting Burke.

Just after one in the morning, a haggard looking

lawyer by the name of Richard Plot entered the small office where Minister Ward was drinking her third cup of coffee.

"I'm here to represent Joseph Burke," said Plot. "My name is Richard. Richard Plot." He stretched out a hand in greeting.

Ignoring the outstretched hand, Minister Ward stood and said, "It's about time you all figured this out."

Without another word, she handed Plot a binder. Plot glanced at it and put it on the table in front of him.

"Take me to see my client," he said.

Ward motioned to a guard who escorted the lawyer down a short hallway to a small block of cells. Burke was the only occupant of the small jail, but his jailers found it amusing to secure him in the furthest cell. Plot shook his head as he walked.

The guard motioned to an overhead camera, and from somewhere else in the facility, another guard remotely unlocked the cell. After opening the door and making sure Burke was not a threat, he glared at the lawyer and stepped back a few feet.

"Is there...um...somewhere more private we can speak?"

"Nope."

Plot smiled wryly. "The government ain't gonna make this easy, are they?"

The guard merely stared straight ahead. Once Plot entered the small cell, the guard closed and secured the door.

Joseph Burke looked up as the cell door swung open. He squinted at the sudden light but resisted the urge to make a break for it as he rubbed his ribs gingerly. He knew all too well these guards were not going to make this an easy experience for him.

"Who the hell are you?"

"Joseph Burke? I'm Richard Plot." Once more Plot attempted to shake someone's hand, and yet again he was rebuffed. "Well, yes. I'm your lawyer."

"Lawyer," said Burke, "I didn't call for one, and I don't need one."

"Be that as it may Joseph, I'm here, and you're stuck with me."

"Have we met? Are we friends?"

Plot shook his head no. Burke stared straight into the lawyer's hazel eyes. "Then why would you *presume* to call me by my Christian name, lawyer scum?"

Plot was taken back slightly by Burke's vehemence. "Apologies, Mr. Burke."

Burke turned his back to the lawyer, who still stood near the door of the cell.

"Now then, um, Mr. Burke, about your upcoming trial."

Burke picked at a scab on his forearm, ignoring Plot.

"Like it or not, in twenty-four hours you'll be standing trial for mass murder and terrorism."

At the word terrorism, Burke spun to face Plot. "Terrorism? Terrorism? Is that what you call this?"

"No, sir, I'm reading from the charging documents."

"This wasn't terrorism. We are attempting to set humans free from tyranny! Were the founding fathers *terrorists?*"

"Well, to the British, yes."

Burke stood and stepped to the door of his cell, and began to violently bang on the heavy metal.

"Guard, get this *lawyer* out of here!"

Seconds later, Plot was roughly grabbed by the guard, and Burke's cell was once again closed and locked. He looked at the guards and laughed.

"That's one tough fella."

The guard nodded and simply walked back down the corridor to the exit as Plot followed.

From the same small office Plot had first entered, Minister Grant watched the exchange between Burke and Plot. She was pleased at how poorly it had gone.

"Good, that'll make my job a whole lot easier."

The Barrens – The Present

ARVESP PACED THE BRIDGE OF *THE AVENGER* AS she waited somewhat impatiently for Admiral Christopher to update her on next steps. They were currently hiding from a large fleet of D'lai ships behind the mass of a small moon in Ryi Bruai. As she didn't have much to do at the moment, pacing seemed like a decent option.

"Captain, perhaps you could go grab some food?"

Arvesp stopped for a moment. "Trying to get me off the bridge?"

The navigator smiled and shook her head. "No, ma'am. You've been up here for several hours without a break."

Arvesp appreciated the sentiment of her navigator

and indeed her entire crew. Since she took command, it felt like everyone on board was more of a family than co-workers.

"I'm good," said Arvesp. "I know that if I leave, something will happen."

The captain continued her pacing as she tried to control her racing thoughts. It's not that she was afraid, but more that she just wanted something to happen. The nearby D'lai made her nervous.

"What can they be doing here?" Arvesp said, repeating her earlier question.

A thought emerged that stopped her dead in her tracks. The runes? Was that what the D'lai were after? Arvesp sat at a work station along a bulkhead and pulled up the schematic she had been shown by Admiral Christopher. She had been unable to decipher them, but she wondered if another look would help.

Looking over her shoulder, her tactical officer pointed at the small screen.

"Captain, that rune right there... the one that looks a little like the letter F."

Arvesp zoomed in on it. "This one?"

"Yes, I've seen that before."

The captain turned to the officer. "Where?"

"Ma'am, in the Negotiator's palace on Naomor."

Inspiration struck Arvesp, and she began frantically typing and moving through screens of information on the console. She pulled up a series of images taken of the palace just after the D'lai abandoned the planet.

"This is it!"

Arvesp instructed the computer to run a comparison between the images from Naomor and the runes from *The Faithful*. Minutes later, she was overjoyed to find eighty percent of the runes matched. She punched in additional search queries to see if the runes from the palace had ever been deciphered. The results pored in on page after page.

Arvesp almost ordered a channel be opened with *The Terran* but one particular piece of text caught her attention. Both she and the tactical officer saw it, looked at each other, and stood. Arvesp read the passage aloud for the crew to hear her.

"We now know the ancients who built the structures in Ryi Bruai also masquerade as the gods of the D'lai." Arvesp stopped reading. "What does that even mean?"

She continued reading. "These ancients, who call themselves The Umawei, exist outside of time and space. Eons ago they planted their Seeds throughout the galaxy and now wait for the final plan to be implemented."

Dread and some unnameable fear filled Arvesp and the crew of the bridge. She turned to face her people and looked at the screen in the front of the bridge. It showed an image of the derelict D'lai ship. She knew that near the ruin sat a hostile D'lai force capable of immense destruction.

"The final plan?"

Every Gathung in the room instinctively understood whatever happened next, the life that filled the galaxy was in absolute peril.

"Oh, no." Arvesp said. "We need to tell *everyone*."

PART 3

PART III - THE FINAL PLAN

CHAPTER 12

Earth – The Present

"General, we have an incoming transmission from *The Terran*."

General Agda looked at her communications officer. "Patch it through."

"This is Admiral Christopher aboard *The Terran*."

Every pair of eyes in the room turned to the large screens. Even though the message was time delayed by at least three hours, the urgency was palpable.

"Moments ago, we deciphered, with the help of allies on board *The Avenger*, the device discovered aboard the derelict D'lai vessel here in the Barrens."

Gallagher smiled at the mention of his old ship.

He turned and gave a thumbs up to Corey Hodges who sat nearby. Hodges had been assigned to assist with maintaining the cloak around the planet.

Admiral Christopher continued his update onscreen. "We now believe that an unknown alien threat exists, and that these aliens have been influencing the D'lai in such a way that they are preparing for a so-called final plan."

The command center grew more tense at the words "final plan." "Indeed, we have recorded at least five hundred D'lai battleships in this sector. We have no information on their plans, but at the current time we believe all of them to be in the vicinity of the ancient ruins. I will update Earth Command when I have further information. Christopher out."

Agda turned to face Gallagher who could only stare at the now empty screen.

"General, what the hell?"

Agda shrugged her shoulders slightly as she barked orders to nearby military personnel. An aide whispered something in her ear, and she turned back to the Secretary General.

"Sir, we can confirm the existence of at least that many D'lai ships. We received a communication from *The Manchester* that they discovered plasma trails of at least that number coming from two planets in the Cathar system."

Gallagher looked at Hodges. "Corey, what is the status of our cloak?"

Hodges checked some information on a pad he was holding before responding. "Well, it seems the cloak is functioning in normal ranges."

Relief flooded Gallagher's face. "That's at least some good news." He turned to Agda, "What of other planets in the alliance?"

"Sir, we believe the cloak is still functioning on Gathung, and..." she checked her notes, "Scree. No other planets currently possess a cloak."

"Right. Mars..."

"No sir, Mars refused the technology."

"Okay. Alert the member worlds of the possible threat. Let them know we'll do what we can to aid them."

The command center busied itself preparing as well as possible against the unknown threat. Gallagher walked over to Hodges and beckoned him to a small office.

"Corey, I don't trust all of this, do you?"

"I'm glad you asked Cormac. I've got a bad feeling."

"Yeah, me too," said Gallagher. "I don't like being on the ground like this without a plan."

"What do you suggest?" Hodges and Gallagher looked at each other.

"I don't have anything, but I feel like I should be out there and not stuck in this damned bunker."

"Cormac, you're the Secretary General of the whole freakin' Earth. This is your place."

"No, it's not. I'm a soldier, not some bureaucrat."

Hodges shook his head. "What do you propose then?"

Gallagher had a wicked smile on his face that Hodges had seen numerous times in the past. "What...?"

"Agda doesn't need me, really. I'm a civilian leader. The military is running the show. She just defers to me out of respect."

"Cormac, if you are going to do what I think you are going to do you are insane!"

"Yep, that's me. Mr. Insanity. The man with a plan."

"When have you ever had a plan?"

"Well, half a plan."

"You're sure buck?"

"Yeah, about ninety percent!"

"Good enough for me then," said Hodges.

Gallagher and Hodges strolled from the tiny office and walked up to General Agda. She ignored them as they came over.

Gallagher cleared his throat. "General?"

Agda lifted a finger signaling she needed a moment.

"General?"

Agda turned, annoyed. "Yes, sir?"

"General Agda, I'm still technically commissioned as a Major, right?"

Agda shook her head in confusion. "Sir?"

"I'm still a Major, ain't I?"

Agda rolled her eyes. "Yes, sir, you are still a major."

Gallagher grinned at Hodges. "Good. I'd like you to give me a ship, a crew, and send me and Hodges out to find out what's going on."

"Excuse me? What?" General Agda could not believe what she was hearing.

"Give me a ship. I'm gonna go investigate and see if I can't help."

"Sir, you've not had enough sleep. Perhaps..."

"Agda, I'm no good down here. You don't need me..."

Agda's face grew red as she prevented herself from exploding with frustration.

"Secretary General Gallagher," she said using his formal title, "I have a million things to do. I don't have time to talk to some space cowboy who wants to go *hunting*."

"Space cowboy? I like that." Gallagher turned to Hodges. "We could name the ship that."

Hodges grinned but wiped the smile off of his face as he noticed the expression on the General's.

"Resign, then."

"Pardon me?"

"Sir, I'll give you a good, fast ship and an awesome crew. If...you...resign."

"Leave the job I never really wanted and get command of a ship?"

Agda sighed so loudly everyone around the three of them started to pay attention to what was going on.

"Sir, yes. You're not cut out for this anyway, and there are tons of others who could step up and fill the shoes."

Gallagher thought for a long moment before a huge smile wrapped his face.

"You know, great idea." Gallagher grabbed a pad

and a stylus. "Write that all down, the part about the ship and the crew and all that."

Agda smiled. "Sir, if I may, this is probably the coolest thing you've ever done."

Gallagher beamed. Margit walked over to the small group. "Cormac, if you are going to do this crazy stunt, you're taking me with you."

Gallagher looked around the room and without thinking, bent over and kissed Margit. "Let's make this official," he said. "Get something, so I can let everyone know."

Agda handed the pad back to Gallagher, and he filled out the document. "I hereby resign as Secretary General, effective immediately."

The room erupted in cheers. No one was clapping because he was resigning. Everyone in the Command Center understood that Gallagher was going to do what he could to be a hero once more.

Arm in arm, Gallagher, Hodges, and Margit left the bunker. If they could, they were going to figure out what was going on and, once again, save the planet.

The Barrens – The Present

ZAT'OL MOVED AROUND HIS QUARTERS impatiently. His armada was just sitting out here, waiting for what? A sign? The Umawei promised to give more information once they reached Ryi Bruai. Where were they? The fleet arrived three days ago, and so far all they'd done was orbit the artifact at a great distance, wary of it activating, and damaging their ships.

To make matters worse, his officers had not been able to pin down with any accuracy whether the ships they detected left the system, or were still lurking about somewhere. Zat'ol was growing increasingly convinced that he was being spied on, and he didn't like it at all. His grand plans for conquering the galaxy and installing himself as the undisputed master hinged on complete surprise.

The vast armada he assembled in secrecy was impressive to be sure, but it would do him no good if all the planets he wished vengeance upon were cloaked and hidden. His scientists had so far proven unable to fully see through that damned cloaking field. The Umawei assured him they would deliver the necessary technology to assist him, but they had not made their presence known.

It grew more and more apparent to the crew aboard *The Spector* that the Negotiator was becoming more erratic as time passed. Already, word passed from commander to commander that they may need to act, and soon. If the promised visit by the Umawei did not materialize soon, the same cabal that plotted against the deceased Ret D'iash would grasp control of the D'lai Authority from Brik Zat'ol.

Nearby, *The Terran* and *The Avenger* waited in silence. Neither ship had dared to send more than short communications between each other since the D'lai armada arrived. Neither Arvesp nor Admiral Christopher were completely sure that the D'lai were still in the area, but they were not willing to take any chances at all.

Scientists on board *The Terran* hatched a plan that might help detect the presence of cloaked vessels, even if they couldn't be sure who they belonged to. The strange radiation in the Barrens behaved unusually enough that they theorized it was possible to measure the displacement of the charged particles that would occur with the presence of the enormous

D'lai battleships. With any luck, that scanning ability would be ready within the next sixteen hours.

On *The Avenger*, Arvesp and a few others had successfully deciphered almost ninety percent of the runes from *The Faithful*. The message that the ancient D'lai leader Am'oll tried to preserve all those centuries ago was growing clearer and more alarming than anyone could have expected. Arvesp doubted even the D'lai were aware of what their leader tried to warn them against.

To make matters worse, communications with Earth had been spotty over the past few days. Earth reported it received the notification from the admiral, and was acting on it. What wasn't clear was precisely what the plans were, and what was going to come next. Neither Arvesp nor the admiral felt very secure. If the D'lai fleet was still here, it was only a matter of time before it left, and neither leader knew if they could track it once it left the Barrens.

"Captain, incoming message from *The Terran*."

"Patch it in."

"Captain Erth, good news," said Admiral Christopher. "My team has done it. We can detect if a ship is present in the Barrens even if cloaked."

"Admiral, that's stellar. Can we see them from behind this moon?"

"That's the rub, Captain. We will need to quietly move out and pray we aren't detected in a similar fashion."

Arvesp nodded. "When will you be leaving?"

"Not us, you."

"What? We aren't a military ship..."

"Correct, Captain. If they catch you, you're just some luckless captain here by mistake. If they catch us, well, that's a whole 'nother pickle."

Arvesp was furious, but he was right. "Wait, won't they have some record of my ships role in the last war?"

"We thought of that too. Simply reprogram your transponder to make it look like you're another ship. Don't use visual communication, so they don't know your Gathung."

"Agreed, admiral. We need time to..."

"You got two hours Captain, Make them count."

Two hours? Arvesp hit the comm and communicated with her engineer.

"Can it be done?"

"Yes, ma'am, give me an hour. The code is archaic. What race?"

"Hmm," said Arvesp. "Oh, right, um...make us Rozk."

"Good one Captain," said the engineer. "The D'lai like them."

Arvesp smiled. "I do have good ideas sometimes!"

The engineer laughed. "Better get to work."

Arvesp hoped the trick would be enough. She also hoped that the cloak would hold out and the D'lai wouldn't have figured out the same thing they had about the radiation in the system.

It was a gamble, but they couldn't hide behind that moon forever. The D'lai may not have been watching, but the Umawei were. They were very interested, in fact.

Ryi Bruai – The Ancient Past

"What is that, a pulsar?"

"Ryäi, if that was a pulsar, we'd be dead." Am'oll said.

"Right, but...look at it!"

The D'lai traveled deeper into the Ryi Bruai system encountering marvel after marvel. Already they counted at least a dozen enormous structures. Most of them they had no clear idea what they were. This artifact looked a lot and behaved like a pulsar.

Am'oll screwed up his face in puzzlement as he thought. "What is all of this? What are we meant to understand?"

The journey from Cathar Prime to Ryi Bruai took eighteen years. Originally, Am'oll and his advisors believed a fifteen-year voyage was to be expected, however, so many obstacles and unexpected accidents occurred en route that of the seventy-thousand souls who left Cathar Prime, only sixty-thousand now survived.

One of the eleven ships in the small armada experienced a devastating explosion in its star drive killing every D'lai on board. The loss of that ship was a major blow and threatened to shatter the morale of those that remained. With time, natural population growth slowly replaced some of the lost numbers, but it put a further strain on the remaining ten ships.

Am'oll kept careful track of all the artifacts discovered so far. Even though he had largely abandoned the *Chäi kia Chlüi* in favor of his more conservative brand of fanaticism, he still consulted the holy book as a guide. It was of particular value now, as they traveled the system where their ancient faith told them the gods resided. He tried to match each new discovery to an entry in the *Chäi* and up until this point, he was successful.

"I take my leave *riaẓ ftialchuaṭ*."

Ryäi knew what Am'oll was up to and it bothered him. His brother was obsessed with the ancient scriptures and the gods. Was it not enough that they made it this far? Perhaps they would find a home somewhere in this system. Ryäi plotted privately with some of the others on the council, and over the past dozen years made plans for the moment they would have to seize control of the armada and remove Am'oll as their leader. Am'oll had no idea.

In his private quarters in the bowels of the ship, Am'oll scanned the pages of the book vainly searching for something, anything, that matched the strange object nearby. When he found it, he collapsed on the hard metal ground. He could not peel his shocked gaze from the pages as he read what he believed was a match.

This particular section of the *Chäi* described the *Hyai kia Chlüi,* or eye of god. According to legend, the *Hyai* blinked as it searched the heavens, searching for the righteous. When the *Chlüi* found a worthy soul, they would snatch the supplicant from mortal life to join the pantheon.

Am'oll was convinced this new relic was the eye of god, and yet he believed his original sin made him less than worthy, meaning he would not be able to join the pantheon. The realization caused him to grow ever more frantic in his religious zeal. He must find a way to atone for his crime, and then perhaps the gods would find him worthy and seat him in their midst.

In desperation, Am'oll continued to search the pages of the *Chäi* for inspiration. Days passed while he did not sleep, eat, or leave his cramped quarters. Other D'lai leaders on *The Faithful* were used to his wild personality swings, so they merely continued exploring the system and cataloging their finds.

None of them had the slightest idea what Am'oll had in mind. He found an inscription in the book that would have devastating impact for all the future generations of D'lai to follow him.

Near Cathar Prime – The Present

Zea Windrow paced her quarters, restless. The past two days her emotions swung between rage, tears, hopelessness, and misery. The gamut of feelings that encompassed this small room was the only company she was allowed.

After Kanner took her ship out from under her, he did what she requested, and locked her in here. Once or twice she tried tentatively to leave, only to find the controls to the door would no longer respond to her. Even when meals were brought to her by some hapless cook, guards accompanied the meal, making escape not quite so easy.

When she was not pacing or crying, Windrow read. She didn't read those trashy romance novels she normally loved. No. She read schematics and engineering documents, devoured technical manuals, and she even furiously skimmed the Three Worlds Alliance charter, looking for loopholes. It frustrated her that an organization she only belonged to as a byproduct of having been born human so easily swept her aside when it suited them.

In all the reading she managed to do with her now boundless time, she found a few little tricks she wanted to try out on Kanner and *The Manchester*. It wasn't that she wanted to hurt her ship or even

Kanner for that matter. He was doing what he was ordered to do. Yes, it did piss her off immensely that he was a damned spy, but she was a smuggler. She never truly bought into that whole honor among thieves trope.

No, she wanted to sabotage the ship just enough that it was useless to whatever objectives the Three Worlds had in mind. The only problem was, none of the tricks could be played while she stuck in this stupid room. She had to either convince the guards to let her out, or she had to find a way out on her own.

So, with all of that in mind, she pored over schematics searching for an escape. The nice thing was, Windrow believed she found one. The designers of the ship built *very* thin walls between the rooms. She often complained to nearby crewman that they were too noisy. Windrow also believed, until a few hours ago, that the walls were made of aluminum and without a laser cutter or something just as effective, she couldn't hope to break through.

She was partly right. The walls were *mostly* made of aluminum. To her glee, a small portion of each main wall was hollow. The computer consoles and wiring had to go through somewhere. With a little muscle, Windrow pried back the console and made a gap just large enough to get through. If she could make a similar gap in the next room, she'd be free. The only problem was, she didn't know if the crewman who occupied this particular room was home or at work.

Windrow decided to throw caution to the wind and squeezed into the very narrow crawl space. Using the light on her comm device, she found where the console was in the opposite room. She braced her back against the aluminum of her own wall, and using her feet, pushed on the opposite wall. After a few heartbeats and considerable strain to her lower back, it moved. An inch. Zea paused, waiting to hear alarm from the other room. Nothing. She resumed her position and pushed some more and gained a few more inches.

It took Windrow nearly ten minutes of pushing, pausing, listening, then more pushing, before she made an opening large enough for her to stick her head through. Cautiously, she inched her eyes into the room and was relieved that no one was inside. She got back into position and pushed more, making a large enough gap for her petite frame to wriggle through.

As soon as she was in the new room, she worked

feverishly to get the computer console as flush as possible with the wall. She was happy to find the occupant of these particular quarters was quite the slob, so she doubted he would even notice.

Windrow approached the door, listening to any noise from the corridor. After she felt it was safe, she exited the room and rushed down the hall, looking for any way to get out of sight. She knew that near her own quarters was a supply closet where she at least might change her uniform. Her face, she couldn't change, but she hoped if she looked like an ordinary crewman, kept her eyes down, and maybe put her hair up, no one would pay attention to her.

She just made it inside the supply closet when she swore she heard Kanner's voice coming from down the corridor.

"Shit."

She had nothing to do but wait. As she did, she changed into the uniform of a food prep worker, used a tie from someone's robe to put her hair up, and sat on a small stool. After a few minutes, when she was sure Kanner was gone, she left and walked quickly but not so fast she'd be observed down the corridor. Her goal was a small maintenance hatch that led to a lower deck.

Windrow had almost made it safely when a hand touched her shoulder. She whirled around to face who she knew must be Kanner. She was relieved when she saw it was an engineer she had a small fling with a few months ago. He smiled at her, puzzlement in his eyes at her outfit. Light dawned on him as he realized what she was up to.

"Shhh," he said, "Kanner is just around the corner."

"Damn, I thought he was gone."

"He's talking to his new First Mate about some personnel matter. I didn't really listen. I followed you from that supply closet."

"Why? I'm just trying to do what I think is best for..."

"Zea, if I was gonna turn you in all I had to do was shout. I said hush. That means listen too!"

Windrow mimicked zippering her lips closed and they both smiled.

"I know where you're heading. I'm gonna help you."

"Why?" Windrow was not sure she wanted help.

"Because," he said as he leaned in closer. "I kinda got a crush on you, and I think Kanner's a dick."

That was all she needed to hear. The duo entered

the maintenance hatch and climbed the ladder down to the lower deck. As they climbed, Windrow filled him in on her plan.

"Devious. I like it."

Windrow grinned. Maybe this was going to work after all. Maybe.

CHAPTER 13

Ryi Bruai – The Present

"Negotiator, we've got it!"

Zat'ol grinned at the news that his crew had successfully recovered the two artifacts from *The Faithful*. Possessing both the original *Chäi kia Chlüi* and the Am'oll Cylinder were among the final objectives Zat'ol needed to attain before he could begin his conquest of his first target.

The Negotiator was aware of what the *Chäi* contained. Every D'lai memorized the book as part of their catechism. He also vaguely knew what to expect in the runes carved into the Am'oll Cylinder. What he did *not* fathom was what was inside the cylinder.

Zat'ol left the bridge and hurried to the clean room where the two objects were now stored. After donning appropriate protective gear, he entered the sterile environment. These objects were ancient, and none among the D'lai wanted to be the one who ruined them or worse. Zat'ol was awed to be in the presence of the original book of knowledge. However, his attention was focused more on the small cylinder. It surprised him that this relic of such renown was so tiny. Measuring at only a foot in length, the runes carved on its surface were cramped together on the silver surface.

The Negotiator picked up the object and turned it over and over. After a few minutes, he realized he was not alone in the room, and he whirled suddenly to find The Emissary hovering in a corner.

"How...what...why are you here Emissary?"

The Emissary pointed at the relic in Zat'ol's hand. *"We were curious how long it would take you to attain the cylinder."* The mind-whisper made Zat'ol flinch in discomfort.

"Yes, our great leader, Am'oll..."

"Stole it from us and desecrated its surface with his marks."

The Negotiator frowned at this revelation. "Stole it, what is it?"

"The mere fact that your organic brain cannot comprehend what it is you hold further proves to us your insignificance." The Emissary reached out as if to grab the cylinder. Zat'ol stepped back away from it.

"This...object...is a Seed?" He received no answer from the Emissary. Zat'ol tried again. "This is a Seed? Am'oll found one?" Awareness dawned in the Negotiator's mind as he realized what must have happened. "Am'oll found this in Ryi Bruai but couldn't have known what it was."

"He knew full well what he found. It is YOU who do not comprehend what you possess."

With a final gesture, pointing to the *Chäi*, the Emissary phased out and vanished.

Zat'ol turned to study the book. Tentatively, he opened it and started to read the pages. It struck him with an almost violent punch to the gut that the words he was reading in *this* book were not the same as he was taught as a young boy. True, the words *similar*, but they were not identical. The Negotiator grabbed a nearby pad and started to compare the texts. After almost an hour passed of this comparison, Zat'ol realized a fundamental truth. The entire D'lai faith he practiced, the very culture he breathed, was a lie. He could not comprehend why.

The Negotiator had a sudden thought and turned his attention to the cylinder in a vain hope that this newer relic would explain the shift. He could read the ancient runes, and spent the next hours pouring over them. Eventually he began to understand that at some point in their ancient history, the D'lai had been deceived by Am'oll. These runes told the story of their original banishment from a different perspective. Am'oll *wanted* his people to leave, and engineered the situation on Cathar Prime.

Zat'ol was stunned, but at the same time he was secretly pleased. He had long understood the cunning deception that his people were capable of. He often used that innate ability to his own advantage. Zat'ol realized that the lies told by Am'oll was a ploy that, in the great leader's estimation, saved his civilization. The Negotiator laughed at the realization of just how similar he and his forebears were to that long dead D'lai leader.

Vowing to further study the relics, Zat'ol left the clean room, and headed to his quarters. He needed some rest and further time to contemplate, but his resolve was now even greater than before. If Am'oll could lie to every living and future D'lai about the true nature of the *Vdo Zämi*, he could use that same ability to make his final goal a reality. Zat'ol would not reveal the true nature of The Seed he possessed, nor the other cylinder en route to his location from Mars. He would not tell his people until the final moment, that his grand scheme had changed.

Zat'ol now no longer planned on conquering just the Three Worlds. The runes revealed one further piece of information that only someone who possessed both the Am'oll Cylinder and the original *Chäi* could decipher. Am'oll discovered a method of duplicating The Seed. Unfortunately for Zat'ol, he was not aware that this knowledge was also the cause of Am'oll's downfall.

Earth – The Present

MAJOR GALLAGHER SAT DOWN IN THE COMMAND chair as he surveyed the bridge of his new ship *Space Cowboy*. General Agda begged Gallagher to keep the original name of the ship, but Gallagher in his typical fashion made a joke and did it anyway. Now, in Earth orbit and preparing to go figure out what was going on, Gallagher felt more free than he had in years.

"Captain, we are ready to depart," said the navigator.

"Major."

The navigator turned in her chair. "Sir?"

"Navigator, say, I don't even have your first name."

"It's Ellen."

"Right. Ellen. I'm not a captain." Gallagher pointed to his uniform. "I'm a Major."

"Right, sir, but when you're on the bridge, and it is your ship, the customary term is captain."

Gallagher's eyebrows arched, and he looked over at Corey Hodges who nodded in agreement.

"Is that so? Well then Ellen, let's get this bucket of bolts underway."

The navigator flinched a little at the command. She was far more accustomed to normal naval protocol, but he was the captain, so she promised herself to not transfer off until she'd given him some time.

"Yes, sir. One hour until FTL insertion."

Gallagher stood and walked over to the workstation Hodges was seated at.

"Say, Hodges, pretty cool ship eh?"

"I'd say it is. This is the newest ship in the Earth fleet." Hodges was clearly excited. "Did you know it has a full battery of..."

"Hey, buddy, I don't need a full run down. I'm sure you and the other engineers and tech nerds will tell me if there is something I need to know."

"Sure," replied Hodges.

The *Space Cowboy* was en route to the Barrens to investigate what was going on out there. Gallagher took full advantage of his security clearances, and made a plan on where he would go first and what he wanted to find out.

"We need to know what those damned D'lai are up to. I don't think we have the full picture."

Hodges nodded. Margit Wold walked over to the two men, a pad in her hand.

"Major, from the looks of these scans, that derelict D'lai ship is the focus of their attention."

Gallagher was none too happy that Margit was calling him by his military title, but he guessed it made sense. "What information is that?"

"Sir, *The Terran* and *The Avenger* figured out how to use the radiation in the Barrens to track the location of cloaked ships."

Gallagher looked at the pad and whistled. "That's

an interesting trick. It's similar to the modifications I made to the FTL drive on *The Avenger*."

"Yes, I believe they used the same principles."

"Ya know, I think that we can use it also." Gallagher started punching keys on the console Hodges was sitting at. After a few minutes, he stopped and looked at Hodges and Margit.

"Look at this."

Both of them read over what Gallagher had input.

"Cormac, that's..."

"Yep. As long as the D'lai are in the Barrens, we can use this to see through their cloaks."

"You know buddy, sometimes you scare me." Hodges said.

"Yeah? How so?"

"Well, for starters, you come across as a guy who doesn't care too much, but then you go and do something like this in what, three minutes?"

Gallagher slapped Hodges on the back. "It's nothing. It was Margit who gave me the idea."

"Me? How?"

Gallagher blushed a little before responding. "Well, remember the other night when you were snuggling with me, and asked me how I figured out the mechanics of the Barrens, and used them to modify the FTL?"

Margit looked mortified, and averted her eyes from Hodges. "Cormac, that was a private moment."

"Yeah, but it got me thinking. That material in the system, whatever it is, wreaks havoc on existing technology."

"A hug is what helped you crack their cloaks?" Hodges asked in disbelief.

Both Margit and Gallagher laughed, drawing the eyes of everyone on the bridge.

"It's my secret weapon," said Gallagher.

"Okay boys, I've got other work to do." Margit was grateful for an excuse to get out of that too revealing conversation.

"Yeah, me too," said Hodges. As he walked off the bridge, everyone could hear him mumbling to himself. "A hug is his secret weapon."

Gallagher returned to his command chair to await their arrival at the FTL insertion point. The *Space Cowboy* was fast. Once it jumped, it would be at the barrens in only a few hours. Then the real work would begin.

Near Cathar Prime – The Present

"Damn, this won't work," said Zea Windrow. "They must've reconfigured it during that stupid refit."

Windrow was attempting to sabotage *The Manchester* in an attempt to make it less than valuable to the Three Worlds Alliance. Her plan was to redirect power to enough minor areas of the ship that Kanner would be forced to dry dock it for repairs.

Windrow and an engineer named Rob were halfway through her list of planned disruptions. The biggest one was to trick the sensors that a large gravity well was nearby, thereby forcing the ship to avoid an FTL jump. Windrow didn't have enough time to read through all the new plans from the recent refit, so she relied on older manuals.

"Maybe we can reverse the polarity on the axial component." Rob said, hoping it was helpful.

"That won't work," said Windrow as she pointed at the cabling. "See this?"

"Right. Well, we could always cut the line."

The two of them continued working on their mischief. Half an hour later, enough subsystems had been damaged that Windrow was confident the ship would have to put in for repairs. She was packing up her tools when she heard voices coming from nearby.

Rob and Windrow extinguished their lights and waited. They were in a small tube system that was nowhere near the main ship components. The voices were coming from another section that was probably the first place repair crews would look.

"Those schematics came in handy," whispered Windrow, "I doubt they'll look here for a good long time."

Rob grinned but felt foolish when he remembered she couldn't see him in the darkness. "Let's see if we can get back. I bet they'll come looking for you soon."

The pair crawled back to the access hatch and rushed down the corridor to Windrow's quarters. At least she could open the door from this side and wouldn't have to go back through the crawl space. She kissed Rob on the cheek and entered.

Kanner was waiting inside, along with two bulky crewmen.

"Well, Zea, it seems you've been up to no good."

Windrow tossed her tools on a chair and sat on the bed. As she glared at Kanner, she rushed over and over in her mind what she would say. When she finally did speak, her response disappointed her and Kanner both.

"Yeah, so?"

Kanner shook his head in annoyance. "I thought you'd be able to be trusted here in these..." he looked around the cramped quarters, "...luxury surroundings." He motioned to the two crewmen who roughly grabbed Windrow by the arms, and stood her up. "I was wrong. Take her to the brig."

Windrow resisted, but it was no use. The two goons who held on to her outweighed her by a hundred pounds each. As they shoved her into the corridor, the grasp on her left arm went slack followed quickly by her right arm. Both crewmen slumped to the ground. She looked up to find Rob holding a small blast gun, and it was pointed directly at Kanner's head.

"I took the liberty of freeing the Captain," he said. "Resist and I'll see what kind of damage this thing does to a human skull."

Windrow hugged Rob. "Gee, I didn't know you're my knight in shining armor."

"Easy there, we aren't finished yet."

Kanner grinned at the pair. "What do you think you're going to do? Lock me in here?"

Rob looked at Windrow and then back at Kanner. "Nope. I think the Captain is going to resume her command of her ship." He looked at Windrow, "what do you think, an airlock?"

"You can't do that! I was following orders."

"Orders? You served under me for *seven years* and then at the first chance you just steal my ship?"

"Zea, hon, I didn't..."

"Don't call me that. It's captain to you." She turned back to Rob. "The rest of the crew...?"

"We are with you, Captain!" Several voices flooded the corridor as her loyal crew crowded around. Windrow's eyes welled up with tears at the sight.

"Um, who's driving the ship if you're all down here?"

The navigator looked sheepish, "Ma'am, autopilot?"

Windrow laughed for the first time in days. The ship was hers again. It felt right to be back in command, even though she knew now Earth would hunt her and her crew down.

"Well, back to work everyone." She turned to face Kanner. "As for you, I should kill you but I won't. You can spend the rest of the trip in the brig."

Windrow turned and left. As she entered her bridge once more, she sighed at the familiar surroundings, but then horror struck her.

"Um, someone is going to have to fix all those little things I did."

The navigator turned from her station to look at the captain. "Ma'am, we already did. You're not very good at sabotage."

Everyone on the bridge laughed. "Fine, fine. Let's take stock of what's going on, and figure out our next move."

The tactical officer chimed in. "Ma'am, perhaps we should follow those plasma trails, see where they lead?"

Windrow pondered for a moment then nodded. "Nice idea. We'll do that!"

The Manchester was in for some adventure, but Captain Windrow was up to the challenge. She sat back in her command chair and closed her eyes in contentment.

"Let's go."

Earth – The Present

"YOUR HONOR," SAID RICHARD PLOT TO CHIEF Magistrate Amanda Givens, "it is an unspeakable violation of my client's rights that this trial is being held so speedily. Under Article XVI of the Code of Justice..."

"Violation?" Deputy Minister of Justice Sela Grant interrupted, "a violation of *his* rights? What about the rights of those who lost their lives as result of Burke's actions?"

Plot turned to the Deputy Minister, "If I may continue," he said, not flustered by her interruption.

Grant inclined her head toward the magistrate, who nodded.

"Thank you. As I was saying, it is a gross violation of my client's civil rights that he has not been granted enough time to prepare an adequate defense." Plot turned to face Grant once more. "An adequate defense, as guaranteed under Article XVI."

The Deputy Minister grabbed a notebook from her table, and held it up high. "Your Honor, may I remind this Court that Earth is currently operating under a Code Black condition." Grant turned to face Burke and Plot. "A condition called *precisely* because of the actions of Joseph Eric Burke."

Joseph Burke was seated in a secure Plexiglass

enclosure in the courtroom. His eyes never left Deputy Minister Grant, not even when his own lawyer was speaking. The effect of his stare didn't seem to bother the minister. She was a pro when it came to trying high profile cases such as this. Granted, she'd never had a criminal of quite the renown of Burke. He and his minions at HCH managed to blow up a good chunk of New York City, and destroy a multi-trillion dollar orbital platform.

Magistrate Givens cleared her throat, and leaned slightly toward the microphone at the edge of her high bench. "Code Black suspends major portions of the Code of Justice, including the sixteenth article."

"Code Black is a violation of the Articles of Federation," said Plot.

"Your Honor, the Articles of Federation include provisions for just such a scenario as Code Black." Grant's smug expression infuriated Plot as she continued. "Try to remember counselor that the Articles of Federation were enacted specifically *because* of a planetary threat."

Magistrate Givens interrupted both lawyers. "It is not in the purview of this Court to rule on the planetary constitution. What *is* in our purview is this case. Code Black is a legally constituted order, and it is enforceable, even in this lowly venue." The Magistrate turned her attention to Minister Grant. "Minister, are you ready to proceed with your prosecution?"

"We are, Your Honor."

"Proceed."

In his enclosure, Joseph Burke continued to follow the proceedings closely. Clad in an orange shirt and orange sweatpants, his hands were handcuffed in front of him so that he could drink water, or take notes. His wrists were secured by a long chain, shackled to his ankles. He had sufficient reach for minor tasks, but most everything else was not possible.

As Minister Grant began her opening statement in his trial, Burke slowly moved his chained hands to his lap. Gradually, his hands moved beneath the waistband of his sweatpants. His eyes panned the room constantly to make sure no one was paying him any particular attention. At one point a guard glanced in his direction, and he froze. Seconds later, the guard's attention was diverted elsewhere, so Burke continued his mission.

Prior to being seated in the court, Burke had been searched and passed through a metal detector. However, the guard missed a small ceramic device beneath his scrotum that Burke implanted prior to his arrest. One squeeze from Burke's fingers would acti-vate it.

His hand found the device, but Burke waited for the best time. The blast radius was small, but it would kill anyone, and do significant damage, to anything within ten feet. As Minister Grant was concluding her opening statement, she approached the defense table to hand a copy of her speech to Burke's lawyer.

Just as she was stepping away from the table, Burke forcefully squeezed the device. Less than a heartbeat later, an intense flash of light filled the courtroom, followed by a shock wave of super-heated air and debris. Burke was instantly killed as the explo-sion ripped through the room, immolating his lawyer Richard Plot, Deputy Minister Grant, two guards, and the court reporter. Almost everyone outside the blast zone was severely burned on any non-clothed portion of their body by the intense heat.

Security and rescue personnel responded almost immediately to the disaster. Numerous people lay on the ground writhing in extreme agony from their injuries. The Magistrate, who was behind a high bench, was one of the few mildly injured survivors. Temporarily blinded and deafened from the intense light, and powerful shock wave, she stumbled about the room searching for an exit. One or two others were lucky as well. Within five hours of the explosion, the official body count rose to twenty-nine.

When Gallagher left his post as Secretary General, Janina Agda assumed the office, until a successor could be approved by the Planetary Parliament and sworn in. Acting as both the Secretary General and the Commander in Chief of Earth's military, she suspended all provisions of the Articles of Federation and imposed martial law planet-wide. All civil liberties, freedom of movement, and freedom of the press would only be restored once the chaos was contained.

In an attempt to not appear authoritarian, she addressed the planet in a broadcast that evening.

"My fellow humans, tonight, in response to the terrorist attacks by Humans for Clear Horizons, including the bombing of Joseph Burke's trial, I have *temporarily* suspended the Articles of Federation. I do this not because I want to. I do this because I must. Earth faces an unparalleled crisis. Not only do we face a renewed threat from the D'lai, we also must address domestic terrorism that is building to unacceptable levels on our home planet. I know this time is frightening and uncertain, but I assure you that Earth is doing all it can to respond in these desperate times. I urge all of you to remember that only as a united people can we face this looming threat. Once we have passed these hurdles to our domestic safety, I will fully restore all that has been lost. Good night, and may whatever god you worship grant you peace."

CHAPTER 14

Ryi Bruai- The Ancient Past

The carving was finished. Am'oll labored over the runes for nearly a week as he attempted to perfect them. This relic would be passed down for generations, and he wanted to make absolutely sure it was done well.

Each rune symbolized a word in ancient D'lai. They conveyed his thoughts, his discoveries, and his plans for the future of his people. Until a few days ago, Am'oll believed without reservation that the *Chäi kia Chlüi* was an inspired text. He built his faith around it, and led his people to greater devotion of these scriptures. It shocked him, therefore, when he found in the original *Chäi* an inscription from his father.

Am'oll's father, the *Vdo D'lai*, was the founder of the entire D'lai way of life. A contemporary of the *Vdo Däk*, both men parted ways in a spectacular rift that was the initial cause of the violent war that ended with the D'lai banishment from Cathar Prime. The *Vdo D'lai* died over a hundred years in the past and in all that time, Am'oll had no idea that his father hid this inscription inside the pages of the *Chäi*.

Even now, as he read the words again, their meaning bludgeoned his brain with anger and paranoia. The three words, "we are deceived" had the power to completely undo his entire belief system. Am'oll dug deeper, searching for more clues and etchings in the book. He assiduously pored over every page until he possessed a complete list.

We are deceived

The Umawei are real

The gods are a lie

Final plan

I am a fool

Am'oll now realized that his entire religion was a lie. His way of life, his reasons for leaving Cathar Prime, all of it a fool's errand, and he, the chief fool, led his people to destruction. He remembered his last meeting with his desperately ill father. The memories filled him with scorn and anger.

"My son... I must tell you..." choked the *Vdo D'lai*. The progression of his cancer was too far along for any comfort to be rendered. Every word was a knife cutting into his abdomen.

"Peace, father. Rest." Am'oll said.

His father's face thundered with agony as he yearned to speak. "Son...the *Chäi*..." His withered hands pointed to the holy book nearby.

Thinking it a mercy, Am'oll put his father's hand down upon his tortured frame. "No, papa, rest."

The *Vdo D'lai* tensed as another wave of pain swept his body. Pointing once more at the book, his eyes implored Am'oll. Just as suddenly as the pain began, it ceased and with it, life and breath left the tortured old man's body. Am'oll grabbed his prayer beads, and he wailed as his father's body relaxed in death.

Am'oll prayed and wished for decades that his father had been able to share his parting thoughts. Now, sitting here in this ancient ship in Ryi Braui, Am'oll believed he latched on to what his father was trying to tell him. The knowledge of their utter betrayal and deception was a knife to his gut. He had to tell his people.

The runes he inscribed on the mysterious cylinder found in the *Hyai kia Chlüi* served as a perfect vessel for his revelation. Once he finished, he didn't know what he would do. Should he repent and fall upon his own sword as penance? Should he convince the D'lai to make the long voyage home, and beg the Däk'in to accept them?

His thoughts so consumed him that he never realized that his *ftialchuaṭ*, his brother, regarded him from a concealed room nearby. Ryäi looked on with growing hatred as his brother descended into what he perceived to be madness. He didn't grasp, and didn't care, what Am'oll was doing, or what he may have discovered. All he saw was a madman leading the people down a dangerous path. He could wait no longer. As he left his hiding place, he reached to his waist to confirm the presence of his *sdiau*. The double-edged blade reflected the dim light as he edged closer.

Hearing the approach of someone, Am'oll whirled to face him. His eyes blazed with fervor as he recognized his brother Ryäi.

"*Riaẓ ftialchuaṭ,*" said Am'oll. "Why are you..."

His eyes were drawn to the *sdiau* on Ryäi's belt as recognition dawned on his face. "You've come to murder me." It was a statement, not a question, as Am'oll innately understood what was about to happen.

"*Riaẓ ftialchuaṭ*," said Ryäi, returning the usual greeting between the brothers. His right hand never left the blade, but his eyes revealed the truth. He moved in upon his brother, inch by inch.

"Am'oll, I do not wish to harm you," he lied. "Your people are worried and lost."

His eyes danced across the room, taking in the presence of the *Chäi*, the engraved cylinder, and the general filth from his brother, who had not bathed or left this room in days.

Am'oll's eyes narrowed, "You were never a good liar Ryäi." He forced a smile to his lips as he spoke. "You do as you must." Am'oll turned his back to his brother. "However, you will not do it while looking into my eyes."

Am'oll knelt before the *Chäi* and the runes, his arms outstretched over them. As he waited for death, he chanted a prayer, even though he sensed deep in his soul that his prayer meant nothing. Ryäi, filled with spite and rage at his brother's abandonment of the D'lai people, swiftly stepped up to his kneeling brother, and plunged the dagger to the hilt in his back. Am'oll did not even cry out as the blade fatally wounded him.

As the life ebbed from him, Am'oll spoke the words he inscribed in the runes, "We are deceived... we are fools...the gods are a lie...the final plan..." He slumped over, blood pooling at his feet as Ryäi withdrew the *sdiau* and viciously stabbed him again and again.

Unable to speak, Am'oll turned his face, and with one final breath, looked into the eyes of his murderer. What Ryäi saw in his brother's dying gaze was not fear or hate or pain. He saw forgiveness. As the light left Am'oll's eyes, Ryäi wiped the blood on Am'oll's *sdawij*, took one final glance at the room, and left. He had no way of knowing that neither he nor any other living being would step foot in this room again for over a thousand years.

The Barrens – The Present

THE SPACE COWBOY ARRIVED RIGHT ON TIME IN The Barrens. Gallagher was unsure if he really wanted to be in this desolate patch of space. The last time he was here while serving about *The Avenger*, he needed to practically re-invent FTL technology to avoid being stranded here.

Relaxing in his comfortable quarters, his arm around Margit Wold. His heart thumped as he held her tight. Her eyes met his and for a moment, neither of them needed to speak. All was right with the world and their hearts were as one. An ear shattering beeping interrupted their moment, and Gallagher groaned as he detached himself from their embrace to silence the alert.

"Gallagher here. This had better be *really* good!"

"Sir, we've arrived in The Barrens," came the voice of his navigator.

"Yeah, so, did you have a point?"

"Um, sir, you asked to be notified the moment we arrived."

Gallagher slapped his forehead in frustration, remembering saying something like that a few hours ago.

"Right. Um...thanks?"

"Sir, did you have updated orders now that we have arrived?"

Gallagher looked longingly at Margit. Her eyes gave him the come-hither look. Gallagher gulped, his Adams apple rising and lowering.

"Navigator, I was just about to um...get in the shower."

"I understand, sir. Ten minutes?"

Gallagher eyed Margit once more. "Better make it twenty."

"Affirmative, sir." The communication ended and Gallagher resumed his position on the couch.

"Was she giving me attitude?"

"Relax, hon, we only have twenty minutes." Margit leaned in closer.

"Right."

Twenty-three minutes later, Gallagher and Margit Wold sauntered onto the bridge arm in arm. Neither of them cared if the whole crew knew they were a couple. Out here, military protocol was not quite as stringent. Beside, Margit wasn't an official crew member. She was a United Nations observer.

"Report." Gallagher said as he sat in his command chair. He chuckled a little, causing some crewman to turn and watch him. "Oh, sorry. I've always wanted to say that."

From his position at the tactical station, the tactical officer spoke up. "Sir, we've reached the outskirts of The Barrens. I've run some preliminary scans of the region and..."

"Let me guess, you found nothing?"

"Sir, not nothing, no. I found what I expected to find." The officer turned to check his pad before continuing. "I found hundreds of plasma trails. All of them lead to *that*." He pointed at the main view screen.

Gallagher followed his finger and stood in surprise. "What is that?"

"Sir," said the tactical officer, "that is a derelict D'lai ship that I believe, based on sensor data, has been out here for over a thousand years."

Gallagher turned to Margit, "Do you think that is..."

Margit grinned with excitement. "Yeah, it must be."

From his station nearby, Corey Hodges interrupted. "Um, it must be what, exactly?"

Margit turned to Hodges. "If I'm right, that is a

ship from the original banishment of the D'lai from Cathar Prime."

"Ah, okay. Well, that figures." Hodges said.

Margit giggled. "It's okay Hodges, you don't have to geek out over it like I am."

"That's a relief," said Hodges.

"So, if that is an ancient abandoned D'lai ship, that explains what?" Gallagher asked.

"Those plasma trails, they are D'lai."

"We can't punch through their cloaks can we?"

"No, sir," replied the tactical officer. "We've received reports from two different ships of a similar number of plasma trails leaving Cathar Prime."

"Gotcha." A thought passed through Gallagher's mind. "We *are* cloaked, right"

"Yes, sir. As soon as we left FTL we activated it. We also contacted *The Terran*."

Further discussion ensued about the discovery of the ancient D'lai wreck and soon it was decided that *Space Cowboy* would move in closer. Minutes later, as the ship was inching closer, proximity alarms began blaring on the bridge.

Gallagher turned to his navigator. "What's up?"

"Sir, another ship...unknown registry."

"Have they detected us?"

"Negative. Our cloak is still active...wait. That's not... Captain, that ship! Sir, it's following us!"

Gallagher whirled to tactical. "I thought we were cloaked?"

The tactical officer checked his monitors. "Sir, we are! They somehow can see through our cloak?"

"Emergency. Navigator, get us out of..."

"Sir, incoming hail."

"Put it on. Voice only."

"This is Captain Arvesp Erth of *The Avenger* to the unknown Earth ship."

"Arvesp? What the hell?"

"Major Gallagher? What are you doing out here?"

"I can ask you the same thing. How is it you knew we were here?" Gallagher asked.

"Major," said Arvesp, "We have figured out a primitive method of scanning another cloaked ship. We don't get much detail, but we can at least figure out enough to know who we might be dealing with."

"Captain, this is UN Observer Margit Wold."

"Hello, Ms. Wold," said Arvesp.

"Margit is fine. Anyway, we are on a fact-finding mission and this new technology, we'd like to know more about it."

"Margit, my ship is observing the D'lai vessels

that are nearby. We only dared to communicate with you using a narrow communications band. Our system is not capable of sharing data."

Margit turned to Gallagher. "Cormac, we need to get this."

Nodding, Gallagher addressed Arvesp, "Continue your observation. We can rendezvous...um... somewhere in the system where we won't be observed."

"Yes, Major. I'm sending the coordinates to a nearby moon where *The Terran* is hiding. We'll meet you back there in..." she paused for a moment, "six hours. Arvesp out."

Gallagher walked over to the navigator and put a hand on her shoulder. "You heard the Captain. Let's go."

If all went well, in six hours Earth would have the technology to detect cloaked ships.

"That'll be a handy piece of tech." Gallagher said as he waited to arrive at the moon.

Ryi Bruai – The Present

"NEGOTIATOR, WE HAVE AN INCOMING transmission from our agent on Earth."

Zat'ol, resting in his quarters, smirked at the news. "Put it on."

"This is Agent Y of Earth. Leader One has left the planet and the cloak is weakened. We await your arrival." The transmission ended. Zat'ol stood and paced the small living area of his quarters, considering the news. Earth, or *Fü*, in the D'lai tongue, seemed to be leaderless and its cloak was damaged. The Negotiator was pleased at the developments.

Even though he was not quite ready to leave Ryi Bruai, he was eager to get the next phase of this war started. He ordered a large detachment of his fleet to disembark and travel with all available speed to Earth.

"Remain cloaked until I give you the order to attack," Zat'ol told his commanders. "As soon as we are ready here, we will join you and the war can begin in earnest."

Despite the misgivings of a good number of his fleet commanders, they were itching for action. The hundred ships now en route to Earth was a good start. Zat'ol continued reviewing his latest attempts at deciphering the runes. Already, he discovered how to replicate The Seed, but there was something more that he wasn't sure he was reading correctly.

The first major portions of the runes were instructions to future generations of D'lai, but the last section seemed to be a warning. If he was reading it right, it said "we are deceived," and "final plan." A few other lines were not quite readable. Time had not been kind and the vacuum of space had damaged the cylinder. Zat'ol was attempting to use the computer to recreate the symbols. He also ran them through the *awch jdiv* to check if the Umawei had any suggestions.

Zat'ol had just deciphered another few words, "the gods," when his comm panel beeped. Annoyed at the interruption, he punched the control almost too hard. "What is it?"

"Negotiator, apologies. We are tracking what seems to be a Rozk ship nearby."

"Rozk, what are they doing out here?"

"Unknown, sir. We are attempting to discern that."

Zat'ol glanced sadly at his work station. "I'm on my way to the bridge."

"Very good sir."

He left his quarters for the long walk to the bridge. Even though he had purposely rebuilt this ship, he wondered to himself why he'd allowed the builders to make the corridors so long. It was a stupid oversight on his part. The original ship boasted these same strangely long halls, and he hated them.

As he finally stepped on to the bridge, concern bloomed on his face at the level of activity. Crew members were gesticulating and moving about the deck frantically.

"What's going on?"

Several crew members didn't seem to hear him so Zat'ol shouted his question once more.

Immediately, the noise died down and a junior officer approached the Negotiator.

"Sir, the Rozk ship scanned us."

"What? How?" Zat'ol ran over to the tactical station. "Are we still cloaked?"

"Yes, sir, our cloak has not even wavered. They can somehow see through it."

"Can we see them?"

"Yes, they are uncloaked and hailing us."

Zat'ol thought for a moment. A Rozk ship, out here and alone. "Tactical, uncloak the ship and lock weapons on that Rozk vessel."

"Yes sir, uncloaking. Weapons lock confirmed."

After taking a couple of breaths to orient himself, Zat'ol said, "Tactical. Destroy that ship."

Seconds passed and nothing happened. Zat'ol faced the tactical officer. "I said, destroy that ship!"

"Sir, I fired and nothing happened."

The Negotiator hit a switch on his command chair. "Engineering, what is going on? Why aren't we firing?"

"Sir," came the voice, "we did fire."

Confusion filled Zat'ol. The order to fire was given, the ship *thinks* it fired, but the Rozk ship was still out there, undamaged.

Suddenly, *The Spector* was rocked by a massive energy pulse. Realization hit Zat'ol as he realized what was happening. The strange properties of The Barrens deflected their weapon fire and, like a boomerang, redirected it back at his ship.

"Sir, we have reports of explosive decompression on two decks. Damage reports coming in from all over the ship."

"That's not all," said the navigator, "we have lost power to the engines and are drifting..." On the screen, Zat'ol could see the derelict D'lai ship coming closer. "We are on a collision course. Impact in two minutes."

The crew worked feverishly to restore power to the ship. Damage control crews were able to stop the ship's momentum, and not a moment too soon. For now, *The Spector* was dead in space, unable to cloak, and vulnerable. It would take the crew hours to repair enough of the ship to full functionality.

Until then, The Negotiator and his entire crew were powerless to stop what was coming next.

The Barrens – The Present

THE MANCHESTER EXITED FTL AND CAPTAIN Windrow ordered a full stop. After regaining her captaincy and dealing with the few crew members, including former First Mate Kanner, she had ordered the ship to travel with all available speed to The Barrens. The plasma trails from the D'lai ships near Cathar Prime was a mystery too interesting to avoid.

"Tactical, scan the region for plasma trails."

"Yes, Captain."

"I'll be in my..."

"A moment, Captain," replied the tactical officer. "Um, my scans detect a lot of very recent activity."

Windrow stood from her command chair and approached his station.

"What's going on, John?"

"Well, ma'am, as much as I can tell from these early scans, not only are there hundreds of distinct trails, but there are signs that several ships have come and gone – all within the past day."

"Hmm. Something is definitely up. We should..."

"Incoming message Captain."

Windrow turned to face the comm station. "From whom?"

"Ma'am, actually, two now incoming. One from a ship called *Space Cowboy* and another from an unidentified ship."

"Put the one from *Space Cowboy* on."

"This is Major Cormac Gallagher of the Earth ship *Space Cowboy*. Zea, is that you?"

A smile broke over Windrow's face as she heard the voice of her old friend. "Cormac, um, what are you doing out here?"

"Zea, great to hear a friendly voice! I've...uh...left government work and traded it in for this old bucket of bolts."

"Well, I go away for a little while, temporarily lose

my ship to *your* former government, and then I find you dozens of lights years from home!"

"We've got a lot to catch up on. I'd offer to grab a coffee with you but, things are kinda crazy. What brings you along?"

"Cormac, we've been following some plasma trails from Cathar Prime. We thought we'd try to see what was going on. Looks like war is on the horizon to me."

"We're doing something similar Zea. I'm sending your navigator coordinates. We're currently hiding behind this giant floating rock, so we can keep an eye on things."

The navigator nodded as she received the coordinates. "We've got 'em and we're on our way. See you in..." Windrow paused, "three hours."

"Swell. *Space Cowboy* out."

"While we make the trip, let's find out what we can." Windrow said as she stood and left the bridge.

Instead of heading to her quarters to grab a little shut-eye, Windrow diverted and decided to visit the brig. She had some questions for Kanner. *The Manchester* had a rather small make-shift brig. It was a converted storage room she used in the past to conceal smuggled items. It was a perfect venue, secure and well-hidden.

Her hands squeezed into fists as she entered. Windrow was still rather peeved that Kanner agreed to steal her ship. She wasn't quite ready to let bygones be bygones. A stocky security officer sat in a too-small chair near the makeshift cell Kanner was crammed into.

"To what do I owe this auspicious honor," said Kanner as soon as he spied Windrow enter.

"You should be honored I've not put you out the airlock yet, Kanner."

Kanner sneered at the comment and crossed his arms defiantly.

"You can't keep me in here forever," he said. "Sooner or later you'll have to figure out something."

"Sure, I'll hop right on that," said Windrow, "just as soon as I deal with everything else you managed to muck up in the twenty-four hours you were in charge."

Kanner glared at her. "Why are you here?"

Windrow sighed as she approached the bars of his make-shift cell. "I just want to know why?"

"Why? Why I obeyed a direct order from Earth?"

"No, why you had to be a damned spy all those years!" Anger bloomed on her face as she spoke. "I mean, god, you were my friend!"

"Friends...there's a good joke." Kanner said. Cruelty tinged his voice as he spoke. "I was never your friend. You're a damn criminal."

Windrow recoiled. "Fine. I'm a criminal. Did you have a point?" She was quickly forgetting her reason for even coming down here. Without waiting for a reply, she said, "did you know about the chaos on Earth?"

Kanner looked at the roof of his cell as he pondered. "Chaos is inevitable when you have a cowboy running the show."

Realizing he was referring to Gallagher, her right eyebrow shot up. "Funny story maybe I'll share if you ever get out of here."

Windrow turned to leave. She understood that Kanner would only toy with her and never share anything of importance. "If this was a military ship, you'd be up for a court-martial. Since it's not, I'll just keep you here."

As she exited the room, Kanner shouted, "Do your worst, Zea. It won't hurt!"

"Maybe I should put him out an airlock," she mused as she walked down the corridor. "One less mouth to feed, anyway."

She just entered her quarters when her comm

panel lit up. "No rest for the wicked around here," she said to no one in particular. Glancing at the message, she frowned and then activated the panel. "Tactical, what's going on?"

"Captain, a large D'lai vessel just uncloaked and appears to have fired at another ship."

"Great. What's the status of that other ship?"

"Well, ma'am, it seems to be okay. I can't say the same thing for the D'lai battleship, though."

Looking around her quarters and especially wishing she could crawl into bed, Windrow exhaled and shook her head. "Okay, I'm on my way up. Save me a seat."

Windrow exited and trod down the corridor once more.

"I need a vacation."

CHAPTER 15

Ryi Bruai- The Ancient Past

Ryäi avoided the glances of his fellow D'lai as he stepped into the massive command center on board *The Faithful*. Moments earlier he killed his own brother Am'oll in a vain attempt to stop his madness. Now, it was time to continue the journey and let the people find a new home.

Already D'lai astronomers concluded that their current system was no good. The few planets and moons in the system were virtually uninhabitable. The D'lai remnant would need to leave this system, and venture off to nearby stars. A candidate star system was less than seven light years from Ryi Bruai. Despite the fact that it would take them at least twelve years to reach this new system, it was important for their long term survival. These ancient ships would not sustain them forever.

"Ryäi, where is Am'oll?"

Ryäi shook his head as he spoke. "The *chtuai* is still below decks reading his scriptures."

The assembled leaders faces were all grave as Ryäi spoke. "We need some of the minerals in nearby asteroids, so we can repair ourselves en route."

Once the D'lai left Ryi Braui and ventured into interstellar space, raw materials would be scarce. They needed to blast apart asteroids and salvage the ore inside as a final step before leaving.

"Fine. Do it."

The massive generation ship moved toward a nearby asteroid belt. Engineers already identified several candidate rocks that should contain enough material. Once *The Faithful* was finished collecting, the other ships in the fleet would enter the field and mine as well.

"Approaching the asteroid," came the voice of the navigator. "Stopping forward momentum."

Ryäi had no interest in the maneuvers, so he

perused some literature that had been written by various D'lai on their long journey. Some of the writing was quite good.

"Firing mining lasers."

Paying little attention, Ryäi continued to read. He looked up when he heard a frantic discussion between an engineer and a tactical officer.

"I did fire!"

"Look at the asteroid. Nothing happened. It's almost as if..."

The deck tilted wildly as artificial gravity and lights suddenly went out. Enormous explosions could be heard throughout the ship as feedback from the mining lasers impacted *The Faithful*.

From their vantage point near the asteroid belt, the other generation ships watched in muted horror as *The Faithful* lurched away from the giant rock they'd attempted to mine. Gas and corpses could be seen blowing out of gaping holes in the ships hull.

"What happened?" Ryäi shouted as he floated free on the command deck. When no one responded, he tried to twist to find someone to answer. Most of the D'lai nearby appeared to be unconscious and a few were obviously dead. Ryäi felt along his body and found he too was severely injured. A jagged piece of shrapnel was lodged in his abdomen, and he knew he would bleed out before help could arrive.

He didn't have long to wait for death. Seconds after he realized the extent of his injuries, a huge fireball erupted on the deck, blowing an enormous hole in the outer hull and blowing Ryäi and every other D'lai out into space.

The remaining ships could only gape as explosion after explosion ripped through *The Faithful*. It was readily apparent that no one would survive the disaster. The nine remaining vessels moved away from the asteroid belt and orders were given throughout the remaining fleet to avoid firing any kind of energy weapons. The survivors hoped the use of ballistic weapons would work, but weeks would pass before they tested their theories.

Seven months after the destruction of *The Faithful*, and with enough supplies to last for the journey, the last of the D'lai left Ryi Bruai and embarked on what they hoped would be their final journey as they searched for a home.

Floating dead in space, the derelict remains of *The Faithful* remained a testament to the foolishness of anyone who did not understand Ryi Bruai and its awesome yet destructive properties. Unseen and hidden, the Umawei waited for the rest of the saga to play out. They'd be waiting a very, very long time.

Earth – The Present

"GENERAL AGDA, WE ARE SITTING DUCKS IF WE can't get that cloak restored." Admiral Kelly Austin said during a meeting of military leaders. "We know the D'lai could be out there."

"Calm yourself Admiral," said Agda, "we are working on the problem."

"General, I'm calm. However, the longer we take to restore our security, the more my men and women are in harms way in orbit."

"Beside the cloak, do you have anything useful to report?"

Stunned, Admiral Austin shook her head no.

"Good, now we need to get on to the matter of internal security."

General Agda was good at pivoting from topics she did not want to discuss. The cloak was not her priority, and she was doing everything she could to keep it working. Inwardly, she was frightened about what could happen to Earth when the D'lai finally made their move.

"The bombing of Burke's trial is an unmitigated disaster," said the Chief of Military Justice. "How can we put on trial any other members of HCH? What if they also are able to commit an act of mass murder?"

"The solution is quite simple, ladies and gentleman." All eyes turned to General Agda. "We do not put any more members of HCH on trial."

The room erupted with voices. General Agda knew what she was doing, so she simply waited for the uproar to die down. After a few minutes, she calmed raised her left hand in the air. At her signal, the room fell silent.

Agda gravely examined each face in the room before speaking. "It is clear we have only one course of action here." She paused for dramatic effect. "Anyone who is a member of HCH must be executed." The room grew wild again so once again she held up her hand. "We are in a state of Martial Law. These *criminals* have disrupted the peace of our planet. What would you do in my position?"

Realization slowly dawned on the faces of the assembled military leaders. The Chief of Military Justice was the first to speak. "General, under the terms of Code Black and Martial Law, you are correct. We deal with criminals in the harshest form necessary to restore law and order."

Agda checked with each leader present. When none objected further to her plan, she nodded. "Commander," she turned to the head of security, "issue the commands."

Despite the fact that it was legally sound to pass summary judgment and execute the sentence during this time, few in the room realized that Earth was now edging toward becoming a full-fledged autocracy.

In dozens of secure prison facilities around the planet, HCH members were dragged from their cells. Most were shot or hanged. None of those who had been previously captured escaped a death sentence.

While these sentences were being carried out, General Agda issued dozens of decrees further strengthening her hold on political and military power. The curfew that was issued planet wide was extended. All non-humans were to be deported off-world immediately. Anyone who protested these orders was arrested and threatened with immediate imprisonment. Despite the human tendency to resist persecution, the population fell in to line with their new reality.

Later that evening in her quarters, Agda stopped working and sat down next to her companion. A Greek expatriate, Alexis Marakos scooted over to give her a little room. The two met when she was taking a short vacation several months ago. His stunning physique and piercing blue eyes instantly ensnared the ordinarily loveless Agda. Her desire to share her life with another human being blinded her to the trap she now found herself in.

After she fell in love with Alexis, she discovered what she believed to be his true nature. At that point however, it was too late. Despite her normal sense of order and decorum, General Janina Agda would do and say anything for his continued attention.

During the past twenty years, dozens of spies were unknowingly recruited by the D'lai, with the goal of insinuating themselves in high places. As no D'lai or Cathari could show their faces on Earth, it was necessary to turn humans to their cause. One such spy, Alexis Marakos, happened to be in the right place at the right time, to trap this particular fly in his own seductive brand of amber.

Alexis lazily massaged Agda's tense shoulders while she stared straight ahead, deep in thought.

Eventually, she sighed with contentment and started to share her day with him.

"I've ordered the retrieval from deep storage of a cylinder that was discovered on Mars decades ago."

This piqued the curiosity of Alexis. "What kind of cylinder?"

The General tilted her head slightly, but her eyes remained fixed on a spot on the wall in front of her. "I'm not sure. We read about it from the journals of that terrorist Joseph Burke. We think it or something found near it was the reason the D'lai attacked Mars." Agda was unsure why she was telling any of this to Alexis. She couldn't resist his allure and was at ease sharing things with him.

"I wonder why it was buried on Mars in the first place," said Alexis. "It must be valuable." He continued to work the tension from her neck and shoulders.

"Mmm that feels nice. I've been so tense lately."

"I can see why," said Alexis. "So much is happening and now with that Gallagher fellow off playing cowboy..."

"Take it easy on Gallagher. He was never suited to the job."

"Still, you have enough to worry about."

Agda felt the tension of the day escaping and closed her eyes. "Let's talk about something else."

Alexis really wanted to talk more about the cylinder. He wasn't the only one on the planet searching for it. He knew that his handler wanted it for his own purposes as well.

"Sure, hon." It frustrated him that he couldn't pry the exact location out of Agda without revealing his true purpose. He really didn't like the woman all that much, but his charm and acting abilities fooled the incautious general. As soon as he got what he needed, he vowed to eliminate the problem.

Near the orbit of the moon, a small D'lai fleet silently arrived. Earth was in more peril now that at any other time in its history, and General Agda would be the primary cause of its downfall if the Negotiator's plan succeeded.

The Barrens – The Present

"WHAT IN THE NAME OF CREATION?" ADMIRAL Christopher was trying to enjoy a steaming cup of tea when *The Spector* nearly blew itself up. Everything had been relatively quiet, and even the unexpected arrival of both *Space Cowboy* and *The Manchester* didn't dampen the admiral's mood.

"The more the merrier," he said to his aide when notified of the two ships arrivals. "I like that Gallagher fellow, he could be of some use out here."

As soon as *Space Cowboy* entered orbit around the same moon as *The Terran*, Admiral Christopher invited Major Gallagher and a few of his officers on board. He particularly enjoyed playing host, even this far from anywhere.

Gallagher, Margit Wold, and Hodges landed on the shuttle bay of *The Terran* and enjoyed a short tour with the promise of a sumptuous dinner, courtesy of Admiral Christopher.

"Why do you think they gave this job to someone as old as the crypt keeper?" Gallagher jokingly asked Hodges when the three of them were alone.

"Crypt keeper?" Margit asked.

"You know, old skull and bones guy from that old show *Tales from the Crypt*," said Gallagher.

Margit shook her head. "Um...no. You've lost me."

Hodges chuckled at her apparent confusion. "I guess he hasn't had much time to make you watch all his ancient shows, what with all the other stuff you two have been up to."

Margit playfully slapped Hodges chest. "Oh stop it."

"No, but seriously, why such an old guy?" Gallagher wasn't ready to let this one go.

"I read up on him before we arrived. It seems he refused to retire a dozen or so years back, and some Admiral named Kelly Austin threw him out here where he could do the least harm."

"Kelly Austin, I remember her. She was pleasant enough."

Margit eyed Gallagher who in turn sheepishly looked away. "Not like you, though!"

"Mmm hmm."

In an attempt to change the subject, Hodges asked, "So what do you guys think about all this seeing through cloak stuff? Pretty cool huh?"

Gallagher was thankful for the reprieve. He glanced once more at Margit before turning toward Hodges. "If it really works, it's a game changer for sure."

"I understand that it only works out here in The Barrens." Margit chimed in. "But I wonder if we can reproduce the conditions in some way to help us replicate the technology elsewhere."

"That's actually something that might work," said Gallagher. "Hodges, what readings have you taken of this region?"

"Oh no, we aren't working tonight boys."

"Damn," said Gallagher. "Just when the brain juices are pumping too!"

The comm started beeping. "Saved by the bell," said Gallagher.

As she went to activate the communications channel, Margit mumbled, "You and your references to the twentieth century."

"Hey, at least you got that one!" Gallagher said just as the voice of Admiral Christopher filled the room.

"I hate to break up your party folks, but we've got a situation. I'd appreciate if you'd come on up to the bridge."

"Sure, Admiral, on our way," said Margit. She ended the communication and looked longingly at Gallagher.

"Always on the clock it seems," said Gallagher. "Come on Corey, Margit, wouldn't want to keep old Skeletor waiting."

As the trio exited the room, Margit looked over at Hodges and mouthed "Skeletor?" Hodges shrugged and kept walking.

Arriving at the bridge, Gallagher and his companions walked over to where Admiral Christopher was leaning on his cane and observing a sizable monitor.

"Major, we've identified a D'lai ship as being a rebuilt version of *The Spector*."

Gallagher stepped back at the name of the ship. "Wow, so the very ship I was a hostage on, that one?"

The admiral frowned, "I'm not familiar with that."

"It's a great story, I'll have to tell you about it sometime."

"Fine. Anyway, it seems it fired on our companion ship *The Avenger.*"

Now it was Hodges turn to be shocked. "Slow way down buddy. You're telling me that both *The Spector* and *The Avenger* are here?" Hodges turned to Gallagher. "Am I the only one with a little Deja Vu?"

"Nope, I'm feeling a little dizzy myself buddy."

"Next thing you know," Gallagher said, "someone is gonna eject me into space and leave me floating."

Hodges rolled his eyes. "It happens *one time* and you never let me live it down."

Both Margit and the admiral stared at Gallagher and Hodges. "I'm sensing there is a bit of a history here we don't know about," said Margit.

"Darn right there is! But anyway, what do you mean *The Spector* almost blew itself up?" Gallagher asked.

"Right, yes. Well, it seems that when they fired their energy beams, it kinda ricocheted and hit them back instead of *The Avenger*."

"I'm still stuck on why they could even see *The Avenger* in the first place," said Hodges. "Was their cloak damaged?"

"No, that's a story for *me* to tell you folks."

Gallagher was deep in thought. "The Barrens does have some strange effects. I theorized that any kind of energy beams would not work here back when me and Hodges were serving on *The Avenger* and we got stuck here."

"Right, I remember something about how you practically reinvented the FTL drive. That was on *The Avenger*?" Margit asked. "Such a small universe!"

"Admiral, what's the status of both ships now?"

"Major, *The Avenger* is cloaked and keeping up her observations. *The Spector* seems to be doing okay, though for a minute there it looked as if it was going to crash into that old D'lai relic."

"Okay, Admiral, clearly all of us need to have a long conversation. D'lai relic? Wow."

"Yes, let's go talk over dinner."

"Yes, let's," said Gallagher. The four of them exited the bridge. It was going to be a rather interesting discussion, of that Gallagher was sure.

Ryi Bruai – The Present

As the remainder of the D'lai armada waited impatiently upon Negotiator Zat'ol to give the order to move out, two cloaked D'lai vessels entered the system. The ships, fresh from their mission to Mars, carried one of the greatest treasures in the universe – an Umawei Seed. Neither ship commander knew precisely what was being transported, but it was apparent from the urgency at which Zat'ol had ordered their journey back to Ryi Bruai that it was incredibly important.

Upon reaching the system, the commander of one of the ships notified *The Spector* of their arrival. On board Zat'ol's ship, crew members and officers were excitedly preparing for their approach. *The Spector* was still repairing its systems from the disastrous attempt to destroy *The Avenger* when it was masquerading as a Rozk ship in order to get a closer look at the cloaked D'lai fleet.

"Negotiator, our cargo and shuttle bays are still heavily damaged. We cannot accept transport from *The Bitter Dawn*."

Zat'ol earnestly believed that no cost was too great to achieve his goals, even the lives of his own crew. He callously ordered that the repairs proceed quickly. Other systems and decks could wait. He *must* have that Seed. From his readings of the Am'oll runes, he learned that in order to replicate the Seed, he must have three of them. The runes were carved on one and *The Bitter Dawn* was carrying one it had captured on Mars. His agents on Earth were working to acquire the third.

"Fix the shuttle bay and get me that Seed." His determination to conquer the galaxy overrode all reason.

"Yes, Negotiator." The crew of *The Spector* realized that failure in this instance was not an option any of them could endure. Zat'ol was ruthless in meting out punishment to those who offended him and none of them desired to experience first-hand the cold vacuum of space.

The Bitter Dawn approached *The Spector* an hour after arrival in the system. The commander had been briefed on the situation aboard the Negotiator's ship. The cabal was prepared to intervene if Zat'ol exhibited further signs of the madness that seemed to be enveloping him.

Nevertheless, the commander ordered that The Seed be placed on a shuttle in preparation for transporting it to *The Spector*.

"Commander, The Seed is prepared. We await your orders."

The commander turned to his tactical officer for an update. "What is the status?"

"Sir, *The Spector* signals that it is ready to receive our shuttle."

"Fine. Launch now."

Aboard the shuttle, The Seed, three security officers, and a pilot disembarked from *The Bitter Dawn* and made the short journey to the uncloaked and still damaged command ship. After a rough docking, a contingent of crewman moved The Seed from the shuttle to Zat'ol's lab. As soon as the two Seeds were in proximity, both of them began to glow a muted green color. Alarmed, the crewman left and secured the room. Zat'ol did not expect a physical reaction with the nearness of the two devices, and he was disturbed. What would happen when all three were together?

He put out of his mind the worry. Re-entering the bridge, he checked to see who was at their stations, and then began barking out orders. "Navigator, when can we depart Ryi Bruai?"

"Sir, we need six more hours before we can safely leave. Our cloaks are not..."

"Repair them en route. I'm ready to get out of here."

"Sir," replied an engineer who was at a console monitoring the repairs, "If we leave too soon, we may not be able to cloak. We need more time."

Zat'ol glared at the engineer for a full, silent minute. The engineer averted his eyes in discomfort, fearing his was going to taste death far too soon for his own desires.

"You have three hours. If we aren't done with necessary repairs by then, we will leave our chances up to fate!"

The engineer breathed a heavy sigh, and got back to work.

No one on the bridge spoke for almost an hour, and none of them wanted to enter the next phase of this mission without the ability to cloak.

Three hours and fifteen minutes later, the repair teams indicated that the cloak was restored.

"Communications, signal the fleet. Set course for the FTL insertion coordinates."

"Yes, Negotiator," said the communications officer.

"Send word to the fleet in orbit around Earth to alert them to our imminent arrival."

The D'lai fleet in Ryi Bruai would break into two smaller groups while the ships under Zat'ol's command would combine with the Earth fleet. The second and smallest group of battleships would travel to Mars. It was Zat'ol's overall plan to take the third Seed by force, if necessary, then after replicating more, attempt to seed Mars. He knew the Umawei failed in their previous attempt, but he felt sure that the recent terraforming efforts by the hapless humans would be of use in his shot at restoring the Umawei home world.

One final command needed to be issued, and this

one, despite Zat'ol's zeal for his objectives, was both the most critical and the most abhorrent of all the planned actions. Before leaving Cathar Prime, Zat'ol and the D'lai Authority selected fifty thousand Cathari and transported them off the surface of Cathar Prime to a waiting freighter in orbit. These imprisoned Cathari would be given to the Umawei as hosts for their planned return to physical form.

"Communications, send word to *The Martian Sword* to get underway," said Zat'ol. Genocide did not bother the Negotiator. He did not care that it was the D'lai, not the Cathari, who needed to answer for their crimes. His hatred overwhelmed his reason, and it would be his downfall.

CHAPTER 16

The Barrens- The Present

"Captain, the D'lai appear to be on the move."

Arvesp glanced up from her pad in alarm. "What? All of them?"

Already on heightened alert after recent indications that two D'lai ships recently entered the system and rendezvoused with *The Spector*, Arvesp was not blindsided that more movement could be imminent. Her previous orders were to alert *The Terran,* and by extension *The Manchester* and *Space Cowboy*. All four ships met up and were ready to form a small convoy if necessary.

"Yes, from our sensor readings, it appears that the entire fleet is on the move."

"Hail *The Terran.*"

"On screen Captain"

On the large view screen at the front of the bridge, Admiral Christopher appeared haggard and not well.

"Admiral, sorry to bother you but we've detected movement in the D'lai fleet."

"Captain, yes, my people have seen that as well." The Admiral faced someone off-screen for a moment and then returned his attention to Arvesp. "I'm patching in Gallagher and Windrow as well.

The faces of Major Gallagher and Zea Windrow appeared.

"Okay folks, it seems to be time to figure out our next moves." Admiral Christopher said. "Things are heating up out here."

"Admiral," said Gallagher, "our ships are closer to an FTL insertion than the D'lai fleet. I say we skedaddle on out of here and get to Earth, like, right now."

"Agreed Major," said Windrow. "My ship is ready to go."

"Captain Erth, your thoughts?"

"Admiral, I'm with the rest of the group. Let's go. We can figure out the rest of our plans en route."

All four ships were capable of communicating with each other while jumping, thanks to a new piece of technology thought up by Corey Hodges and Margit Wold. While the various ship commanders were preoccupied with watching the D'lai threat, Hodges and Margit decided to solve one of the biggest problems in FTL travel. Communication had always been possible while jumping, but only with a stationary relay. Hodges figured out how to imitate that process with a virtual relay. Margit and Hodges tested the idea numerous times, and it worked perfectly.

"Fine, how long until we can all jump from The Barrens?"

"My crew says we are less than thirty minutes out." Gallagher replied.

"And the D'lai? How long for them?"

Windrow chimed in. "They are close to several of those gigantic artifacts. It will take their fleet more than three hours to get out."

Admiral Christopher nodded. "Good. A benefit is we are only four ships, and so we can jump quickly. It will take much, much longer for their massive fleet to do the same."

"Agreed," said Gallagher. "Oh, one final thing, some of my crew are on *The Terran* Admiral. Can they hitch the ride with you?"

Christopher laughed. "Of course, Major."

"Good. Let's go."

The communication ended and each commanding officer ordered their ships to disembark from orbit and travel at full speed to the FTL insertion point. The newest ship in the bunch, *Space Cowboy* arrived ten minutes faster than the others. While he waited, Gallagher and Hodges did some final calculations.

"That D'lai fleet will take six hours to jump. That gives us a nice head start," said Hodges.

"Yeah, but what will we find on the other end?" Gallagher asked. He had heard rumors of problems on Earth. "Agda is doing some funny stuff from what I hear."

"Cormac, do you think we can fully trust Christopher?" Margit asked. "I mean, he is part of the military and...well...it worries me."

"Babe, er, Margit, I'm military too."

Margit blushed at the word babe. "Yeah, but you're...oh I don't know."

Gallagher understood what Margit was trying to say and touched her arm. "Why do you think I left some of my crew over there? It wasn't an oversight on my part."

"You're one sly devil, buddy." Hodges said. "If I didn't know any better, I'd say you have a plan."

"Well, I have eighty percent of one," said Gallagher. "But that's always worked out in the past!"

The men laughed. "I don't get it," said Margit, "but at least I know I can trust you."

"Major," came the voice of the navigator, "the rest of our ships have arrived"

"Good, coordinate with them. We all need to jump together to make this all work out."

"Yes, Major."

All four ships smoothly entered faster than light travel. Within seven hours, they'd be in the Sol system. Then the real fun would begin.

Earth – The Present

"General Agda," came the voice of Hirota Renzo, "we've found the whereabouts of the cylinder and are moving to secure it."

"Excellent news, Minister."

A team of military analysts earlier discovered references to the device in NASA records. Michael Wyatt's suicide, and the link to Joseph Burke, were tantalizing clues that led the researchers to discover where Josh Burke hid the cylinder. The immense secure warehouse where NASA stored thousands of artifacts and research materials was a perfect location for Burke to hide the Seed in, just as the overwhelming vastness of the facility made it easy to conceal the technology from future generations.

Burke, however, made one mistake. A trained scientist, he could not stop himself from logging its location in his journal. Even though he also hid that journal, his now dead son Joseph obtained it as part of his father's estate. It wasn't clear if Joseph knew what was contained in its pages, but after his arrest, military intelligence searched and seized anything that was even slightly relevant to the dismantling of HCH. The journal was part of that seizure.

"General, what are we going to do with it?"

"Minister, I believe this device was the primary reason why the D'lai attacked Mars."

"That makes sense," said Renzo. "After all, from our records, it was buried in approximately the same location."

"Yes, Minister. We need to figure out what this thing is and how it can be of use."

"Once we have it in hand, let me set some of our scientists to work on the problem."

"Fine. Just remember, time is of the essence. We don't realize what we have or why the D'lai seem to want it."

The communication with the minister ended. Agda picked up her tea, intent on finishing it. Living in England had its perks. The English knew their teas. Her favorite, English Breakfast, was taunting her while she worked. As she picked up the steaming cup, her communications console beeped again.

"What now? Never a moment's peace." She took a small sip of her tea before answering. "Agda here."

"General, I have an incoming message from Admiral Christopher."

"Christopher?" It took her a moment to remember his role in all of this. "Yes, isn't he out patrolling The Barrens?"

"He is, ma'am."

Agda adjusted her shoulders. That massage had not done much good. "Put it on."

"Yes, ma'am. Playing it now."

The voice of Admiral Christopher filled the room. For such an old man, his voice was certainly loud, and she needed to lower the volume. "General, moments ago the D'lai fleet began moving out of The Barrens. We are not at present clear on their intended route of travel. We will be monitoring to the best of our ability, but once they leave the region, all of our jury rigged sensors will not be able to detect them if they remain cloaked. I will report more when I can. Christopher out."

Agda felt increasing alarm at the news that the D'lai were on the move. Numerous tasks filled her head as she contemplated next moves. Standing, her tea forgotten, she stormed into the command center.

"The D'lai are moving," she announced to the room, "what is the status of our planetary cloak?"

"Ma'am, the cloak is active but the satellite is aging. The failure of the new orbital platform..."

"Will it hold?" Agda demanded.

"Yes, we believe it will hold."

"General," said a nearby colonel, "we believe it is

possible the orbital location of the cloaking satellite has been compromised. I suggest..."

"Compromised? How?"

"Ma'am, military intelligence intercepted a communication from Earth to an unknown deep space location with data that appeared to be orbital tracking data."

"Colonel, what are you saying? The D'lai know where it is? Can they use that information?"

"Yes, if someone knew the precise location, a targeted shot would take it out and bring our protective cloak down. However, it is possible to move the satellite."

"Then why don't we move..."

"Apologies, ma'am. If we move it, we must first deactivate it."

"How much time is required?" Agda was peeved that she was just finding this information out. These people were supposed to report things to her if it was at all relevant.

"General, six hours."

Agda turned to speak to a navigation specialist. "If the D'lai are just now leaving The Barrens, how long can they reasonably be expected to take to travel to Earth, if we are their intended destination?"

The specialist did some quick calculations. "Presuming their FTL technology is similar to what we have records of, it will take them no less than ten hours."

"What if they've made improvements?"

"There is no way of calculating. Perhaps, six to eight hours?"

"Damn. The window is tight." Agda thought for a few seconds. "Colonel, we need to move that satellite, but we only have four hours."

"I'm on it. I'll see if we can cut any corners."

Agda plopped down heavily in a nearby chair. Events were moving almost too fast to keep up. Between domestic terrorists, the D'lai, and that Martian cylinder, she had no patience left for any more disasters.

Mye Bruai – The Ancient Past

A DOZEN YEARS AFTER THE DESTRUCTION OF *THE Faithful* in Ryi Bruai, the remnant D'lai fleet finally arrived in the Mye Bruai system. The central star was a relatively cool blue giant. D'lai scientists estimated at least several hundred million years would pass before the star would explode, giving them the chance to settle down, albeit temporarily, on one of the rocky planets in this system.

The remaining D'lai were weary from their journey. Cathar Prime, nearly thirty years travel time distant, was becoming a distant memory with thousands of children and young adults that had never set foot on that planet. Priests and mystics continually reminded the people of the reasons for their departure, and the mythos of the *Vdo Zämi* was kept fresh in their minds. None of the D'lai had any reason to suspect that their entire plight was based on the lies of their greatest leader Am'oll.

During the preceding decade, in the absence of a central leadership, a new group of D'lai began to take control of the remnant. Calling themselves the D'lai Authority, they instituted new rules and worked to change life aboard the generation ships. Each ship elected its own leader, called a Negotiator, to represent their interests in the authority.

Owing to the slow pace of travel of the ancient ships, it was possible for the various Negotiators to travel frequently for in-person meetings of the ruling council, or *Iuv*. Within a few years, the *Iuv* started to resemble a legislative body, with each Negotiator having a vote. The D'lai Authority continued to evolve, and by the time of their arrival in Mye Bruai, the D'lai had a full-fledged government in place.

The first glimpse of their new home, however, brought dismay and fear. Mye Bruai had three rocky worlds, but only one of them possessed liquid water. The problem was that their new home, which the D'lai Authority named Resh, was barely habitable. The D'lai were unwilling to continue to search for a new home, so the government ordered all nine remaining generation ships to land on the surface. Their ships would act as temporary cities, until the planet could be further transformed into something more conducive to a long-term settlement.

The first years on Resh were hard. Native organisms on the planet resisted the terraforming of the planet. Fortunately, higher life forms did not exist, so over time the D'lai learned to deal with the harsh conditions, and Resh became more livable.

The D'lai Authority oversaw the expansion of the nine cities and the growth of the population. Upon arrival on Resh, their civilization could boast just under one hundred thousand persons. Within ten years, that number doubled and over time, the planet was filled with D'lai. The *Iuv* passed more laws, and soon life on Resh settled into a predictable pattern that would continue for the next thousand years.

The D'lai never forgot their exile, and despite the passage of centuries as Resh became more and more suited to their needs, they began to plan and prepare for the time when they could take by force all that was lost to them. As time passed and the civilization grew, they built new, more versatile ships, and began to explore their new system. Mye Bruai had three rocky planets, two massive gas giants, and one distant ice giant.

Despite their earlier misgivings, the D'lai discovered that the system was abundant with the raw minerals that would be necessary for the building of a massive space fleet. D'lai scientists soon discovered faster and more efficient means of space travel and star ship design. Eventually, the D'lai were capable of traveling between the stars faster than light.

As they prepared for their impending conquest plans, they kept an eye on their ancient foes. Despite the vast distance and time required of their earliest ships, the D'lai Authority dispatched a small fleet to remotely monitor Cathar Prime. They watched with growing anger and resentment as their Cathari brethren expanded outward, and formed their precious Cathari Alliance. The D'lai vowed that whatever the despised Cathari did, their ascendancy would be terminated with extreme prejudice. As the centuries rolled by, the D'lai increased in strength and advanced technologies, and finally, after close to five hundred years on Resh, they blasted into space to begin their assault on the galaxy.

The D'lai Authority began conquering lessor civilizations, including Gathung'l. They kept secret their ancient origins, revealing to no other conquered race their true history or appearance. They knew that in the fullness of time all would be revealed, but to reveal their Cathari origins would be a devastating blow to their ultimate goal of reclaiming their lost home. It would take great effort on their part, but soon the entire galaxy would fear the name D'lai.

Deep Space – The Present

WHILE THE HUMAN AND GATHUNG SHIPS WERE en route back to Earth after departing The Barrens, Zea Windrow, Margit Wold, and Arvesp Erth were in close contact with each other. The three women had some ideas on how to solve the cloaking problem, and even though none of them were scientists, all of them brought some unique talents into the discussion.

"I recall that the radiation from The Barrens is almost entirely gamma radiation, and we had some success on Gathung'l in using it when we were helping to develop planet cloaking technology." Arvesp said.

"Right, do we have any information on the similarities between our cloaks and those of the D'lai?"

"Yeah, Margit, we do. In fact..." Arvesp paused for a moment to look up some information on her pad. "Yes, here it is. The cloaks the D'lai were using also rely on gamma radiation."

"It could be that because they spent time in The Barrens centuries in the past, they figured out how to manipulate the strange behaviors of the region." Windrow said. "In fact, I think that my FTL jump trick worked precisely because of the type of radiation it uses. Can we use that?"

"I'm not sure," said Arvesp, "but this is all an interesting path to explore."

The women ended their conversation but all of them mulled over the possibilities. Margit went to talk to Corey Hodges and probe his thoughts on the subject.

"No one on board this ship knows more about cloaks than you, so I was wondering if gamma radiation was a disruptor or something?"

"Hmm, let me think." Hodges said. "My cloaks do use it, but we rely on different technology. Me and Gallagher discovered an exotic form of radiation we called the stuff."

"The stuff? That's...interesting."

"Yeah, right? Neither of us could think of a better name and it didn't matter. The stuff works. Anyway, we figured out that the stuff interacts with light and actually slows it down. We used that to help build our cloaks."

"Slowing down light, that's esoteric to say the least."

"I don't know about esoteric, or even what that means really, but I do know that gamma radiation reacts badly to the stuff and causes...oh...wow!"

Hodges stopped talking as his fingers played across the console in front of him. The pages were moving too fast for Margit to keep up, but she had hopes that his ideas would become something useful.

"I'm gonna need a few minutes," Hodges said as he rushed from the room.

"Okay," she said to the empty room. "I'll be here."

Margit plopped down on a nearby sofa and lifted her own pad to do some reading.

Thirty minutes later, Gallagher and Hodges entered, and startled Margit out of a light snooze.

"Um, I guess I must've fallen asleep," she said. Seeing the looks on both men's faces, she stood. "What...?"

Gallagher's face lit up as he fumbled over his words. "We did it!"

Hodges clapped Gallagher on the back. "Did what?" Margit asked. "Broke the cloaks?"

"Better," said Hodges, "we figured out how to not only break the D'lai cloaks, we can do it without them even realizing it!"

"We've gotta notify the Admiral and the others," said Margit. Both men looked at each other and then back at Margit. "Don't we?"

"Um, well," hesitated Gallagher, "we probably should." Gallagher glanced over at Hodges before continuing. "It's just that, we don't fully trust Admiral Methuselah. When I was Secretary General, I read some...discouraging reports of his loyalty."

"You don't think he's loyal to Earth?"

"Oh, no. He's super loyal. Uber-loyal. No, he's... um...well we don't know who he is loyal to. Earth, or General Agda." Gallagher said. "We, Hodges and me, think we should keep the tech from him."

"We should at least tell Windrow and Arvesp, after all they helped..."

"Oh, yeah, we trust those two girls." Hodges said.

"Women."

Hodges blushed, "Yeah, sorry. Women."

Gallagher chuckled. "Hey, Margit here is super woman's rights and..."

"Okay, let's keep going boys." Margit said.

Everyone laughed as they started working on a plan for how best to use the technology.

"You do realize, at some point, we have to ditch *The Terran*." Gallagher said. "If we are going to use this thing, we can't do it with him nearby."

"That's a pickle," said Hodges. "Let's set up a comm with Windrow and Captain Erth and...say, I just got it. Her name, it rhymes with..."

"You just now got it? You're slower than I thought!" Gallagher said.

Margit gave both men her best disapproving glare, and they both returned to the work at hand. "You two in a room and its all jokes." She turned her head away from them to avoid them seeing how hard it was to keep up the stern look.

After an extended conversation with Windrow and Erth, a workable plan was devised. As soon as the four ships left FTL, *The Manchester* would simulate engine trouble. *The Avenger* would render aid, and *Space Cowboy* would pretend to make a supply run to the Saturn space hub. Gallagher would encourage Admiral Christopher to get back to Earth to report to Agda. Once *The Terran* was out of range, the three ships would rendezvous at Titan.

"Let's hope Christopher doesn't see through it all," said Windrow. "I hate it, but we have to keep Earth in the dark on this one."

"Great. We have a plan. Let's get to work." Margit said as the communication ended. Gallagher and Margit walked down the corridor and stole a kiss. "When this is over, I'm taking you on a vacation."

"Okay, but you must recognize I only like the best hotels," said Gallagher.

"We won't even leave the hotel."

Gallagher grinned as the couple headed to the bridge. "Sounds fun."

"Yes, I'm a lot of fun." Margit stuck out her tongue. "Too bad we have to work."

"I bet we could find five minutes."

"Only five?" Margit said.

"Okay, ten."

"Deal." No one would miss them for ten minutes. They hoped.

CHAPTER 17

Earth- The Present

Alexis Marakos was supremely frustrated by the slow trickle of information from that hag General Agda. He put in so much time and energy in cultivating a relationship, and he expected a return on his investment. His handlers demanded constant updates, and began to threaten his life if he didn't come up with something useful soon. In desperation, Marakos was rifling through papers on Agda's desk when the door behind him opened. He whirled to face the General. Agda had a puzzled look on her face that soon turned to anger. He was busted.

"Just what in the hell do you think you are doing Alexis?" Agda demanded.

Stalling for time, Marakos said "You remember that restaurant we ordered from the other night? I was trying to find the..."

"Don't lie to me!" Agda took two huge steps into the room and viciously slapped Marakos across his unshaven face.

Never one to turn down a good fight, Marakos pulled back his fist, but stopped suddenly when he made out that in her left hand, Agda held a small blast gun.

"Whoa, take it easy..." Marakos said.

"I've known for some time there was a spy somewhere near me. All this time, I never imagined it was *you*." Agda said. Wiping tears from her eyes, she continued. "You were supposed to be my person, my love. You're a fucking traitor!"

Marakos let slip a sadistic smile. "Correction, *both* of us are traitors. I just told someone all the juicy little details you couldn't wait to share with me."

Agda flinched as if she had been slapped. "I'm not a... I never..." Her hand fell to her side as she attempted to come to terms with his accusation. That was all the opening Marakos required. He swiftly grabbed Agda by the throat, both hands wrapping around her neck. His hands squeezed until she could breathe no more and her struggles subsided. Her body dropped to the floor.

Marakos felt giddy. He loathed the general and was glad he wouldn't have to deal with her anymore. As he was scanning the room for clues to where she kept her pad, a sudden realization paralyzed him with fear. He had just killed his only source of information. His handlers would not be pleased.

Disregarding his search, he ran from the room and slammed headlong into a maid who had just entered the spacious suite. She saw the dead body of General Agda on the floor and screamed. Marakos didn't make it far. As the leader of the planet, her security was never far off. Two muscular guards grabbed Marakos and efficiently subdued the fleeing murderer.

Hours later, as Marakos sat alone and shackled in an interrogation room, his thoughts were running quite dark as to how his handlers would dispose of him now that he was no longer of any use. A sudden movement from the door startled him, and he looked up into the face of his contact. His insides watered as he knew his time was likely up.

"So, Alexis, tell me how it is that you killed the

Commander-in-Chief and Acting Secretary General of Earth?"

"I didn't realize you were the police, Saul."

Saul Rowe, a Detective Chief Inspector for the Metropolitan Police, was an imposing man. Standing at six feet six inches, he towered over most other people.

Saul's eyes flashed as he flipped a chair around and sat, resting his arms on the chair back. "You killed your cash cow Alexis."

"I didn't mean to, you gotta believe me. She..."

"Oh, I believe you, Alexis." Saul smiled. "The trouble is, it doesn't matter if I believe you or not."

Hanging his head in resignation, Alexis didn't respond. Instead, a single tear fell from his eye as he contemplated the end.

Saul reared his head back and laughed. "Crying? Really?"

Alexis met the cold eyes of his interrogator. "I don't want to die."

"No one does, slime." Saul said. "And yet, everyone does, sooner or later."

"How will..."

Without giving a response, Saul stood, turned the chair back around, gave Alexis a once over glance, and left the small interrogation room, whistling.

The sudden exit unnerved Alexis and he began sobbing uncontrollably. He never wanted to be a spy, and he hated every moment.

"Why didn't I just run," he asked himself. He knew he'd never receive a response.

Without warning, the door was opened once more and a different man entered. Unlike DCI Rowe, this man was definitely not with the police. In his right hand he held a lighter, and in his left he held a cup brimming with some kind of liquid. The man poured the liquid over the head and shoulders of Alexis, and he screamed in terror. Gasoline. The executioner flicked the lighter and lit a trailing edge of the puddle on the floor of the interrogation room. Hungry flames erupted and consumed the shrieking spy as he left the man to burn.

Near Saturn – The Present

GALLAGHER AND THE REST OF THE SMALL FLEET arrived in the Sol System several hours before the

D'lai fleet. Almost at once, the communications arrays on the four vessels were overwhelmed with a staggering amount of chatter.

"Major, this is...hard to sort." The comm officer said as soon as she began sifting through the feeds.

Gallagher marched over to her station, his face draining of color. "Something happened, we need to find out what." He shifted his stance to steal a closer look at the list of incoming transmissions. "That one," Gallagher said, pointing at the screen.

The comm officer opened the message and put it on speakers. "This is Earth Command, Admiral Kelly Austin, to all Earth ships." Everyone on the bridge craned their necks to hear the dispatch more clearly. "An hour ago the body of CinC General Agda was discovered. A suspect has been apprehended. Earth is now on full lock-down. All future communications will be via coded channel and on a need-to-know basis. Austin out."

Gallagher whistled at the news. "Agda is dead? I leave the store unattended for a week and all hell breaks loose!"

Margit Wold approached Gallagher. She reached a hand out to comfort him but Gallagher pushed it away. Hurt, Margit stepped back. She understood he was worried but being rebuffed still stung. Nevertheless, she vowed to herself to help wherever she could.

Gallagher threw himself into his command chair and stared straight ahead for a long moment before speaking again. Everyone on the bridge waited his next orders. Prior to their arrival in Sol, a plan had been hatched to ditch *The Terran*, but no one was sure if that plan would still be implemented.

Turning his attention to Hodges and Margit, Gallagher said, "We stick with the plan as much as we can. This only helps as Christopher will want to make haste back to Earth."

"Buddy, you sure? How well did you know the General?"

Gallagher squared his shoulders and his face became more determined than usual. "What matters is not how I *feel*. What matters Corey is that we still have a mission. The D'lai are on their way."

Hodges simply nodded his agreement and gave a short glance at Margit before turning back to his own work.

"Comm, send the prearranged signal to *The Manchester*."

"Yes, sir." A few seconds passed before the comm

officer responded again. "Signal sent and acknowledged Major."

Gallagher massaged the back of his neck as he waited on Windrow and Arvesp.

"Sir, the distress signal just came in from *The Manchester*. Admiral Christopher is hailing."

"Put him on."

"Major, we just received word of engine trouble from Windrow." Admiral Christopher said as soon as the channel opened.

"Yeah, so did we. My engineers are in communication with *The Manchester* and *The Avenger*. It looks like Captain Erth is closer, so she will render immediate aide." Gallagher pretended to look at and speak with a nearby crewman before continuing. "I'm taking *Space Cowboy* to Saturn for some parts she needs."

"Mmm, sounds like a plan, Major. Have you had time to listen to some of the comm activity in the system yet?"

"Yes, we're working through it all now. Looks like you should head back to Earth on the double."

"My thoughts exactly Major. Let me know if you need any further assistance. I'm gonna go get to the bottom of all this nonsense."

"Safe flying sir," said Gallagher.

Nodding, the admiral ended the communication. "Christopher out."

"Well, that went better than I expected," said Margit. "The crisis on Earth certainly helped."

"Yeah, now we have to find out if our plan is going to work," Hodges replied. "We've only tested it on simulations."

Gallagher glanced at a chronometer mounted nearby, "Well, we have a few hours. Let's make final preparations." He stood and swiveled his head around the room, "I need a few minutes. I'll...be in my quarters."

"Of course," Hodges said. "We'll let you know when we need you."

Without a word or a glance at anyone, Gallagher rushed from the bridge.

Margit and Hodges huddled together to fine-tune their preparations. Margit kept glancing back to where Gallagher had been only a moment earlier. Concern was clear on her face as she worked. She hoped the news of Agda's death would not ruin the plan, but she understood why Gallagher was so upset. After all, he'd left the planet in her care after leaving his post. The two of them worked together for several years prior to that.

In his quarters three decks below the bridge, Gallagher allowed himself a few minutes to mourn his friends death. He wasn't a man who easily showed his emotions, but this hit him hard. After ten minutes he resolved to get back to work. Glancing at his work station, he glimpsed a private message from the General waiting for him. He punched the icon and settled back to hear the last communication from his friend.

"Gallagher, I recognize you won't receive this for several hours, so I'll make this brief," said Agda. "We've discovered why Mars was attacked and are working to understand a strange cylinder discovered at the site decades ago."

Gallagher's eyes lifted in surprise. Agda continued, "I've kept this information from the regular chain of command. I'm not sure why I'm telling you even, but I think this has something to do with the imminent war." Agda glanced off-screen a moment then turned back. "Also, you need to be careful. Spies are everywhere. If you get this and want to know more, make contact with Renzo. He's in charge of the cylinder."

The message ended and left Gallagher even more confused than he was before. He noticed the comm came with an attachment. Gallagher opened it and his screen filled with an image of the cylinder covered in odd runes that somehow looked familiar at the same time. He stood and smoothed out his uniform.

"No time to grieve," he muttered to himself as he left his quarters and tramped back to the bridge.

Deep Space – The Present

FIVE HOURS AFTER DEPARTING RYI BRUAI, ZAT'OL scanned a list of orders to be issued as soon as the armada arrived in the Sol System. It was imperative that Earth and Mars have no idea that the D'lai were in system. All his plans hinged on the element of surprise. If all was going according to plan, both planets would be defenseless and his two fleets could quickly take control.

"Negotiator, what are your plans for The Seeds?"

Zat'ol hated being questioned by subordinates. In response, he glared at the science officer and went back to reading his pad.

Frustrated, the science officer tried a different approach. "Sir, the Seeds, they seem to be active."

This surprised Zat'ol. He put his pad on his lap and looked back up. "What do you mean, active?"

"Sir, both of them are...glowing."

Grunting with frustration, Zat'ol stood and walked toward the exit. "Show me."

The science officer led the way to the science lab where the two Seeds were currently being housed. Without any external illumination in the room, the dull green light emanating from the Seeds gave off an eerie glow.

"That's interesting," said Zat'ol, "when did this start?"

The puzzled science officer gaped at the Negotiator. "Sir, this started in Ryi Bruai. I personally notified you."

Zat'ol was aware that his mental acuity was slipping recently. He chalked it up to his work load, but he began to wonder if something else was at play. Each time there was a new development with the Seed, he felt a small piece of himself shift. The Negotiator refused to own up to this, however, so he waved the science officer away and approached the glowing cylinders. Instinctively, he reached out with one hand

and touched one of the two devices. Not only was it glowing, it was warm to the touch.

The instant his fingers brushed the warm metal, Zat'ol's mind flashed with memories of planets and civilizations he had never before seen. The images raced by in quick succession, causing Zat'ol to collapse under the sheer weight of images flowing through his brain. His hand left the cylinder and the barrage of scenes dissipated. Breathing heavily, he looked up at the two glowing objects as trepidation filled his mind.

He could not fathom what he just witnessed, but he knew something was off. Doubt and fear flooded his heart as he wondered what would happen when he had possession of the third Seed. Zat'ol sent a communication that he was not to be disturbed. He needed to consult the *awch jdiv* for any clues about what he just experienced. Surely the Umawei would have warned his people.

The Negotiator flipped through page after page of notes and abridged references the Emissary input into the fake brain. Hours passed as he searched. His body protested at the lack of food and sleep, but Zat'ol refused to stop until he found something, anything, that might shed some light on the experience.

Howling with rage, he finally gave up and collapsed onto his small bed. How could there be no references to what just happened? Why were the Umawei silent? As he fell into a tense sleep, he vowed to attempt to communicate with the Emissary but his body would no longer cooperate and it shut down.

After what felt like only a few minutes, a loud beeping emanated from his comm unit. Zat'ol swiped the channel open, annoyed at being disturbed.

"I told you not to disturb me."

"Apologies Negotiator. I believed it important to notify you that we have arrived in the Sol System."

Zat'ol rolled over on the bed, his eyes opening slowly as he adjusted to the light. He hadn't even bothered to turn off the illumination before he fell asleep. It took a few moments for his eyes to adjust to the brightness before he sat up, the comm channel still open.

"I'm on my way to the bridge."

"Yes, sir." The comm unit went silent as Zat'ol stood, unsteady, and looked in a small mirror over his bed.

"I need a bath," he muttered to himself before shrugging, spritzing some deodorant over his no-doubt smelly clothes, and left the room.

Upon his arrival on the active bridge, he slouched in his command chair and called up the list of orders he had made the day before. It took him a second before he realized that not only was his hand shaking, but everyone on the bridge was staring at him, slack-jawed and confused.

Zat'ol looked around the room. "What?" No one responded. "Why are you all staring at me?"

A brave junior officer approached the command chair. "Sir, your hair. It's white."

"What?" Zat'ol asked in surprise. He realized that while he was observing himself in the mirror in his quarters, he'd seen the white hair but it didn't register to his sleep-deprived brain. The physical shock of contact with the Seeds must have caused it.

Ignoring the rude stares, Zat'ol barked out a few commands. It took a few seconds, but the well-trained crew started to get back to work. One crewman, however, did not stop his observation of the physically modified Negotiator. In a corner of the deck, a senior security officer didn't hide his attention. His eyes moved to the pad in his hand as he thumbed an icon. The Cabal would be very interested to know what happened. The officer gave a half-smile as he turned back to his console.

Near Saturn – The Present

CAPTAIN WINDROW SURFED THE BLAST OF communications everyone received upon exiting the FTL jump. She was looking for one particular message in the pile from her contacts on Earth. Her officers already briefed her on the most important messages concerning the chaos and the death of the General.

Prior to leaving on her current mission, while still in The Barrens, Windrow made surreptitious contact with a rather shady friend in Earth Command. She told herself she wasn't recruiting a spy, but essentially that was what she did. Life as a smuggler taught her the valuable lesson to always have a fall-back position, and to never trust anyone in a position of power. Her contact in the government was tasked with one simple thing: root out other spies and, where possible, feed them disinformation.

Windrow knew that Gallagher was too much of a stand-up guy to do this for himself, so she acted as his spymaster. Now, she hoped her efforts would bear fruit, and she could help the effort in an unexpected manner.

A few minutes of searching and Windrow found the message she was hoping to find. It was in code, naturally, so she got to work deciphering it. Every sentence unraveled made less and less sense. She knew that spies were everywhere. That was, after all, a byproduct of governing. What she didn't expect was that a spy was actually *living* with the now deceased General Agda. To make matters worse, her contact believed he was spying for the D'lai.

Apprehension filled Windrow as she finished deciphering the coded message. Not only had the spy been feeding information to the enemy, apparently he was also the chief suspect in her death.

"Odd, why kill your source?"

One piece of the communication puzzled her more than the rest. Agda found an odd device from Mars that no one knew what it was used for. Her contact included an image of the cylinder, and as soon as she saw it, Windrow jumped from her chair and yelped. It was almost identical to the cylinder Arvesp Erth studied while they were all in The Barrens.

"What the hell?"

She hailed *The Avenger,* and after making sure

she was speaking only to Arvesp, told her about the discovery on Mars, and the similarities to the cylinder found on the derelict D'lai ship.

"Send the image to me Zea," Arvesp said.

"Already on its way."

Arvesp's eyes moved off-screen and froze. "My gods, that is identical!"

"That's what I thought also. What do you think this means? Two of them in opposite corners of the galaxy? That can't be a coincidence."

"It does explain some of the cryptic lines from the *Chäi kia Chlüi* I found in The Barrens." Arvesp said. "I couldn't understand why Am'oll referred to the device in the plural when he only had the one."

"That's interesting. Did Am'oll know what he had?"

"Yeah, that part makes more sense now too." Arvesp pulled up a copy of the *Chäi* and read a few lines of it. "Am'oll called it a Seed, uppercase S." She paused as she read some more from the book. "Here's something else, he did indeed use plural, but he also referenced...whoa..." Arvesp stopped talking and Windrow could see fear cloud her face.

"Arvesp, what? What does it say?"

"I didn't understand this before, but the translation has been refined by the computer while we've been in transit."

"Okay, what then?" Windrow said a little impatiently.

"The first time I read it, I translated the passage to refer to life, lower case L." Arvesp continued reading and speaking at the same time. "I thought it was in reference to the concept of life, you know, the meaning."

Windrow felt herself go tense as she waited, halfway expecting what was coming next.

"The computer further refined it, and now it reads Life, uppercase. Proper noun stuff. Life as in ALL life."

"Arvesp, I'm not all that good with grammar, so I'm a little lost."

Arvesp attempted, and failed, a reassuring smile. "Am'oll, a thousand years ago, discovered that the Seed in his possession was *the source* of life. Not just *a* source. *The* source."

Understanding bloomed for both Arvesp and Windrow at almost the same time. "My god. What you are saying is this ancient D'lai dude believed he had found the actual source of all life in what, the galaxy?"

"Yes," said Arvesp. "And there is more than one of these. The Seed in The Barrens, and…oh wow…another Seed on Earth!"

Windrow came to an instant decision. "Get in a shuttle and get over to *Space Cowboy*. I'm heading there now." Windrow stood. "This needs to be discussed face-to-face. If this is all accurate, we have a much bigger problem than just the D'lai."

"Agreed. Erth out."

Rushing from her quarters to the shuttle bay, Windrow's heart threatened to beat out of her chest. "What the actual hell is going on?" She didn't have to wait long to find out. The D'lai were in the system. The final battle was coming.

CHAPTER 18

Earth- The Past

A week after Michael Wyatt killed himself in front of Josh Burke, Burke was released from custody and allowed to return home. The investigation was still ongoing, but no one seemed to realize the full extent of what happened. Seconds after the gunshot took Wyatt's life, Burke rushed from the small office and packed up all the notes and materials that were related to their illicit study of the Martian cylinder.

In a flash of inspiration, Burke sealed the device Wyatt had opened in an unmarked canister and shoved it in the back of a small store room. Only a few minutes after concealing the evidence, military police took him into custody for questioning. The trip from the laboratory to the secure facility gave Burke time to come up with a cover story about why he had left the corpse of his dead friend.

"I panicked. I'd never seen someone blow his brains out before." Burke said to his questioner.

The interrogator appeared to believe Burke, even though he wrote down something in his small note-book before proceeding. "Now, tell me why, again, Dr. Wyatt shot himself? Did you threaten him?"

Burke was stunned at the line of questions. "Threaten him? How? He was my closest friend."

The interrogation lasted several more hours. Burke held his emotions in check as much as possible and eventually he was allowed to eat a light meal and get a few hours rest on a hard bunk.

As soon as he was released from custody, he took a quick shower, went through a drive-thru for a burger and fries, and returned to his lab. He was relieved to find the unmarked canister was where he left it. He had no intention of opening it. It drove his friend to suicide, and Burke had a family that relied on him too much to lose him.

Burke took the canister with him when he left the

lab at the end of the day. No one even gave him a second glance, which he found weird. If he encountered someone who was in the vicinity of a suicide, he'd be more curious than these folks were. However, it was a relief that little attention was paid, and no one wondered what the scientist was doing, carrying an unmarked canister to his truck.

Right after he had been arrested, he sent his wife and kids off to visit her sister, and they were still gone. This gave him a little breathing room, and time to plan his next move. He knew he needed to dispose of the relic. It couldn't remain in his house. Burke made some notes in his journal, and early the next morning, visited NASA's secure warehouse. It was easy enough to gain access, and after making sure he was alone, he stuffed the canister behind some dusty boxes containing meteorite fragments that didn't look like they'd been touched since the Apollo era. He noted the location in his journal, and quickly left the warehouse.

An hour later, Burke hid the journal among some files from a study he had conducted a few years back. He presumed that even if someone knew of the journal and the cylinder, they'd not look there. Finally able to relax, he fell into a dreamless sleep and only woke when his young children bounced on the sofa he crashed on.

Burke's wife Anna knew that something wasn't quite right with her normally clean-shaven and well-dressed husband, but chose to give him some space. She understood that the trauma of watching his friend die would be a good excuse for a little untidiness.

Later that evening as they were in bed together, Anna snuggled up to Burke. "Honey, you doing okay?" Anna spoke in a low, and she hoped soothing, tone of voice.

"Yeah, honey, I'm still in shock, I think, but I'll be fine."

They had been married for nearly fifteen years, and Anna knew when her husband was prevaricating, but she chose to overlook this small sin as well.

"I can't imagine, first Mike kills himself and then those MP's arrest you," she said. "Why'd he do it?"

"I don't know," lied Burke, "I couldn't stop him."

Anna laid her head on his chest, his heartbeat and steady breath always reassured her in the past. Now, it reminded her of the shortness of life, and she rolled off of him. Burke didn't even notice. Even after Anna's breathing evened out, and she slipped into sleep, he lay there, eyes open, thinking.

The next morning when Anna woke up, Burke was gone. So was his truck. She searched but found no note, or any hint of where he was, but she knew deep in her spirit that he was gone. Anna never saw Burke again. He simply vanished from her life.

Joseph, his oldest son, vowed then and there that he would never stop searching for his father, and the reason why he left. Three years after graduating from high school, Joseph found his father in a mental ward in upstate New York. Burke told Joseph some crazy story about an alien cylinder from Mars, and droned on about the voices. Joseph tried to understand what his father was saying. He'd never thought of his dad as a mad man, but this story was straight out of science fiction. His father had always made sense when he spoke, but this gibberish only confused Joseph.

A nurse approached with a tray of medicine, and gave his dad a small cup with three or four pills inside. Burke didn't even hesitate as he swallowed them without water. This shocked Joseph. His dad had never taken a pill other than the occasional aspirin. He must truly be sick to blindly down this medicine.

As he was leaving, Burke pressed some papers into his son's fist. His eyes went glassy as the meds took effect. Joseph left the facility, tears welling up in his eyes. No way was he going to tell his mom where his dad was. The news would kill her. She'd suffered enough over the past seven years.

As he settled behind the wheel of his car, he opened his hand and read the note. His dad gave him directions to some boxes in the back of his mom's garage. As soon as he got home, Joseph rifled through them, searching for clues as to what happened. That was when he found his father's journal.

Joseph scanned the cramped handwriting, searching for what, he didn't know. His eyes settled upon an entry from May 2061, seven years earlier. He read the entry, and closed his eyes in contemplation. His dad found something alien, two years before the Cathari arrived. Joseph didn't know if he could actually get his hands on the device, but his father's journal entry pointed to more evidence and information. It took him a week to gather everything, but when he did, he realized that his father had stumbled upon an even greater truth than anyone on Earth could have realized.

The next day, he and a few friends formed Humans for Clear Horizons, and got to work to change the course of human history. Earth was not alone in the galaxy, but there was also something much bigger going on than those smug Cathari let on. Joseph and his new organization vowed to not only find out, but to work as hard as they could to stop it. They had no idea that forces far beyond their comprehension, were working against them.

Earth – The Present

Chaos seemed to be the order of the day in Earth Command. Admiral Kelly Austin swirled around the room, checking with aides and commanders on the status of so many different crises that she was afraid her head would spin off its shoulders.

A helpful lieutenant noticed her confusion and attempts to keep things clear and offered to help her.

"That would be a great relief lieutenant," said Austin, "up until three hours ago, I wasn't in charge of the whole planet!"

"No problem, ma'am," said the aide, "things are definitely in flux right now."

"You've got that right," said Austin, "now about the line of succession..."

The lieutenant signaled a nearby civil administrator. "We need to get the Admiral sworn in as the acting Secretary General," he said.

The administrator glanced at his pad and then raised his gaze to the steely eyes of the flustered admiral. "Admiral," he pointed in the direction of a small office, "this way please."

Once the formalities were concluded and Admiral Kelly Austin was given a short briefing on succession protocols, she returned to the main conference room to address the military leaders and civilian ministers.

"Okay everyone, let's get down to business. Our first priority is to ensure that the planet is safe." She consulted a prepared list of planetary leaders, "Minister Renzo, as the acting head of Earth defenses, where do we stand?"

Minister Renzo cleared his throat and, after a moment of consulting a nearby assistant, glanced at the admiral. "Ma'am, the cloak is not activated. We have no intelligence that the D'lai or any other potentially hostile force is in system."

"Good, what about friendlies?"

"Admiral, as of our last update, several Gathung and Scree vessels are in system," he paused and checked some notes, "most of them are situated at the Saturn Space Hub."

The Admiral rubbed the back of her neck as she consulted her list once more. "General O'Connor," she turned to face the aging head of planetary security, "what about HCH..."

Before the general could respond, Minister Renzo interrupted, "Excuse me, Admiral, I have an update..." Everyone nearby focused their attention on the minister, "Ma'am, *The Terran* and three other ships just exited FTL and are en route to various positions in system."

"*The Terran?*" Admiral Kelly Austin asked, shock obvious in her tone of voice, "they are supposed to be in The Barrens."

"Yes, ma'am," said Minister Renzo. He flicked a switch on his console, "we've received word that Major Gallagher on *Space Cowboy* and two other vessels are with him."

"Gallagher?" The admiral sat straighter in her seat, "we could use him right now. Hail him."

"Yes, ma'am," said a communications officer. "On voice only."

"Major, Admiral Austin here, I must say I'm concerned as to why you are back in Sol."

"Admiral, nice to hear your voice," said Gallagher, "we...uh... We had some interesting stuff happen the past few days, and we need to report in."

On board *Space Cowboy*, Margit and Hodges faces reflected their surprise at Gallagher's response. He winked in their direction before continuing.

"The D'lai, it seems, are on their way here."

Nervous voices erupted all throughout Earth Command at the news. Admiral Austin moved to silence them to no avail. She moved closer to the communications console before continuing.

"Major, that is not good news," she said. "We will need a full report when possible."

"Sure, Admiral. I think that Admiral Christopher on *The Terran* is on his way to Earth as we speak. He'll fill you all in."

Admiral Austin audibly sighed, "Okay, Major. What is your status?"

Gallagher filled the Admiral in on their plan, omitting any mention of their discoveries. He and the others planned to keep that to themselves until they could figure out who to trust on Earth.

Austin and the others in Space Command waited on a report from Admiral Christopher as they handled the various problems erupting all over the globe. HCH was not dead, despite the best efforts of General Agda, and despite the cloak still being functional, it was currently off-line as it was repositioned.

"What is the status, how long until the cloak is ready to be re-activated?"

"Admiral," said Renzo, "we need another two hours."

For the first time that day, Admiral Austin whirled in anger to face the minister. "Two hours may be too late! The D'lai may already be here somewhere!"

"I'm sorry, Admiral, we are moving as fast as we can. Too fast and we risk damaging the satellite."

Admiral Austin didn't reply, instead she checked her notes once more and then proceeded to get updates from the other department heads in the room.

Several thousand miles from the moon, the smaller D'lai fleet was joined by the larger group under the command of Negotiator Zat'ol. The D'lai were pleased to see Earth in the distance. The blue sphere was a sight to behold and Zat'ol was ready to implement his plan.

"Navigator, bring us in closer." Zat'ol ordered. "Tactical, prepare our weapons and shuttles." His face lit up with pleasure. "Let's go get that third Seed."

Mars – The Present

SEVERAL HOURS AFTER GALLAGHER AND HIS group arrived in the Sol System, a more ominous and much darker vessel also jumped in. The *Martian Sword*, carrying fifty-thousand Cathari prisoners settled into a high orbit around the planet Mars. Each of the prisoners on board were unaware of their ultimate destination, but none of them were fooled that the D'lai had anything but evil intentions for them.

The journey aboard the converted freighter was not comfortable for anyone, including the crew. Not only were the D'lai rough and abusive to the unfortunate Cathari, a more malevolent force was present as well. Several members of the Umawei race, wraith-like and frightening, accompanied the *Martian Sword* on its journey from Cathar Prime. Even the guards and crew were frightened by their presence, but none dared disobey Negotiator Brik Zat'ol or anger the seemingly omnipresent Umawei.

"Signal the Negotiator," said the captain of the *Martian Sword*, "inform him at once of our arrival at Mars."

"At once, commander."

Several crewmen approached the dais where the commander had his command chair, "Sir, what are our orders?"

Impatient to get this mission completed, the commander addressed his D'lai crew. "We are on station at Mars to deliver upon orders the Cathari prisoners to the surface. Once we have fulfilled those orders, we will rendezvous with the main fleet and await further instructions."

This small speech did nothing to allay the fears of the crew and only increased their wariness. None of them were comfortable with the Umawei hovering around every corner. Add to that the constant battle to keep fifty-thousand souls restrained, and the ship was rife with a mutiny-like air.

The commander was aware of his crew's fears and tried his best to keep things as normal as possible. It wasn't working. The *Martian Sword* felt more like a hell-bound ship than a prisoner transport.

"Commander, I have the Negotiator on communications," said a nearby officer.

"Put him on."

"Commander, your orders have not changed," said the voice of Negotiator Zat'ol, "remain cloaked and in orbit. Once we've recovered the third Seed from Earth, we will proceed to the next phase."

"Yes, Negotiator." The commander said. His face was grim as he considered his next statement. "Negotiator, things on board are tense. When can we expect to..."

"Arrogant *chtuai*, you have your orders."

The communications channel closed, leaving everyone who heard it puzzled and unsettled even further. The commander tried to put a brave face on but it was obvious to anyone who could see him that the strain of this mission was breaking him.

Prior to receiving this ignominious assignment, he had been stationed aboard *The Spector* as second-in-command. He wished to his core he was back in his old posting. This new task filled him with despair and made him feel dirty. He believed wholeheartedly in the mission of the D'lai, and he despised every living and dead Cathari. It was the presence of Umawei that made his skin crawl.

"I can't imagine why the Negotiator would

involve our civilization with these wraiths," he said to his friend and tactical officer.

"You will obey orders and will not question the plan," came the mind-whisper of the Umawei. Every D'lai and Cathari mind on the ship was invaded by the unholy voice. As soon as the message was received, loud wailing began anew among the prisoners, and each D'lai shivered with unnatural predatory fear.

"Commander, please, don't anger them," said the tactical officer. "It's too..." He trailed off in palpable discomfort.

The commander could only shake his head. He had always feared the D'lai Authority, but he was far more frightened by these Umawei guests than anything Negotiator Zat'ol could do to him.

Earth – The Present

THE SECURE NASA WAREHOUSE, LOCATED IN THE outskirts of Orlando, Florida, was a massive structure. The 250,000 square foot facility housed thousands of artifacts and antiquated technology used and discarded by NASA in it's one hundred and twenty year history. Among portions of rocket fuselages and prototype capsules could also be found meteorite samples and discarded experiments from orbital facilities.

The sheer size and scope of the warehouse made it the ideal location for Josh Burke to hide the Seed after the death of his friend and co-worker Michael Wyatt. It would be virtually impossible to find a small canister measuring only three feet in such a place.

At the direction of Minister Renzo, a team of forensic and intelligence officers scoured the journals of Burke for clues. While he did provide a location, it was only a clue and needed to be deciphered. After an extensive effort, the team found what they believed to be the location and moved in on it.

The search party spent hours moving through the facility before coming upon the location they believed contained the cylinder. Moving several dusty boxes out of the way, Captain Alex Trujillo grabbed what looked like a small hard shell suitcase from the shelf.

"Sir, I believe this may be the device," said Trujillo. He started to open the clasps but his hand was stopped by a strong grasp.

"Careful, son," said Colonel Waters, "we don't know what's inside that."

"Yes, sir," said Trujillo. As he was placing the container on the ground, a jumble of images and imagined voices filled his head. Frightened, he dropped it and backed away from the case.

"Captain, what in blazes," said the Colonel before his hands shot to his head as if trying to shake off something. "What the..."

Both men convulsed as they were overcome by the alien force inside the canister. Colonel Waters hand moved to his belt, unholstered his pistol, and raised it to his forehead. The sudden gunshot alerted nearby guards who rushed to the scene. The colonel's lifeless body lay on the ground next to the still seizing captain.

As soon as he arrived on the scene, the sergeant lifted his radio and called for backup. "SitCommand, SitCommand, this is patrol. Shots fired in the northeastern sector, send for emergency personnel. Over"

"Copy that, patrol. Please advise on casualties and SitRep, over."

"Two down, one apparent gunshot. No active shooters. Over."

"Copy. Emergency personnel incoming. Facility lockdown active. Over."

"Patrol out."

The sergeant attempted to render first aid on the colonel, but he was already dead. He moved to assist the captain and in so doing his hand brushed the sealed container. A wave of vertigo and nausea overcame him before he picked up the canister by its handle and moved away from the scene. He was not aware of his actions as he avoided the incoming emergency crew and rushed to a secluded section of the cavernous warehouse.

The sergeant placed the container on a work station and after taking out his communications device, snapped some images of it. Without even realizing it, he pulled up a communications app on the device, keyed in an address, and sent the images off. He then sat on the floor, waiting for something. He had no idea at all what he was doing as his mind was filled with images and sounds he could not comprehend.

In orbit, a communications officer aboard *The Spector* received an incoming message from the planet.

"Negotiator, we are receiving a transmission from Earth."

Startled, Zat'ol turned to face the officer. "Source?"

"Unknown, sir. It appears to be coming from an area near active launch facilities on the surface."

"Is it audio or visual?"

"Neither, sir. It is an image."

Curious and not knowing how else to respond, Zat'ol said, "Send it to my pad."

The Negotiator opened the flashing icon on his device and a puzzled look blossomed on his face. "What, this is..." He checked the faces of the others in his immediate vicinity and stood from his command chair.

"Tactical, trace the source of this communication."

"Yes, Negotiator," came the response.

On the Negotiator's pad was an image of the sealed canister containing the third Seed. Zat'ol had no idea what was inside the case, but he knew enough about the effects of the Umawei technology to suspect what he might have in his hand.

"Negotiator, the communication came from a personal comm device of an active military officer. I believe the transmission emanated from a large warehouse on the surface."

Zat'ol broke out in an enormous smile. "This must be it! The third Seed!"

His mind was racing as he tried to figure out how he would get it off the surface. He didn't have long to think as he was interrupted by the communications officer once more.

"Negotiator, another incoming message. This one is audio."

"Put it on."

"This is..." the voice was muffled and hard to understand. "The canister is..." The audio message ended abruptly with the sound of a man screaming in tremendous pain.

Zat'ol came to an immediate decision. "Dispatch a cloaked shuttle to the location of that communication. Let's get inside that facility, now!"

Furious orders and activity filled the bridge as the crew worked to obey the Negotiator. A few minutes after the order was given, a small shuttle undocked and entered the upper atmosphere of Earth. Despite the cloak, the fireball of re-entry would be visible to anyone watching.

The crew of *The Spector* monitored communications channels and kept weapons aimed at the planet to defend the shuttle if necessary. With any luck, any observers would believe a meteorite or some space junk was the cause of the fireball. After several tense minutes, the shuttle was through the most violent portion of the landing and the cloak kept it hidden as it approached the warehouse.

Zat'ol was on pins and needles as he waited on reports from the landing crew. The D'lai were experienced in getting in and out of facilities or ships without being detected, so he was not concerned that his men would be able to obtain the device. Nevertheless, he knew that humans were tenacious, and anything at all could happen.

An hour after departing orbit, a coded message came in notifying the Negotiator of success. The shielded and cloaked D'lai soldiers had secured the container and departed the surface without being detected. Zat'ol was anxious to have the shuttle back in the shuttle bay and could not wait to get his hands on the third device.

Three hours after the first communication from Earth, the Seed was placed next to the other two. Unlike the previous encounter when the two Seeds began glowing, there did not seem to be a visible reaction. That didn't mean there was no reaction at all. As soon as the third Seed was in proximity to the others, an invisible circuit closed, and every Umawei on board the *Martian Sword* began to rejoice. Their ancient plan was nearing completion, and the entire galaxy would never be the same.

CHAPTER 19

Near Saturn- The Present

"What do you mean, it's gone?" Arvesp said, "gone where?"

"That's just it," said Admiral Kelly Austin over a secure comm channel, "we don't know."

Arvesp shook her head in frustration. She stole a glance at Gallagher and Windrow. Neither human wore a pleased expression.

"Admiral, how can a canister that has been hidden for decades suddenly end up missing," asked Major Gallagher. "I mean, it's not as if anyone could have *known* about it until recently."

"Major, we are working to figure that out." Admiral Austin said. "I'm only notifying you out of courtesy."

Ten hours earlier, the trio decided that they had to start trusting someone on Earth. Gallagher was in favor of Admiral Kelly Austin, and the two women consented. They presented their information on cloak breaking technology and their discovery of the true source of the cylinder to the Admiral. It took her ten hours to get back to them, and now she was telling them it was gone.

"We found three soldiers, all dead, in a NASA warehouse." Admiral Austin explained. "The team was dispatched to recover the object. One died of a self-inflicted gunshot wound, and the other two from massive seizures."

Arvesp interrupted the narrative, "Admiral, one moment please." She muted the audio and turned to Gallagher and Windrow. Her wide eyes looked at them in alarm. "From what I was able to ascertain from the ancient texts, the devices or Seeds have some way of mind-control."

"I bet that is why those men are dead," said Margit Wold from a corner of the room. "Those poor men and their families."

Gallagher shook his head in anger. "We don't have time to mourn the dead, but I know what you mean." He unmuted the channel and addressed the admiral. He asked Arvesp to explain her work with the ancient texts.

"Some ancient voodoo from a long dead D'lai is what we are trusting?" Admiral Austin asked. "Um... okay then."

"It's not voodoo," said Arvesp, "this Am'oll guy is the earliest known contact with these things."

"Fine," said the Admiral. "I don't suppose those texts will tell us who stole it?"

"I might have some thoughts on that one, Admiral," said Gallagher. "Years ago I was on *The Avenger*," he glanced at Arvesp before continuing, "well, I was *outside*, but that's another..."

"Yes, yes, Major. Get to the point!" Admiral Austin snapped.

Gallagher smiled in embarrassment, "Yeah, sorry. Anyway, I think the D'lai could have done this. They do have the ability to sneak onto unsuspecting ships, so why not secure facilities?"

On the screen, the admiral fixed her gaze off camera and whispered to someone. A moment later her attention returned. "We did detect a fireball over the Caribbean and Florida around the same time as the incident. My people chalked it up to a meteorite."

"That was the D'lai," said Arvesp firmly. "They took it."

"Damn it," exclaimed the Admiral. "We have to get our cloak back up!"

"That's a good idea," said Gallagher. "They wouldn't have been able to land otherwise."

Admiral Austin ended the communication. Gallagher turned to face Arvesp, "Say, you don't by chance still have..."

Knowing what he was going to ask, Arvesp's face lit up. "Yeah, I couldn't bring myself to take it off-line. We need to get to Earth, now!"

Confused, Margit Wold asked, "What are you two planning?"

"It's simple, really. Decades ago we used *The Avenger* as a temporary planetary cloak for Gathung'l. Since the cloak around Earth is still offline, we can..."

"Use *The Avenger* to protect Earth," chimed in Windrow. "Brilliant!"

"We don't have time to get to our own ships. I'm so glad we decided to meet on *The Avenger*, instead of one of the other vessels!" Gallagher said.

They all rushed up to the bridge. Arvesp issued a series of commands and within minutes, *The Avenger* was en route to Earth. With any luck, they'd arrive before any more plans could be implemented by the D'lai.

Near Mars – The Present

ACTIVITY ON THE *MARTIAN SWORD* RAMPED UP when the three Seeds came together. The D'lai on board grew ever more apprehensive as the Umawei stopped pretending they were simple onlookers, and began taking control of the ship and the minds of any soul on board they wished.

Realizing too late the danger his ship and crew was in, the captain began composing a message to Negotiator Zat'ol, warning him of the new danger now facing them. It was fortunate for him that the Umawei, though it seemed they were omnipresent, were not also omniscient. He discovered early in the voyage that the Umawei did not ordinarily appear near the large engines of the massive freighter. Taking advantage of this blind spot, the captain secreted himself away and wrote his urgent appeal.

Not daring the risks of transmitting the message via ship to ship communications, the captain recruited a low level security officer to use one of the escape pods, and jettison himself into space. Both the captain and the crewman understood this was likely a suicide mission, as the *Martian Sword* was too far from Mars, or any other planet for a safe landing of the pod.

It was also a stroke of luck that the freighters decentralized design meant that escape pods were strewn all over the ship. The security officer was able to take the encoded message aboard a pod near the engine room, and escaped the ship undetected by the ever present Umawei wraiths.

As soon as the escape pod was far enough from the *Martian Sword*, he transmitted the encoded message to *The Spector*, still in orbit of Earth. Now that he was done with his task, all he could do was wait. The small craft didn't have engines, and using only the maneuvering thrusters to get away from the ship burned up any fuel on board. The captain promised that if he could, he'd bring the pod back aboard, but that was a long shot.

The message was received by a communications

officer on *The Spector,* and routed at once to the Negotiator. Zat'ol read the message, as twisting fingers of fear clawed his guts. He dropped the pad he was holding onto the hard metallic floor of his quarters, and threw himself onto his small bed. What was he going to do? He had endangered his entire civilization by wedding his plans to those of the ancient Umawei. He had believed that he and his people were the true heirs of the ancients, and their mission would bring about a lasting D'lai dominance.

As he lay there, almost paralyzed with growing fear, an idea filled his brain. In fits and starts, a nascent plan grew, and he realized with full surrender what exactly he needed to do. He must abandon the long laid plans of the D'lai, and destroy the Seeds. There was little else he could do. The Umawei deceived him, and he had been an utter fool to trust them.

Zat'ol rose from his bunk and ran at full speed down the endless corridors of *The Spector.* Time was of the essence, and he needed to act before he could be stopped. As soon as he was within a few paces of the lab housing the three Seeds, a cold dread filled him. Floating in the corridor in front of him was the

Umawei Emissary. Zat'ol realized at once that the Emissary must be aware of his plan.

"We have need of these Seeds. Our plans must come to fruition." The whisper-like voice of the Umawei pierced his brain.

The Negotiator halted his forward momentum. He hadn't expected to see the Emissary. Of course, he did not have much of a plan at all. The ideas were still being worked out as he ran.

"Yes, Emissary," was all that Zat'ol could say. "I understand."

As he turned to return the way he came, Zat'ol's mind filled with a flurry of images, scenes, and words he could not comprehend. The Umawei was attempting to flood his mind in an effort to stop him. Having experienced this barrage once before back on Cathar Prime, the Negotiator built up some temporary mental barriers that forced the images to recede. He picked up his pace and ran as fast as he could away from the wraith who did not follow. The Umawei was content merely to guard the passageway.

Zat'ol returned to his quarters and collapsed onto his bed once more. His body ached from the physical effort and sweat stained the sheets as he worked to control his breathing and pounding heartbeat. He needed time to think and to figure out how to thwart the villainous Umawei before it was too late and their plan was completed.

Their final plan was in place, and despite eons of a bodiless existence, the Umawei would not be stopped easily. It would take a miracle to save the galaxy now.

Earth – The Present

"Admiral," shouted a security officer from his station in Earth Command headquarters, "I don't understand how this is possible...but... Ma'am, Earth just cloaked!"

"What? How?" Admiral Austin asked, startled. "Did we finish moving the cloaking satellite?"

"Negative, Admiral."

Austin rushed over to see what the officer was pointing at. Sure enough, an obvious cloak was just raised around the planet.

"That's not possible! Who ordered..."

She was interrupted by a communications officer. "Ma'am, we have an incoming hail from *The*

Avenger." The officer checked his panel, "Admiral, it's Major Gallagher"

Admiral Austin rubbed the back of her neck in confusion. "Put it through."

"Admiral, this is Gallagher aboard *The Avenger*," Gallagher began, "you probably noticed the cloak. We used the ship to wrap the planet up tight."

"Major, I can't say I'm not surprised."

"Uh huh, well, we also don't know who is out there and maybe monitoring communications traffic, so we...uh...decided on our own to do it."

"Thank you, Gallagher. Please let Captain Arvesp know how grateful we are."

"She's right here and listening Admiral," said Gallagher. "We can hold our position for...eighteen hours."

"That should be enough time. We are almost ready to re-engage our own tech."

"Good. Now, about those D'lai, we should..."

Alarms began blaring from several stations in the headquarters. Admiral Austin held up a finger to the screen as she tried to ascertain the problem.

"What now," she said in clear frustration. The past few days had been exhausting.

On a large screen in the center of the room, an

image appeared that looked like a large planet. The only problem was, no one in the room had even seen this particular one. It resembled Earth, but the continents were all wrong. Austin approached the screen, forgetting the communications with Gallagher entirely.

She snapped her fingers to get the attention of a nearby scientific advisor. "What is that?"

"Admiral, I've never seen that planet before." The advisor checked some information on his pad. His face froze in confusion as he moved his eyes back to the view screen. "Admiral, that...can't be there," he said, "that planet is in orbit of...Mars."

"Excuse me?" Admiral Austin whirled on the advisor. "You're telling me that..."

"Yes, it also looks very much like a research model of Mars we've been using in a hypothesis of what the planet might have been like several billion years ago."

Still on the communications console, Gallagher interrupted. "Uh... Admiral... I think I have an idea."

Admiral Austin threw up her hands. "What now, Gallagher?"

"Um, ma'am, Captain Windrow here...she experienced something similar near Cathar Prime."

The Admiral made a gesture and an observant

aide put Gallagher's communication on the main screen for everyone to see.

"Yes, what is it then?"

"Ma'am," said Windrow, "we saw a large projection like this near Cathar Prime of Mars. I sent that report in..."

"A projection?" The scientific advisor asked. "Can you explain?"

"Not well, but if you took readings you'd find it has no real mass."

"A moment," said the advisor. He hastily ran some calculations on his pad and an instant later, his face relaxed, and he smiled. "Yes, that isn't a planet at all."

After several more tense moments of discussion, it was decided to dispatch *The Terran*, now in orbit of Earth, to investigate. The cloaking satellite was in position. It took the technicians far longer than originally estimated, but now Earth could rely on its own cloak, and not be tied to *The Avenger*.

Admiral Austin had an idea and decided to broach it with everyone. "Gallagher, can we get *The Avenger* out to Mars? They have no cloak. Let's see if we can do it for them?"

"A good idea," said Gallagher. "But first, we need

to talk more about the cloak breaking tech we came up with."

"Right," said the admiral, "we've had a look at it. Too much has been happening, so we've not had a chance to implement it."

"Understandable." Gallagher said. "We'll get out to Mars."

For the first time in several hours, Austin was able to relax and get a bit of food. The non-stop troubles weren't gone, but she could at least relax for a while as Earth was now safe from a D'lai threat.

As she sipped some tea, she felt like she wasn't alone in the small office and craned her neck to see who had followed her in. No one. She picked up her tea once more and froze. A dark, ghostly figure hovered in a corner of the office. Rising, she started to press a panic button when her hand stopped in midair. Unable to move it, she stared at the unresponsive limb. A moment later, the wraith vanished, and her hand fell to her side.

"What in creation was that?" Unknown to any human, the Umawei just made their first appearance, on Earth.

Earth Orbit – The Present

ONE OF THE MOST PERVASIVE CHARACTER FLAWS of the D'lai civilization was their innate inability to trust anyone. Their paranoia and disaffection tainted everything about their culture. It also had one unintended benefit. The D'lai always built in back-ups for their back-ups. *The Spector* was no different. Despite not being able to get to the lab where the Seeds rested, Zat'ol knew that, in principle, he could do anything he needed from just about anywhere on the ship, as long as he had his pad and his wits with him.

The Negotiator was aware of the Umawei's intolerance for even low-level radiation, and the engine room of a large space-faring ship was full of the stuff. Even though it was not deadly in normal quantities, Zat'ol recognized that if he could get to engineering, he could safely do what he must, without the interruption of the Emissary or any of his legion.

He took a rather circuitous route, but after what felt like an hour, Zat'ol finally got near enough to the engines that he was confident he could work unmolested. Grabbing his pad, he used the backup codes he memorized before the current mission, and worked his way deep into the subsystems of the ship. It took some effort, but he finally found what he was looking for.

It was not enough to jettison the three Seeds into space. Any ship could simply scoop them up and the Umawei could continue their haunting mission. Zat'ol knew he needed to completely obliterate them. That would take an immense source of energy. He racked his brain, trying to imagine what could possible work, when it struck him. Sol. If he could get *The Spector* close enough to the central star, it would do the work for him.

The only problem was, Zat'ol had a fleet of over five hundred battleships primed for war, and a prison ship full of frightened Cathari. Never mind that the entire solar system was on red alert, and the Umawei were no doubt ready to implement their final plan.

It was a good thing, then, that in addition to the security overrides at Zat'ol's disposal, he could send untraceable and unbreakable commands to any D'lai ship within communications range that could, in theory, send them back home. Despite this, Zat'ol knew deep in his core that even if he managed to destroy the Seeds and send the D'lai back to Cathar Prime, the cycle would continue, and his people would again attempt to conquer the galaxy in the future.

He had to do what Am'oll could not bring himself to do. Zat'ol knew he must reveal the greatest lie in his people's history. He needed to expose Am'oll as a liar and criminal.

In his study of the *Chäi kia Chlüi* and the runes etched onto Am'oll's seed, Zat'ol discovered the truth. Deciding on a plan of action, he opened a wide-band communications channel that would broadcast to not only every D'lai ship, but to anyone in range, on every planet and vessel in the Sol System. If he was going to expose the truth, he was going to tell everyone.

Embedded in the communication was a series of commands to uncloak and disarm the entire D'lai fleet. It would also dispatch *The Spector* on a collision course with the sun. Zat'ol hoped that the message would be received as intended, and his people would be able to surrender in peace. As his finger hovered over the icon to send the command, his body was filled with the most horrific pain he could have ever imagined. Zat'ol screamed as his blood and organs started to cook from the inside out. His skin began to bubble, and Zat'ol was on the verge of losing consciousness when, in a final burst of strength and determination, his finger twitched and touched the icon, sending the command.

A wailing keen of intense grief, anger, and hatred from the disembodied Umawei shattered his eardrums. As Zat'ol collapsed to the floor and burst into flames from the Umawei attack on his body, every creature in range of the communications blast received his message.

Alarms blared on ships and planets as the massive D'lai fleet was exposed. The D'lai panicked at their inability to hide or flee as the message exposing Am'oll filled their screens and exposed their darkest secret to the galaxy. Despite the obvious fact that everyone in authority knew the D'lai were nearby, no one realized the true extent of the intended invasion.

On the bridge of *The Spector*, the navigator panicked as she could not control the flight path of the massive vessel. "Sir," she shouted in alarm to the watch commander, "we are on a course for the central star."

Still reeling from the Negotiator's message, the watch commander jumped from his seat and stood behind the navigator. "What? Stop the ship!"

"I can't, the controls are not responding."

Everyone on the bridge knew what was going on.

It was an open secret that the Negotiator could control the entire fleet, but no one seriously expected him to do it.

Left with no other options, the commander ordered, "All hands, abandon ship. Repeat, all hands abandon ship."

Hundreds of D'lai crew members fled to waiting escape pods in a desperate bid to escape the impending fiery collision with Sol. Still smoldering below decks, the body of Negotiator Brik Zat'ol and the disembodied Umawei Emissary were the only witnesses as *The Spector* raced toward the sun. As the gravity of the massive star clutched the ship in its grip, another keen of grief shook the now empty corridors.

From his vantage point en route to Mars, Gallagher watched as *The Spector* drew ever closer to the sun.

"Why would they send their ship there?" He asked.

"Probably to destroy the Seeds." Arvesp mused.

"It's a shame, I'd like to know what those cylinders contained," said Hodges. "We could really increase our knowledge and..."

"Are you out of your mind?" Margit shook her

head in disbelief. "Those things are dangerous, if what we know about them is true."

Everyone stopped chatting as *The Spector* began its dive into the star's corona. Seconds later, the battleship exploded with enormous ferocity. The Seeds, now exposed to the white-hot star, fused and detonated. The intense burst of the ancient technology caused a massive solar flare that swept out from the star. Many hours after the destruction of *The Spector*, most of Europe and Asia would go dark, and radio communications planet-wide would be interrupted by the burst.

On board the *Martian Sword*, every Umawei faded away at the destruction of the last known Seeds in the galaxy. Foiled, bodiless, and powerless without their technology, the race of ancient beings could no longer maintain a grasp on the plane of existence they so desperately wanted to rejoin. The ancients would never again gain the strength to meddle in the affairs of the living. The race that began it all, died out with a whimper, leaving almost no trace of their civilization. Their only legacy were the countless beings, on countless worlds, who had no idea they ever existed at all, or owed their very existence to the Umawei Empire.

EPILOGUE

EARTH – THE PRESENT

Gallagher and his friends exited the shuttle, and stepped into the bright sunlight outside London. After a short trip back to Earth from Mars on board *Space Cowboy*, Admiral Austin summoned Gallagher and his fellow adventurers for top-level discussions on what to do with the D'lai, still in orbit of Earth and Mars.

None of the battleships were able to resume normal operations after the Negotiator sent the kill-switch command that disabled their cloaks, weapons, and propulsion systems. Earth really had little idea how to handle the presence of five-hundred dead in space ships, so a little creative thinking was in order.

Admiral Austin extended her hand, but

Gallagher, never shy, grabbed her and embraced her. Stiffly, she returned the embrace and pulled away as quickly as she could.

"Admiral, good to be back on the surface again," Gallagher said, "and this time, no one is asking me to run things."

Admiral Austin shot a furtive glance at Margit Wold, who returned her gaze with a slight frown. Both women knew what was coming, and also knew that Gallagher would not be as pleased as they were.

"Well, that's the rub, Sir," said Austin.

Gallagher's brow furrowed at the formality. "Sir?"

"Yes, you see, when you resigned as Secretary General," at this, the Admiral used air quotes when she said the word resigned, "well, um, you didn't *sign* the document."

Gallagher's jaw literally dropped. "What?"

Behind him, Hodges burst into laughter. "So, you're telling us that Gallagher is still..."

"Yes, Cormac Gallagher is still the Secretary General of Earth."

"What, so all that stuff Agda and you did was..."

"Yes, less than legal."

"Well, wait..." said Gallagher as realization hit him, "so that means that I get to..."

Reading his thoughts, Margit touched his shoulder, a large engagement ring sparkling on her left hand. "Yes, hon, you have to figure out how to clean things up."

Gallagher was far from pleased that he was still in charge. He had no idea whatsoever how to deal with the stranded D'lai, or the stunning revelation from their ancient past.

"So, I'm open to some advice," he said. "Anyone?"

No one said a word as they walked toward a waiting air transport. Gallagher swore as his old security detachment surrounded him once more.

"Damn."

D'LAI GLOSSARY

- aiṛ - cloak
- awch jdiv - fake mind
- Çäi - Celebration of Summer
- Chäi kia Chlüi - Book of Knowledge?
- chleng uikir - skinned alive
- chtuai - fools
- Däk'in - Followers of Vdo Däk
- Däz jdiä - welcome friend
- dü va chtuai - stupid fools
- ëmshu chäi - blood oath
- flaibrawch - heretics
- Fü - Earth
- Hyai kia Chlüi - Eye of God
- keṭ - grazing animals

- küad - deceive/lie
- riaẓ ftialchuaṭ - my brother
- Riaẓ jdiä - my friends
- riaẓ ḷong - my love
- roiṣ - help
- sdawij - traditional garment
- sdiau - dagger
- Sriam Yë - secret Gathung group on Earth
- Vdo chlüi, ḍoi fud riaẓ uisdaẓ. Jdaw riaẓ yuak flaibawṛ, vro ble riaẓ uisaṭ. Oh great god, to you I pray. Save me from the liar, and grant me victory.
- Vdo D'lai - Great Believer
- Vdo Däk - Great Priest
- vdo hyëb - spirit
- Vdo Zämi - Great Exile
- viug - father

A Trio of Worlds

Book One of the Three Worlds Chronicles